RECEIVED

DEC 07 2022

THE MAGICIANS OF VENICE, BOOK 2

THE SEA OF THE DEAD

AMY KUIVALAINEN

bhc
press™

Livonia, Michigan

Editor: Amanda Lewis
Proofreader: Jamie Rich

THE SEA OF THE DEAD

Published by BHC Press

Library of Congress Control Number: 2020933936

ISBN: 978-1-64397-133-9 (Hardcover)
ISBN: 978-1-64397-134-6 (Softcover)
ISBN: 978-1-64397-135-3 (Ebook)

For information, write:
BHC Press
885 Penniman #5505
Plymouth, MI 48170

Visit the publisher:
www.bhcpress.com

For Dr. Edward Bridge who labored diligently
to teach me about The Dead Sea Scrolls...

I told you I was going to write a book.

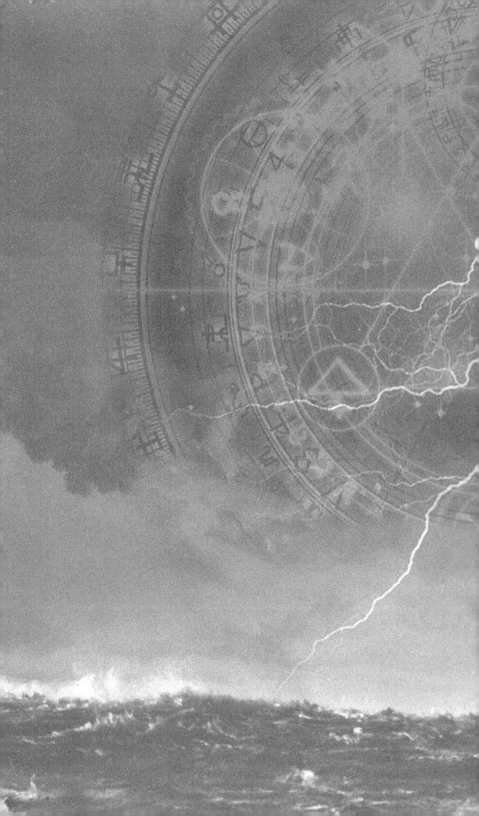

THE SEA OF THE DEAD

PART ONE

MAGIKOS

Greek, noun:
"One of the members of the
learned and priestly class."

PROLOGUE

THE DAY BEFORE Tim Sanders went mad, his biggest concern had been the purple sunburn on the backs of his knees. He had passed out on the sand of Kalia Beach, lazily dreaming beside the Dead Sea with only the palms and bright pink bougainvillea for company. Since arriving in Qumran, he'd spent most of his time squatting in dark caves, so the placement of the sunburn was a particularly painful reminder of why beer and sun didn't always mix.

The days were becoming warmer. The breeze off the Dead Sea wasn't as chilling as spring came to the desert. Tim was alone for the first time in months, the rest of his crew on leave for a month to visit family or partying hard in Tel Aviv to blow off some steam. They thought he was overzealous staying behind to go over the cave for the hundredth time.

"I admire your stamina, Doctor, but anything valuable that Cave 12 may have held is long gone," Professor Abraham Schaal had said, giving a shake of his head. One of the foremost Dead Sea Scrolls scholars in the world, Professor Schaal had been the one to bring Tim onto the site as soon as Cave 12 had been discovered. They had known each other professionally since Tim had come to Israel as a grad student, filled with all the zeal of youth over the Dead Sea mystery. Abraham was leading the dig and even he had gone back to Spain to see the extended branches of his family. Despite the professor's urgings, Tim still couldn't bring himself to leave.

"Are you sure you want to devote your life to a site located in the West Bank?" his friend, Penelope, had asked one night as they camped in the middle of the desert. "I can't explain it, Pen—it's like I'm meant to be here," he'd replied. And when she had persisted in her warnings, he'd lightly scoffed, "You're one to talk, Atlantis Girl." It was what had first bound them together in their undergraduate years—their single-minded obsessions with discovering impossible finds.

And here Tim was ten years later, scratching around an empty cave for something that might not even be there. He knew he was close, knew he would sacrifice everything to get his big, career-making find.

When Cave 12 was first found the year before, it had yielded pottery, carnelian beads, and scraps of crumbling parchment and fabrics. There was evidence the cave had once held more, but looters had reached it in the years before them. The cave's contents had probably been hocked on the antiquities black market, but Tim hoped that the looters had overlooked something in their haste.

The Essenes, who had written the scrolls, had been an extremely private people who valued their writings and knowledge. It was possible they had hidden more, with modern scholars simply having no way of spotting the signs in their original place due to the combination of erosion and the secrecy of the extinct people.

While it may have seemed painfully obvious to anyone else that all that remained in the cave was dirt and rock, Tim couldn't—*wouldn't*—let his dream of a great discovery go until he was satisfied that there was none to be had. He could barely explain the reasoning to himself sometimes, but it felt as if the cave was calling out to him.

His ex-girlfriend, Carolyn, would have called it intuition. She would have said he was "following the energies to his destiny." When they were dating, he'd always been too scientifically minded to meet her halfway in her beliefs, but lately, he was starting to think she'd been onto something. The desert air was tense, like it was holding its breath, and Tim knew he was getting close. He just needed to wait for it to relinquish its treasures to him.

Did Schliemann give up when he searched for Troy? Did Carter give up when he was told there were no pharaohs left to be found in the Valley of the Kings? The voice in his head sounded a lot like Penelope's. However, he was willing to bet that even her legendary patience would've been tested by Cave 12. He'd wanted her to come with him on the dig, but she'd turned him down, still unable to let go of Atlantis.

"You two are like Howard Carter and Jacquetta Hawkes; Tim's too cocky and will probably meet a bad end, and Pen's too clever and a woman so she'll never get the recognition she deserves," Carolyn had once said to them. They'd been stuck with Carter and Hawkes as nicknames ever since. Yes, his Hawkes would have understood the tingling between his shoulder blades and the butterflies in his stomach.

Tim took a break from chipping away at the back of the cave, and sat down on the three-legged camp stool, stretching out his aching legs. He hoped there had been a cave-in at some point in the past and that some of the clay jars containing more scrolls had been caught in the slurry. A fool's wish perhaps, but stranger things had happened in the history of archaeology. Hell, Cave 12 had been right in front of their noses for the last sixty years, but they had only found it last February.

Tim checked his watch and set the alarm for when he would run out of decent light to set up camp. He hadn't told anyone of his plans to sleep overnight in the cave, but he thought it would be a good chance to get some solid immersion therapy. How often would he get the chance to work alone in the silence, to lie under the desert stars and hear what they wanted to tell him?

Carolyn had never understood his fascination for the arid beauty of the desert or its cultures, from the Bedouins of today to the Essenes of the past. The desert appealed to those with a contemplative mind, and the very sands of Israel were packed with secret, untold history. No matter how many times Tim left, his return was as inevitable as the tide.

IT WAS almost midnight when a faint, golden light pulsed at the back of the cave. Tim had set up his swag and other camping gear at the mouth of the cave and was enjoying the final beer of his six-pack when an unexpected beam of light made him sit bolt upright.

"What the hell?" he murmured.

Very faintly, the light flickered again. *Did I leave a lamp on in there?* He rose unsteadily, turned on a torch, and headed back into the cave.

Light shone through a crack in the wall he had been working on all day.

"What the hell?" Tim leaned down and put his eye to the opening. The torch clattered from his hand.

Inside was a chamber, and a man in a *thawb* was writing frantically on parchment, a single oil lamp burning on a rock beside him.

"Hey! How did you get in there? Are you okay?" Tim called through the gap. The mountains were riddled with caves... Was there another entrance he didn't know about?

"Help me... You must help me stop them!" the stranger said in urgent Hebrew, which Tim struggled to translate in his inebriated state.

"Tell me how to get to you, and I'll help," Tim fumbled out, hoping he was getting the words right.

"It is too late. The caves are collapsed," the scribe replied and turned back to scratch out words on the paper. "They are all dead. Everyone is dead. I'm the only one left to pass it on."

"You're not dead yet! I can help get you out. Just...just wait there. I'll be right back with some tools," Tim assured the stranger as he hurried back to his gear. He grabbed the pickax and carried it back down into the cave. "I'll get you out. Just stay away from the wall, so nothing falls on you."

The man started to sing a strange lilting song as Tim struck the clay and rock with the sharp hook of the pick. He couldn't hear enough to make out the words, but it sounded like a hymn.

He struck the wall over and over until it crumbled and gave way. Tim dropped the pickax and leaned in to look.

But the golden light was gone, and so was the man.

"Hello! Where are you?" Tim called as the dust settled. There was no other tunnel the man could have escaped down. Something crunched underfoot, and Tim swung the torch around. *Bones.* "What the fuck is going on?"

As he tried to move into the space, he stumbled and slipped backward onto the broken rocks. Panting heavily, he shone the torchlight around him.

The cave was bare except for the skeleton beside him, a scattering of writing implements, and a clay oil lamp. Tim squatted, looking over the remains of the man and the clay jar clutched in his hand.

Tim's heart pounded; he needed gloves and a camera to document and photograph every inch of the scene. He needed to call his team, rouse Professor Schaal from the arms of his beautiful Spanish wife, and demand he leave his holiday in Madrid for the Dead Sea at once.

Why? So they can get the credit? Tim hesitated and then instead of following procedure, he took off his shirt, wrapped it around the jar, and plucked it gently from the scribe's hand.

The sun was beginning to rise as Tim stepped from the cave. How long had he been in there?

He placed the jar carefully into his backpack and gathered up the rest of his gear. Thirty minutes later he was driving his beat-up Jeep down the packed dirt roads, heading for Kalia at a reckless speed. He contemplated calling Schaal again, but another look at the jar in his bag made him hesitate. Schaal and the others would be back soon enough. They had laughed at his theories that the cave held more secrets, but he had been right. A scribe had walled himself inside to protect whatever he had written. It *had* to be important. It was Tim's discovery and he didn't want to share this moment—or his prize—with anyone before he had to.

LATER, SAFELY locked behind the door of his hotel room, Tim showered and contemplated what he should do with the jar. Did he dare open it without Schaal? He wondered how badly he would get his ass kicked, weighing whether it would be worth it as long as he was the one who saw its contents first. Tim eyed the jar through the foggy pane of the shower door. He was reluctant to let it leave his sight for even a moment, part of him afraid that he would wake up on the cave floor and realize he'd passed out from too many beers, that it was all just a dream.

God, he wished he could call Carolyn about his vision. She always knew exactly what to do when faced with the spooky and mysterious. A ghost would be right up her alley.

Alas, their last phone call had not ended well. Tim never could control his temper, and he had pushed Carolyn one step too far, losing her friendship as well as her love. The last four months in the desert had given him time to think, and Tim had come to the horrible conclusion that he had been a complete and utter prick to her.

Can't worry about that now. Not when he was so close to proving it had all been worth it.

Tim wrapped a towel around his waist and carried the jar to where he'd set up a makeshift office using the room's small dining table and bedside lamps. He took out his battered leather field journal and started recording his notes on how he'd found it. Almost immediately, the details of the vision flooded back to him, everything from the description of the man to the rhythm of his language.

The scribe had been scared of something. Or someone. He had said that they were all dead. Learning why and how the Essenes had vanished was one of the reasons why Tim was here. How could a whole community just vanish? He carefully recorded the placement of the body and the other items that had been scattered in the cave.

God, he had just left the body there. A body that could very well be over two thousand years old and hold fresh insights into how the

Essenes lived. The site was restricted, but there wasn't any security in place to ensure no one snuck in. He knew that as much as he wanted to keep the discovery a secret, he also needed to cover his ass.

Tim grabbed his phone and typed out a text message to Schaal: Didn't want to disturb your holiday but found a body in Cave 12 behind a weak wall.

It was still early, he figured he had time before the phone calls started. He would let the jar and its mysterious contents be a surprise.

Tim picked up the jar, turning it over in his hands. His body broke out in goose bumps. "What secrets are you hiding, my pretty?"

The jar had been sealed with a mixture of mud, wax, ink, and rust smears that could have been the scribe's own blood. Tim cleared the table, covered it with a fresh white bedsheet from the cupboard, and set up the bedside lamps around it to give him maximum light. He rested his iPad on a stack of books, so the camera captured the jar and pressed record on the video.

Taking out a small toolset, he selected a scalpel, and began to slowly scrape at the seal.

FOUR DAYS later, bleeding and stumbling through the streets of Tel Aviv, Tim Sanders clutched a precious package tightly to his chest. He kept glancing backward, checking around corners, and peering into parked cars.

They were coming for him. They were always there, moving in the corner of his eye. They had been following him for days, forcing him to hide where he could, stealing food when his money ran out. He had to keep moving. Tim couldn't remember the last time he'd slept or how he'd managed to get from Qumran to Tel Aviv. Only the scroll's message mattered now.

Have to get it somewhere safe. Have to get it somewhere safe.

Tim knew he had to part with it—it was the only way to keep it out of their hands. He couldn't keep running, he needed to get the scroll as far away from him as possible.

Finding a post office, Tim gently boxed up his greatest treasure and sent it to the only person left on earth he could trust.

ONE

$\mathcal{T}$HE WAREHOUSE AT the docks of Palermo smelled of fuel and fish and old blood. Alexis's magic hummed on the surface of his skin, mingling with his pent-up frustration. He had been hunting for weeks with Aelia and Phaidros, with no success. They had searched all of Italy for signs of Abaddon, the head of the snake that he desperately needed to cut off. Every lead they had was taking them further away from Venice where he should be. Abaddon and Kreios had simply vanished from the country without a trace.

Phaidros and Aelia had been uncharacteristically well-behaved, neither picking fights with the other, as if they could feel Alexis's temper and how close he was to exploding. *If only they knew.* The tide of magic was rising, and his power was building inside him with all the pressure of a storm.

Since Venice had nearly been consumed by dark magic a month ago, Alexis had been searching for the new priesthood of Thevetat. After failing to locate Kreios or Abaddon, he'd turned his attention to their hired underlings, the *Sanguine de Serpente*, the Blood of the Serpent. He'd taken out every one of the gang's headquarters across Italy until they had reached Sicily and their hometown of Palermo.

Alexis didn't want to be here. He wanted to be back in Venice where he could keep his eyes on Penelope and the new magic swirling inside her. He needed to ensure that Abaddon would never return to the palazzo to finish what he'd started the night of the storm. Penelope had Zo and Lyca—two of the best warriors he'd ever met—guarding her, but no matter how good they were, he remained uneasy being apart from her.

As if on cue, Alexis felt Penelope's presence with him. The sense of her bloomed inside him so strongly, he swore he could almost smell her perfume. It meant only one thing; she was touching the *moíra desmós*, the metaphysical knot that tied their fates together.

"Defender! Why have you stopped?" Aelia whispered tersely, her *gladius* sword drawn in the dim light. They were at the back of the warehouse, ready to charge in, and he was hesitating.

"Wait…just wait," Alexis said as he typed Penelope a short text message, and the pressure in his chest disappeared at once.

"Now is *not* the time to be sending love notes," Phaidros growled beside him, struggling to pick the lock of a service door.

"Shut up and focus," Alexis snapped, drawing his daggers.

A moment later, Phaidros had accomplished picking the lock, and together they crept inside.

"Their security's appalling," said Aelia in disgust. Alexis took note of the white plastic casing covering the alarm system beside the door but said nothing as a small, red light began to flash.

"It's probably because anyone local isn't stupid enough to break in here," Phaidros replied. "They—"

Aelia pressed her hand over Phaidros's mouth. "Over there." She pointed.

Two men with guns were standing beside another door. Before the men spotted them, Alexis let his daggers fly, and the guards dropped without a sound.

"Phaidros, check the office. Aelia and I will keep searching," instructed Alexis.

Phaidros headed for the door as Aelia followed Alexis down a set of metal stairs. The burning rage in him hardened into something cold and dark as the smell of blood and suffering grew stronger. The slaughterhouse stank like the temples of Thevetat had when he'd raided them for survivors. Alexis had never forgotten that smell, even if he wished he could.

"This doesn't feel right," Aelia murmured. "I can't sense them."

Alexis knew what she meant. In the past, the priests' magic had always felt like a sticky, foul tongue on his skin whenever he encountered it.

"It could be different this time around," Alexis said. "Thevetat's power could've changed, or the priests aren't adept enough in wielding it."

The next door they came to was made of thick iron and covered in rust. A heavy bar kept it locked. Alexis worked to lift the bar as Aelia watched his back, her magic coiled, ready for a fight.

Alexis opened the door and lights flickered throughout the cavernous concrete basement. Bile crept up the back of Alexis's throat when he saw the bodies strung up with wires, naked and mutilated.

"Alexis, over here," said Aelia, her voice icy cold.

A group of dirty, starved women were crowded up against a far concrete wall, their stares vacant as if they were waiting to be executed.

"You are going to be okay," Aelia told them, her musical voice laden with magic to keep them calm. "You're safe now. We are here to rescue you." She repeated the phrases in Russian and English as the women came forward.

Alexis turned back to the sacrifices: two women and a man. Both had died horribly. As gruesome as their deaths must have been, there was no essence of magic lingering in them.

"You are right, Aelia. This wasn't done by a priest of Thevetat," he said. Somehow that made it so much worse. The priests performed ritual sacrifice because it fed Thevetat and gave them power. This was done for the sport of it, something to keep the women scared enough to behave. He was so angry he could barely breathe.

"Alexis?" Aelia sounded wary. Unlike the women huddled around her, she knew the signs when he was about to lose control. Magic fizzed in his blood, begging to be let out.

"Stay with them and don't bring them up until Phaidros comes to get you," Alexis commanded. Then he shut the iron door and headed back up the metal stairs.

He knew a silent alarm had been triggered when they had entered the building and had purposely done nothing to stop it. He'd had enough of chasing these evil snakes. He wanted them to come to him…all of them.

Now men were filing into the building, their guns ready and knives out. *Good.*

"I found their boss. He's trying to be an acolyte and has had no real training. He's trafficking people and his accounts…" Phaidros halted when he saw the look on Alexis's face and was given further pause by the magic and light spilling out from his skin. Phaidros took a step out of the way as Alexis drew out his *yataghan.*

"Go and protect Aelia," Alexis ordered.

"Defender, think this through. If you kill them all, they won't be able to tell us what we need to know," Phaidros reasoned.

"You say that this boss knows Abaddon?" Alexis stepped into the office. It was trashed from the fight with Phaidros, and a fat, middle-aged man was sweating from fear in the corner of the room.

"Do you know who we are?" asked Alexis.

"You're dead men. When the Master learns what you have done here, we are all dead," he said through busted lips. Phaidros's handiwork, no doubt.

"Are you training to be one of Thevetat's Vessels?"

"No, I wasn't worthy enough. It must be enough for me to serve."

"By trafficking women like they are objects?" hissed Alexis.

"Don't be naïve, magician. They are a means to an end, and at least if they are sacrificed, their useless lives will have meaning."

"Alexis, don't—" Phaidros shouted.

Too late. Alexis brought his sword down, cleaving the man's head from his shoulders.

"Go and help Aelia. I won't ask you again," Alexis said, flicking the blood from his blade.

"Don't lose yourself when Penelope has only just found you," warned Phaidros before obeying Alexis's instruction and hurrying from the room.

Penelope. They had thought they could sacrifice her too. That her life didn't mean anything and her worth only lay in feeding Thevetat's power. The *Sanguine de Serpente* would end tonight. Alexis stepped out into the darkness and unleashed his fury.

TWO

OTHERE WERE FEW things in the world that Doctor Penelope Bryne truly hated more than someone telling her, "You can't do that." Incidentally, it was her father's favorite phrase.

"You can't do that," Stuart Bryne had said when she had called her parents a month ago to say that she had accepted a position as the curator of a rare, private manuscript and antiquities collection in Venice.

"Actually, Stuart, I *can* do that. I have. It's done. This is a courtesy call to let you know I'm not going back to Melbourne," Penelope responded in a tone she would never have had the confidence to use just a few months ago. It had been an illuminating seven weeks, and Stuart Bryne's perpetual disapproval of her life choices no longer intimidated her.

"This had better not be about bloody Atlantis, Penelope. What's in this collection? More fake maps and theories about its location for you to waste your life chasing?" Stuart argued, his Irish brogue growing thicker the angrier he became.

"Would it matter? I'm not like you. I don't want a job in a comfortable university teaching ungrateful kids. I'm going to be paid extremely well, and I'm living in a private palazzo with access to a collection that would rival the Bodleian. As a parent, that should be enough for you not to worry about your *adult* daughter." *Goodbye, patience, you were fun while you lasted.*

The silence that followed was long and full of judgment.

"Jesus Christ—this isn't about a man, is it?" Stuart finally said.

"No." *Not entirely anyway.* "It's my decision to stay, and I'm not going to change my mind, so save your breath. If I find anything interesting that relates to you or Mom's research field, I'll be sure to let you know."

Stuart Bryne sighed in defeat. "Did you catch your serial killer at least?"

In her mind's eye, Penelope saw the knife fly through the air and Tony Duilio's throat reduced to bloody ruins. Her hand gripped her phone tighter.

Penelope made sure her voice was steady as she said, "I did. He was killed in the cross fire. I'll send you links to some articles if you're interested in reading about it. It was a bit of a media storm here in Venice for a while. I've got to go."

"Pen? Please be careful."

The line went dead, leaving Penelope shocked that Stuart had bothered to show any concern for her at all. In the past, she had gone off to the West Bank without so much as a flicker of unease from her father.

Penelope let out a long, frustrated sigh and tossed the mobile phone onto her new desk. Everything in the office was new because the Archives had made it especially for her.

The day Penelope had taken a small piece of Nereus's magic inside herself and accepted her role as the Archivist, the Archives had undergone multiple changes to accommodate its new master. Penelope had stepped out of the elevator and found Nereus's lab and office gone, replaced by a newly minted space cut into the stone of the cavern and surrounded by glass so she could see out over the bookstacks.

Inside the office, Penelope had found a long desk of dark wood, a comfortable chaise lounge for reading, and her laptop and notebooks arranged and ready for her. Lamps with stained glass shades filled the room with a warm glow, while paintings of daily life in Atlantis hung on the walls. Best of all, her shelves were filled with books that the Archives thought she might enjoy. It was as if the magic of the place had plucked her dream workspace out of her head and created it for her.

Maybe it had.

Penelope had learned weeks ago that questioning the magic of the Archives, or the palazzo, got her nowhere.

"If we knew definitively how magic worked, there wouldn't be much need of magicians. Magic is about exploration and experimentation. You need to surrender to the flow and mystery of it all; otherwise, you'll only drive yourself mad," Alexis had told her with a consolatory kiss on her forehead.

Alexis Donato: the only thing that rivaled the Archives in mystery and magic. The magician whose heart she could hear singing to her.

Because it belongs to you, he'd told her weeks ago. Since then, their entire world had changed.

Think about something else, Penelope prompted herself. She spun a bronze-and-silver astrolabe on her desk, the intricate engravings blurring. It had also been left for her by the Archives, and she knew even before she touched it that it had belonged to Nereus. It was something else Nereus wanted her to have, though Penelope couldn't figure out why.

Penelope turned it over in her hands, trying to keep busy, so she didn't text Alexis. Phaidros and Aelia had gone with him to watch his back, but Penelope still worried. The Serpent members had tried to kill her on more than one occasion, and she was still having nightmares about being strapped to a chair and thrown into a canal. She sometimes woke up sweating and shaking, her mouth tasting like oily brine.

Stop thinking about it. Penelope focused back on the device in her hands. She ran a finger around the border of the astrolabe, studying the designs layered over each other. Light danced under the skin of her hands, and the line of figures shimmered and rearranged into words.

"*Be the star whose light guides them home,*" Penelope read aloud. "Seriously, Nereus?" She could practically hear the old woman's cackle in her head.

There was a soft snick as the astrolabe suddenly unlocked. Penelope stared in disbelief before banging her head against the desk. She'd been trying to find the way to open it for the past three weeks. Alexis had simply smiled and told her it would open when she needed it to. *I bet he'd seen the sealing spell on it too, the bastard.*

With a deep breath, Penelope gently lifted the lid until it folded out flat. Astrolabes had been employed throughout history for purposes ranging from scheduling prayers to astrology, navigation, timekeeping, and surveying. The astrolabe in Penelope's hand was the same in principle, but it looked far older and more intricate than others she'd seen. Parts of the dials emitted a dull glow, which told her magic was definitely involved.

Penelope twisted a small knob on the side of the device, and seven metal rings rose out of their positions. Each ring had symbols etched into it that changed as different dials moved.

"What on earth are you tracking?" Penelope asked it. None of the symbols were astrological or alchemical that she could recognize.

Hoping it didn't blast her with magic, Penelope touched one of the dials with her index finger. It glowed gold, sending a line of electricity through the back of her hand, and the aroma of olive groves, old wine, and apricots filled the air. Penelope had encountered that particular perfume before.

"Phaidros," she whispered. No one knew where the talent had come from, but Penelope had discovered she could smell magic when it was being performed. Each of the magicians had their own signature and her knowing when they were doing magic had made them cautious of trying to trick her in any way.

Penelope removed her finger from the glowing ring before touching another. The symbols glowed fuchsia pink, and she guessed its owner before the aroma of rose petals and frankincense hit her senses. *Aelia.*

"Seven dials, seven magicians. You were keeping track of them by charting their magic. Clever, clever, Nereus," murmured Penelope.

She fiddled with another dial and the seven rings spun until they perfectly aligned and folded down into the lid of the device, revealing another series of dials underneath. She bent her head, straining her ears until she heard the faint ticking of tiny gears.

"What else are you monitoring?" she asked. Penelope jerked her head back as the air pressurized around her, the dials glowing as the engravings changed.

"*The Tide*," she read slowly.

Tony Duilio's unwelcome voice slithered through her head like an oily snake. *It has taken ten thousand years for the tide of magic to rise again.*

"An astrolabe that monitors all magic as well as the magicians. Only you, Nereus!"

Except now it was hers—a riddle to solve and use in the conflict to come. She was undisputedly the Archivist, but Penelope was quickly learning that her new role also included Nereus's other duty: being the calm in the tumultuous storm that was the palazzo at 39 Calle dei Cerchieri.

Closing her eyes, Penelope reached deep inside herself and felt out the threads of light that tied her to Alexis. *Still there, still safe.* She had promised not to touch it while he was off on the mission in Sicily, the sensation a dangerous distraction. It didn't stop her from checking a few times a day to ensure that he was still alive. The worst of her recent nightmares was always a repeat of those desperate moments when she'd pulled an unconscious Alexis from the sea, the CPR she had tried utterly useless. She couldn't handle not knowing if he was safe.

In addition to the destiny knot, Penelope could now feel two other things lurking beneath the surface of her skin. The Living Language that had leaped into her from Alexis's stone tablet five weeks ago still purred inside her mind, translating languages and sending her unexpected warnings. It was continuously useful but still largely a mystery.

The other part of her gift had been the small amount of power that had belonged to Nereus. What exactly it did, if anything, Penelope had yet to discover. The other magicians thought it would simply integrate with her other magic, perhaps having no greater purpose than opening the Archives. It wasn't hurting her, and that was enough for the magicians.

They might not be worried about it, but Penelope was. Nereus had been the eldest of all the magicians and the most powerful. Brief contact with Alexis's magic had left her with special abilities, and she highly doubted Nereus's gift would simply absorb and disappear. From the letters she'd left, Nereus had seen her death, and she wouldn't have only given Penelope enough magic to open the Archives. That was something she could've left instructions for Alexis to do.

Penelope had thought Nereus's journals would be a good place to learn what her thoughts were in her final days and uncover clues to what Penelope was meant to do with the magic. But all the journals were gone and no amount of begging persuaded the Archives to produce them. She knew she was overthinking it because she wanted to help, to be a good Archivist. But, as Alexis had told her many times, that wasn't how magic worked.

"What if I wake up with a tail? You'll be worried then," she had argued.

"Will I? I happen to think you would look rather cute with a tail," Alexis teased back with a smile. "Have patience, Penelope. Magic is a journey."

Alas, patience was something Penelope lacked. As if in response to that thought, the phone on her desk started vibrating. Q4R10S3B7, the message read. Penelope's face broke into a smile, and she hurried out of the office and into the stacks.

"Quadrant four," she said, locating the correct pillar with the golden Atlantean symbol for history crowning it. "Row ten. Shelf three…from the bottom." She ran her fingers along the spines. "Book seven." She pulled it out eagerly. It was a thick tome bound in blue leather. The symbols on the cover rearranged to read, *The History of the Founding of the Citadel of Magicians.*

"You aren't playing fair at all, Alexis Donato," Penelope said, sighing.

Every few days she received a list of coordinates that took her on a treasure hunt. It hadn't taken her long to realize that Alexis was purposely leading her to titles he knew would distract her the most. The more distracted she was, the less she worried about where they were and if they were safe.

Penelope clutched the book to her, hoping it would alleviate the hard ball of longing in her chest. How could she have thought she could permanently walk away from Venice?

It was a day of pain and clouded memory. Nereus had been found dead, Galenos was wounded, and Alexis and the other magicians were left reeling by their loss and the cold knowledge that they were going back to war. Penelope had been hurt, not knowing if she had a place among the magicians, or if she could help them. She had convinced herself that leaving would protect Alexis and used it as an excuse to run from what she had really been feeling. When Penelope had walked back in, the magicians had all looked relieved, and hadn't held her moment of doubt against her.

Since then, however, the energy in the palazzo had changed to tense alertness as the magicians searched for leads on their enemies, and Penelope hadn't had a chance to talk to Alexis about what happened. He treated her with the same affection, but there was a tightness around his eyes that she hated. There had been no time to smooth things over before he, Phaidros, and Aelia had left for Sicily. So, she had done what she'd always done when she couldn't process her feelings: she threw herself into research.

With Galenos still confined to bed, Penelope hadn't been game enough to try out his high-tech computer lab, and so she'd stuck to books and her academic databases. She didn't know how long it took for a magician to heal, but she knew she wasn't going to get anywhere significant without Galenos's help.

A loud clang on the other side of the cavern snapped Penelope out of her misery. It was followed by two heavy strikes of metal on metal.

"What in God's name is that?"

Still holding her book, Penelope hurried toward the sound, hoping the Archives wasn't renovating again.

THE ARCHIVES twisted deeper into the rock as Penelope searched for the source of the consistent banging. The air grew hotter, and as the bookshelves ended, she found herself in a museum of weaponry.

Swords, shields, whole suits of armor from every time period, spears, lances, daggers, and other short-range weapons were displayed neatly on stands of gleaming death.

With her mouth hanging open, Penelope found Lyca swinging a hammer at a forge. Lyca's black skin gleamed with sweat, as she shaped hot metal and shoved it back into a glowing bed of coals.

"Did you make all of these?" Penelope asked, eyes wide.

"I wouldn't trust a weapon in a battle that I didn't make myself," said Lyca sharply.

"Are all of these yours?" Penelope looked at the neat stands of armor, helms, and shields.

"They are all of ours. That Roman breastplate was Alexis's in the fourth century; that shield was Zo's from when he was a mercenary in Babylon. Even Aelia has a section over there from when she started to learn how to protect herself and stopped being so useless."

Penelope swallowed hard. Lyca had accepted Penelope as the new Archivist only after checking both letters from Nereus to ensure they weren't forged. She was probably seen as the useless one now.

Lyca had spent the last few weeks tending to Galenos, and Penelope had been too nervous to intrude. When they did encounter each other at the dinner table, the conversation was tense no matter how hard Penelope tried to be friendly.

"These are incredibly beautiful, Lyca. I didn't know you were a weaponsmith as well as a magician."

"I've been working a forge longer than I've been working magic," Lyca replied before taking the piece of plate from the coals and raising her hammer once more. Penelope's senses tingled, and she could smell hot blood, steel, and desert air. Whatever she was making, Lyca was weaving magic into the metal, layer upon layer.

"Can I ask what you're making?" Penelope risked another step toward the workbench. Other small pieces of plate were sitting on top of complex sketches.

Lyca grunted. "A new arm and leg for Galenos."

"No wonder you're putting so much magic into them. Will magic be used to power them over animatronics?" Lyca gave her a sharp look and Penelope instinctively stilled, her heart racing.

"I keep forgetting you can do that."

"Sorry. I didn't mean to pry. I'm just curious—"

"It's fine." Lyca shoved the plate into the water before placing it on the bench with the other pieces. "I'll make the parts and Galenos will add whatever technology he needs. The magic is to strengthen the metal while also ensuring he can still channel power throughout his body." Lyca twisted the plans toward her and Penelope studied the hundreds of intricate parts.

Penelope let out an appreciative whistle. "Tony Stark, eat your heart out."

"Who is Tony Stark? Is he a friend of yours?"

"He's Iron Man. You don't know... He's a guy I know who made a suit like this."

"Iron would be the incorrect metal to use on the arm and it would dull the magic," Lyca replied, matter-of-factly. She lifted two other items from the bench. "These will be new daggers for Alexis."

"I thought he would have plenty by now."

"Not ones like this. You need special weapons to kill priests of Thevetat, imbued with magic that can cut through their defenses. I have not made such things since Atlantis."

"It must be hard for you to have to make them again."

Lyca gave one of the daggers over to Penelope. "Not as hard as it will be for Alexis to wield them. He's hoping that Kreios and Abaddon are the only ones out there. I told him if he thinks that, he's a fool. The priests always bred like filthy maggots. There will be more, and I'll make sure we are ready for them. Once Galenos is healed, I will hunt the scum to the ends of the earth."

The hair on Penelope's arm stood on end at the promise of violence in Lyca's tone. She was so eager for revenge, she almost vibrated.

"I'm sure the others will be grateful for your forethought, Lyca. I saw your weapons in action against Kreios. Nothing else could hurt him."

Lyca's smile was vicious. "I'm going to make something special for him. Alexis is about defense, but I'm about offense. I need to get these parts done for Galenos so I can begin my hunt."

Penelope turned one of the unfinished daggers over in her hand. "Do you think they've found anything?"

"Of course they have. Alexis will want to keep you out of the details to protect you. I'm not sure if they've found priests, but they have flushed out more than one snake."

Penelope's stomach tightened, hoping for the thousandth time that they would be okay. After holding Alexis dead in her arms only weeks beforehand, she didn't think she could handle seeing him hurt again so soon. *If ever.*

Lyca made a sound of frustration in the back of her throat. "You shouldn't be so worried about them. Alexis is the best warrior I've ever trained. The other two are good enough to watch his back and stay out of his way."

"Were you a warrior before you made weapons?" asked Penelope, wanting to change the subject.

Lyca looked down at the tongs in her hand, her expression darkening. "My father was a mercenary. He taught me to fight. And when he needed new weapons for a large contract, he sold me to an armorer in the city of Atlas."

"How could he do that? You're his daughter!" Penelope had her issues with Stuart, but even she didn't think he'd stoop low enough to sell her.

"It was a big contract. My father thought he would be able to buy me back once it was over. You are a typical starry-eyed historian romanticizing the past if you don't think Atlantis had problems like slavery and oppression."

"I'm not starry-eyed. I was only shocked that a father thought it was okay to sell his daughter for weapons."

Lyca's face went carefully blank. "Men have sold their daughters for less. He saw it as an enforced apprenticeship, an opportunity. I like to hope that he didn't know how big of a bastard my master was. I guess I'll never know."

"He never came back for you?"

"No. He died with a blade in his belly. I remained a slave and learned the craft."

"When did you meet Nereus?"

"She had discovered that the priests of Thevetat had murdered a magician. He had foreseen the war and wrote to her before they had the chance to kill him. She knew how powerful they would become if they remained unchallenged. She came for weapons, but when she saw the magical ability within me, she bought me from my master and took me with her to the Citadel."

"No wonder you protected her for so long."

"She gave me a new life, and I always tried to show how grateful I was for that. I didn't serve her because she was the Archivist. I won't be protecting you the same way just because you have taken her place."

Penelope looked her in the eye. "I don't have any expectations of you, Lyca. You need to avenge what happened to Nereus and Galenos. Alexis needs to track Abaddon and Kreios down, not babysit me. I'm not delusional. I know I'm not going to be useful in a fight, only in a library."

Lyca put down her hammer. "I only wanted to establish where we stand. You are your own responsibility."

"As I've always been." Penelope turned to leave, but Lyca stopped her.

"Do you have a picture of what that Stark man built? I'd like to see it." It was as close to an olive branch that Penelope was ever likely to get from the warrior magician.

Trying to explain superheroes to Lyca would take too long, so Penelope fished out her phone and Googled it for her. She was just pulling up another set of pictures when the wards in the palazzo sounded around them.

The corner of Lyca's mouth twitched up. "They are home."

THREE

$\mathcal{A}$LEXIS DEPOSITED AELIA and Phaidros into the foyer of the palazzo before portaling back into his tower. He didn't want Penelope to see him before he had a chance to clean the blood and ash from his body. She knew him as the scholar, not the rage-filled beast fresh from battle.

In his bathroom, Alexis stripped off his jacket and unbuckled the heavily warded breastplate he wore underneath. His phone buzzed on the marble counter; Inspector Marco Dandolo was persistent for more information about the night's efforts. He'd have to wait. Gisela Bianchi and her DIGOS team would inform Marco what had happened. Alexis wasn't in the mood to talk about what he'd seen in Sicily.

Climbing into the shower, he scrubbed himself all over in an effort to rid himself of the crawling dread scratching and biting under his skin. All those weeks tracking the *Sanguine de Serpente* operations, and they weren't any closer to finding the hole that Kreios and Abaddon were hiding in.

Alexis touched the center of his chest, the pulse of the *moíra desmós* sending an ache of want through him.

A part of him knew that he needed to take things slowly with Penelope to ensure she didn't run again. Another part wanted to lock her in the tower with him and not leave for a hundred years; demons, priests, and the world be damned.

Don't forget she chose to come back, Alexis reminded himself. He didn't know if she made the right choice or not. He wanted her, so much it was enough to drive him mad, but it was driven by his own selfish desire to have something—*someone*—that he belonged to. Someone that actually saw *him* and not the Defender.

The timing for a relationship couldn't have been worse. Alexis didn't want to see that bright joy in her eyes dimmed by a war with Thevetat. He didn't want her to see what he would become before it was over. Penelope deserved more than that, but the thought of her leaving again nauseated him.

After finishing his shower, Alexis took the time to clean his armor and weapons. He didn't know if Penelope was still awake. It was late and waking her felt selfish.

It was hunger that finally drove Alexis out of the door of his tower. He was still buttoning up a crisp, white shirt when he reached the bottom of the staircase and found Penelope pacing, arguing with herself under her breath. She looked up at him and stilled, her hazel eyes rapidly taking in every inch of him, assessing for damage. *Penelope was worried, and you were hiding in your tower while she suffered. What a stupid thing for you to do.*

"I wasn't sure if you were awake or if you wanted company—" she began uncertainly, taking a step toward him.

The *moíra desmós* inside his chest vibrated with emotion, and they collided together. Alexis buried his hands in her thick curls, his face resting in the groove of her neck so he could breathe in her clean scent of jasmine and sea salt, letting it chase away the smell of the warehouse. Penelope's hands slid under his shirt, running up his back and then down his chest.

"Are you hurt?" she asked urgently. Her hand rested over Alexis's heart, and she took a deep, steadying breath as she felt its strong pulse.

"I'm okay, Penelope. I don't have a scratch on me," Alexis tried to reassure her. Her concern hit him deeply; he was the Defender. No one ever assumed he wasn't okay. If he was home from a mission, that was enough for them.

You keep forgetting she's not like them. She cares differently.

The other magicians knew Alexis needed time alone to think and process after a mission. Penelope didn't. Anxiety radiated off her. He lifted her face and kissed her cheeks gently.

"I'm fine, *cara*," he repeated, looking her in the eyes. "How are you?"

"I'm glad you're back. Zo's been acting like a mother hen and won't let me go anywhere without an escort," Penelope huffed.

Alexis smiled. "That's because he knows I'd get upset if anything happened to you."

"*Dio.* I do it because I don't want her getting kidnapped again, not because I'm scared of *you*," said Zo from the other side of the room. He was leaning against the doorway with his arms folded across his broad chest. He looked like a bodyguard, and something inside Alexis relaxed a little further, knowing Zo had kept his word to watch over her.

"Here I thought you just enjoyed my company so much that you had to follow me everywhere like a little puppy dog," teased Penelope.

"It is good company for the hour a day when your nose isn't stuck in a book. The rest of the time I might as well be talking to a wall. Hurry up and finish kissing her, Alexis. The food is going cold." Zo gave them a lascivious wink before leaving the room.

"Yeah, Alexis, hurry up and kiss me." Penelope's lips quirked, and he bent down to put his mouth to hers. The claws that had been scratching at his insides retracted, and he drew her closer. When they pulled apart, her cheeks were red enough that her adorable freckles stood out. He liked that she still blushed every time he kissed her.

"Come on, *Signore* Donato, before I decide I'm not going to let you out of this tower after all," she said.

Despite the late hour, Zo had the kitchen table set and wine poured. Phaidros and Aelia were already drinking and snickering together. They had remained civil for the last six weeks which was suspicious but a relief. Alexis didn't have time to hunt priests and stop them from killing each other.

"I didn't think Zo would manage to get you out of that tower once you saw Penelope," Phaidros teased him. Penelope kissed the top of Phaidros's golden curls on her way past.

"Nice to have you back, even if you are a dick," she said affectionately.

"I kept them from getting killed, just as I promised," Aelia said, wrapping Penelope in a rose-scented hug. "Although I was tempted to kill them myself a few times."

"Liar," Phaidros retorted with a smile that Alexis had seen melt women. Aelia, being Aelia, merely rolled her eyes at him.

"Maybe you could've let them take a few pieces off Phaidros," said Penelope. "Make him less pretty."

"Doctor Bryne, I'm shocked that you would condone violence against me. *Me*. Who has loved you since you came to us like a bloody wet rag out of the canal," Phaidros replied.

"That's funny. I'm sure I remember you telling Alexis to kill me."

"I saw what trouble you were going to be, and I was right," he said, kissing her hand.

"Can you believe this rubbish?" Penelope asked Alexis.

"I'm appalled. Get off Penelope, you letch," Alexis said, flicking Phaidros's hand so he was forced to release her.

"This is the thanks I get for watching his back and cleaning up his messes."

"A part of the job," Alexis replied as he sat down.

"What job? If it were a job, I'd be paid."

"Penelope needs wine!" Zo declared, handing her a glass.

"She definitely does, so you all need to stop manhandling her," Penelope replied, taking a large swig.

"You look pale—what have you been doing while we've been gone?" asked Aelia as she rearranged Penelope's curls.

"Hanging out in the Archives, searching and studying."

"And moping. With sad sighs and long stares into the distance." Zo hugged Alexis around the neck. "You should've seen how devastated she was without you."

Penelope stared daggers at Zo. "You're so full of shit. Don't listen to a word he says, Alexis."

"I never do. You have nothing to fear, *cara*."

"Hmph. I can see someone is getting grumpy because he hasn't eaten."

"Well, feed me, man, and stop annoying my Archivist," said Alexis.

"Out of the way," came Lyca's sharp voice, and Penelope and Aelia scattered.

"Thank you," Galenos said as he came in, leaning heavily on a crutch. Alexis hurried to pull out a chair and help him into it. He sent his magic into Galenos's hand, checking on his healing and removing some of his pain.

"I'm glad to see you up and about, old friend," Alexis said.

"He shouldn't be out of bed at all," growled Lyca as she sat beside him.

"She worries," Galenos said, giving them a wink. "I'm so bored in that room. Tell me about your trip." Aelia and Phaidros both looked at Alexis as Zo banged a serving spoon heavily against the table.

"Food first, then drama," he declared. "I won't have Thevetat spoil my tagines."

"You must've really missed me to make tagines," Alexis said with a laugh.

Zo gave him a knowing look. "I had to entice your appetite back somehow when you got here."

Alexis could've kissed him with gratitude as Zo scooped spiced couscous and steaming lamb onto a plate and passed it to him.

"Oh, this takes me back," Aelia said after a mouthful. "I did love Byzantium."

"I could tell by all the emperors you made fall in love with you," Phaidros commented.

"Which emperors?" Penelope's curiosity perked up.

"*All* of them. Even Mehmed mooned over her," said Galenos.

"I'll tell you about my favorites later and maybe even the ones I managed to bed," Aelia told Penelope with a wicked smile.

"Constantine was so smitten, he tried to marry her," grumbled Phaidros. "At least twice."

"I didn't say yes," Aelia said as she reached for flatbread.

Alexis had heard this argument too many times to count, so he ignored them and reached for Penelope's hand under the table. Her warm fingers gently stroked the underside of his wrist, and the sensation muted everything else out to a pleasant buzz.

"Defender!" Lyca snapped.

Alexis glanced up to find everyone at the table looking at him. "What?"

"I asked what happened in Sicily. Was there anything there worth pursuing or do you need me to go and take a look?"

Phaidros came to Alexis's rescue. "The Serpents are still puppets for Abaddon. The ones we interrogated didn't know where he and Kreios are, or that Tony Duilio was the Acolyte. They were used for hired hands, money laundering, that sort of work."

"The only one that knew anything about Thevetat was killed by one of his men, probably something Abaddon had insisted on as a failsafe if they were ever raided so he couldn't be interrogated," said Aelia irritably. "Although what we found in his building made me want to skin the bastard alive."

Phaidros shared a look with Alexis and wisely kept his mouth shut. Phaidros knew exactly who'd killed their leader and it hadn't been one of his men.

"We don't need to talk about it," Alexis warned, his eyes darting to Penelope.

Aelia glared. "Penelope needs to know as much as the rest of us!"

"What did you find?" Penelope asked, her hand tightening over his. The small gesture was enough for Alexis to give Phaidros a small nod to continue.

"He was trafficking women, though I don't know if the rest of the Serpents outside of Palermo knew about it," Phaidros said grimly.

"He imagined himself a priest in training and had constructed a few wannabe sacrifices in the basement where he held the women. Something to keep them afraid. The sick…" Aelia cursed long and elaborately in Greek.

"But you got them out, right?" asked Penelope.

"Of course we did," Alexis assured her. "Aelia called Gisela Bianchi, and she got ahold of the Sicilian authorities. We were gone by the time they got there. The women are safe."

"Alexis lost his temper and burnt down their warehouse," Aelia said with an approving smirk. "I haven't seen vengeful Alexis for a long time."

Alexis stilled, waiting for Penelope to pull away from him in disgust. Unbelievably, she moved closer, comforting him.

"Good," Penelope replied coldly. "The only reason Abaddon can hide so successfully is that he has the money and protection to stay that way. I know you guys believe in going old school and hunting them using magic, but we might be more successful hunting down their assets and shutting them down. It could flush them out."

"She has a point," Galenos said. "I can get started on tracking the Serpents accounts and it might—"

"No. You need to heal," Lyca said. Alexis had seen kings and generals pale when she used that tone on them. Galenos, quiet, gentle Galenos, lifted the terrifying assassin's hand and kissed it.

"I'm healed enough. Besides, you are going to fit me out with a magnificent arm and leg in the next few days. One arm will do in the meantime. I miss my computers and being back at them means I'll find Abaddon sooner for you."

Lyca's silver gaze softened, her red mouth twisting into a savage smile. Galenos knew exactly how to win an argument with his lover.

"You're smithing a new arm and leg?" asked Alexis, wanting to keep the conversation on life and not death.

"Yes, but after getting some ideas from Penelope today, I'm rethinking a few aspects," Lyca said thoughtfully.

"Is that so?"

"Her friend, Tony Stark, made an interesting set of armor. I think I can use some of those components."

Phaidros choked on his wine. "Your friend, Tony Stark, eh?"

"Shut up. It was a good idea," Penelope said stubbornly.

"I agree. It would be an excellent idea to combine that design with Lyca's magic and skill."

Lyca's expression darkened, unable to follow Phaidros's amusement. "It *is* an excellent idea." Her tone was enough to wipe the smile off his face.

"It is good to be home," whispered Alexis to Penelope.

"Are you sure?" she asked, her brow lifting in the direction of the brewing argument.

An hour later Alexis rose from the table, wanting his bed and Penelope in it, when Galenos rested a hand on his arm.

"Don't forget to feed the Guardian. I have heard her singing in my sleep," he said quietly.

"What? She hasn't done that in centuries."

"Zo was too afraid to see her. I think she is lonely."

"I am not! Reitia just likes Alexis better. She'll barely bother to turn up if he's not there," Zo defended.

"Another woman infatuated with Alexis. Why am I not surprised?" Penelope gave an amused smile.

"This woman is exceptionally bad-tempered when she's not visited and fed. I have something ready for you," said Zo as he carried the dirty plates to the sink.

"Now I'm *definitely* intrigued." Penelope looked at Alexis expectedly.

"I don't know if I should take you," he said. God knows how Reitia would react to a newcomer after such a long time.

Zo snorted. "Do it. I bet Penelope has never seen a sea monster before."

FOUR

"*A* REAL SEA monster? Or is this some kind of pet name that Zo has for her because she scorned him once?" Penelope asked as she followed Alexis and Zo through the kitchen and into a large, cool room.

"Reitia isn't a monster. Zo's saying that because he's terrified of her," explained Alexis.

Zo pulled on a heavy, steel door. "With good reason! She's tried to eat me on more than one occasion."

"It's how you know she likes you." Alexis winked at Penelope, and she hid a grin.

"I suppose I shouldn't be surprised that you're friends with a leviathan."

"*Cara*, you have only known me for a few short months. I would be worried if I stopped surprising you in such an embarrassingly short period of time." Alexis bent down to give her a soft kiss, and Zo made a frustrated sound at the back of his throat.

"Kiss Penelope later. I got Reitia a lamb. She likes lamb, doesn't she?"

"She likes pork better," said Alexis.

"Probably because it tastes more like human flesh." Zo pointed to a carcass hanging from a hook. "You need help carrying it?"

Alexis gave him a long, disbelieving look before he started unbuttoning his shirt.

Penelope tried not to stare as Alexis's golden-brown muscle was revealed, along with his magical, ever-changing tattoos. Completely unaware of the effect he was having on her, Alexis passed her the still-warm fabric. She placed it over her arm with a smile, fighting the urge to lift it to her nose and inhale the spicy cinnamon and sandalwood aroma that she had missed almost as much as the rest of him.

With an easy strength, Alexis lifted the carcass off the hook and slung it over a shoulder.

"Let's just hope she's around tonight," he said as Zo and Penelope moved out of his way.

"So how does one become acquainted with a sea monster?" Penelope asked as she followed Alexis out of the palazzo and through the inner courtyard.

"Reitia is the goddess of Venice. She was living here in this series of inlets long before any of us," he explained. "After we came here from Alexandria in 49 BC, we started to hear rumors of the goddess from the Veneti. They would leave offerings to her of flowers and food on certain days and would seek her counsel in matters of dispensing justice. If the crimes were bad enough, she would act as executioner. Offending such a goddess wasn't in our best interests, so we sought her out. We have an understanding; if she doesn't attack humans, we keep her fed on the meat that she can't obtain for herself. Despite what Zo says, she's always protected the seas around Venice and has never had much interest in eating its fishermen."

"If she's been here that long, where has she been hiding? A creature that big would be noticed."

"At one time, she was living in a secret cavity under the Punta della Dogana on the Grand Canal. She's a wily old creature and doubtlessly has more than one hole to hide in."

"That's kind of terrifying."

"She's a sweet thing, really, once you get to know her. The only real malice she has toward anything is the cruise boats."

"Like all Venetians," said Penelope.

"Don't laugh. I've spent quite a lot of time trying to convince her not to attack them. She didn't like it when the Arsenale started their production of the Venetian fleet either, so it's been a centuries-long battle with her."

"You're lucky she doesn't eat *you* for your impertinence, always telling her what to do."

"What can I say? I'm convincing in an argument." Alexis smiled over his shoulder, and Penelope knew exactly how convincing he could be.

They walked through the floating gardens until they came to a series of steps that led down into the dark, choppy waters of the canal.

"Try not to scream when she comes." Alexis flashed her a smile before stepping down into the canal.

Penelope's heart began to race, seeing him enter the water. Suddenly, she was back at the Lido inlet, pulling his cold body from the sea. Her fists clenched tightly at her sides as she tried to control her rising panic. *He's going to be fine.*

Something inside her stilled as Alexis's magic pulsed out into the water. The waves and wind died around them, though Penelope could still see boats being tossed about across the canal. Her own scrap of magic fizzed, and lights flashed under her skin, leaving a word on her hand; δράκων. It shivered and changed again, *Drákōn.*

Before it changed a third time, she heard a voice in the wind. It started off as the faintest whisper, and as she strained to hear it, she realized it wasn't entering through her ears but dropping directly into her mind.

"Alexis?" she asked uncertainly, looking around.

"It's okay, Penelope. Trust me." He had stopped moving, the water lapping at his waist. He didn't look cold, even though she was shivering from the damp wind. He stood perfectly still as the water around him began to shudder.

The song in Penelope's head grew louder as a long line of ripples stretched out and shadowy fins rose to the surface. Penelope's breath caught in her throat as a dark, blue-and-black head the size of a small car emerged from the water. Large, golden eyes studied them with a curious glow.

"Dragon…" Penelope whispered.

Defender, the voice in her head purred. *Home for mere hours and you are already bringing me treats. This is why you are my favorite.*

"My lady, I apologize for the lamb. Zo has been distracted of late."

Why does he not visit me? I like his scent on my tongue. A huge tongue licked her lips, and Penelope smothered a laugh. The sea dragon had a crush; no wonder Zo was afraid.

Reitia took the lamb from Alexis all the same, chewing it with a crunching of bones before she carefully licked the blood off his shoulder. Ever the gentleman, Alexis gave her a bow of thanks.

I see you have finally found your lover, Defender. Reitia's large, golden eyes rested on Penelope. On her list of things that would never happen to her, being assessed as girlfriend material by a sea dragon was at the top. Not knowing what else to do, Penelope gave the dragon a short bow.

"It's an honor to meet you, goddess," she said politely. Reitia swam closer to where Penelope stood, and she tried not to run away as the fanged mouth hovered over her head. Reitia bent down and sniffed her.

She loves you, Defender. That is good, considering the light that binds you together. She smells of the sea and new magic and female arousal. You chose well.

"She chose me," Alexis corrected.

Your male smugness tells me you are pleased about it, too.

"All men should be so lucky to find such a woman."

Neither Penelope nor Alexis had mentioned the L word, and as for female arousal…Penelope contemplated throwing herself into the canal before she died of embarrassment.

Defender, what is happening in my city? I feel darkness growing within it, Reitia said, her long tail curling around Alexis.

"We rooted it out weeks ago. There were priests of an old religion doing magic here, but they have left now."

No, it is still here, and it's growing.

"Can you tell us where it's coming from?" asked Penelope.

Cannaregio. Even the fish are not swimming near it now.

"We will find the source, I promise," Alexis said, placing a hand on Reitia's slick scales.

Bring them to me for justice, Defender. This is old magic, and it will be settled in the old ways. It wasn't a request, but a command, and Penelope felt the edges of the creature's teeth in it.

Without a goodbye, Reitia slunk beneath the waves and disappeared into the night. With a curse under his breath, Alexis climbed from the water.

"She likes you," he said, but his deep-blue eyes were filled with worry.

"I'm not the one she licked. You smell like a fishing boat." Penelope wrinkled her nose.

His lips rose in a cheeky smile. "Well, Reitia was very clear on what *you* smell like." Before she could protest, he pulled her close and they portaled back into her room.

"Ew, now I need a shower," Penelope complained as she pulled away from him, her sweater smeared with sea dragon saliva.

"Me too. Come to find me after," Alexis said before disappearing once more.

IT WAS almost dawn by the time Penelope pulled a robe over her pajamas and went to find Alexis. The palazzo had expanded her rooms, and now she had a reading alcove filled with her books from Melbourne along with the rest of her possessions.

It turned out that Zo was a master of overseas relocation, and Penelope's things had arrived within a fortnight from the cluttered flat she had shared with Carolyn. Seeing all of her gear unpacked had caused Penelope a momentary heart attack, the full realization of what she had done hitting her. The discomfort had lasted only as long as it took for her to reach the Archives, its existence a solid reminder of one of the reasons she'd stayed.

Penelope found her other reason sitting on a meditation cushion on his balcony, looking out over the city.

Sitting in profile, his shoulder-length black hair tousled by the wind, Alexis seemed out of place in the modern world. It was easy for her to forget how old he was, how many empires he had seen rise and fall, how many of his friends he had buried, and yet he couldn't always hide it from his eyes.

Without a word, Alexis lifted the corner of the blanket around his shoulders and Penelope snuggled under it, tangling her arms and legs with his.

"Are you okay?" she asked softly.

The other magicians hadn't seemed to notice the shadows under his eyes or how uncomfortable he looked as they had discussed Sicily. She had felt his tension while the others spoke of war, knew the burden placed upon him. Now, he had Reitia's warning about Cannaregio to worry about as well. Penelope could sense his anger and grief through their tie, but she didn't know how to alleviate it.

"I thought we could watch the sunrise together. I won't be able to sleep until the sun comes up anyway," he said, pressing his lips to her temple.

"Sicily was that bad?"

"Yes, and I've seen enough wars to know that it's only the beginning."

Penelope tightened her arms around him. "I've got your back, magician. No matter what. I might not be good in a firefight, but you know I'll help you any way that I can."

His eyes closed at her words, and he kissed her hand. "Thank you, *cara*."

They watched the sun spread fingers of light over the terra-cotta roofs and gray-blue water, before Alexis carried a drowsy Penelope to bed, curling around her and finally falling asleep to the sound of the first church bells.

PENELOPE EXPECTED to wake that afternoon draped over a gorgeous magician. Instead, she woke alone. A note on the bedside table explained how Alexis had gone to train with Lyca. Her phone buzzed on the bedside table, and she read over the message with bleary eyes. With a sigh, she pressed the dial button.

"*Buongiorno*, Marco," she said with a yawn.

"*Dio*, are you only just waking up?"

"I stayed up and watched the sunrise with Alexis."

Marco made a disgusted sound. "I don't need to know what you and Donato were up until sunrise doing. We need to talk. What are you up to now?"

"Nothing. Do you want to swing by the palazzo for a late breakfast?" Penelope asked. Marco had been a visitor on more than one occasion in the past few weeks. The palazzo's wards let him in, and generally behaved while he was around.

"Is *la Dea* home too?" Marco asked hopefully.

"Yes, the goddess Aelia is here. So is Phaidros, by the way," Penelope warned. Aelia was a shameless flirt when it came to Marco, and Penelope worried about her leading the inspector on and breaking his heart. He was Penelope's friend, and she didn't want Phaidros stabbing him with the nearest sharp object because Marco smiled a little too much at Aelia.

Marco merely clicked his tongue. "He'll get over it. I'll be there soon."

PENELOPE WAS making coffee in the kitchen when two arms snaked around her and a whiskery kiss pressed against her neck.

"She finally wakes," Alexis teased.

Penelope turned in his arms and ran an appreciative eye over the navy-blue knit sweater he wore. "You don't look like you've been training."

"I trained and showered *hours* ago, that's why."

"Of course you did. Why didn't you wake me?"

"You were tired, and Zo said you've barely been sleeping. Would you like to talk about that?"

"No, I don't. Zo needs to stop gossiping like an old *nonna* and mind his own sleeping patterns."

"You shouldn't have been so worried about us—"

"Don't tell me not to worry—you died in my arms a month ago!" Penelope exploded, the frustration she had been carefully holding in for weeks unexpectedly bursting out of her. "I know I'm not some magical warrior like Lyca, and I can't go on these missions with you. I know you have to fight if we're going to stand a chance of stopping Thevetat... Just don't expect me to pretend that it doesn't bother me that you're risking your life out there. Don't say it doesn't matter that you could be hurt, because it's your mystical, bullshit higher calling to be the *Defender*. I don't give a damn about that, I give a damn about *you*—"

Alexis's eyes glowed hot as he pulled her to him, kissing her so deeply that she dropped the jar of coffee she was holding. She pushed her hands through his dark curls and pulled him closer. *He's okay he's okay he's okay.* She repeated the words like a mantra, hoping she would soon believe it.

A discreet cough from the doorway made her jump back.

"I was going to ask you for a coffee, but you seem to be all out," said Marco with an amused expression.

"We have more," Alexis replied, his eyes still fixed on Penelope even as he snapped his fingers and the coffee grains from the floor vanished.

"Handy trick. Don't feed me floor coffee, *per favore*. My day has been bad enough." Marco chuckled.

Penelope moved Alexis's hand from where he gripped the bench behind her, freeing herself so she could go and kiss both of Marco's cheeks.

"What's wrong? You look tired," she commented.

"Some of us don't get to sleep all day, *Dottore*."

"Why don't you two go and sit in the day room, and I'll make the coffee," Alexis suggested, waving them out. His eyes were still hot, and he looked as if he were struggling to be polite about the interruption. Penelope gave him a flirty smile behind Marco's back as she led him out of the kitchen.

"How's the construction work on the Arsenale offices progressing?" Penelope asked as they sat down on the soft lounge chairs.

"They are up and running again with the new renovations, the builders making quick work of it. Donato's anonymous donation has ensured any damage from the bombing is taken care of. Even though Duilio's dead, the bombings have had their effect on Venice. DIGOS is reassessing the city for potential target areas, and we still can't find the place Duilio did his magic. We turned up nothing from what was left of his apartment."

"Keep looking," Alexis said, bringing in a tray with their coffees and biscotti. "I heard from a source last night that there is still a dark presence in the city."

"Anything else? Some Venetians would say a cruise boat is a dark presence."

"Focus on Cannaregio," Penelope replied before sipping her coffee. She took a moment to savor it before swallowing. No one made coffee like Alexis; he had tried to teach her, but she didn't get anywhere close to the same result.

"We are still trying to sort out the scandal and financial trail Duilio left behind, and nothing has pointed to investment properties there. I will see if anything is flagged in his real estate portfolio, if I can get a copy of it."

"If you do find a property listing, don't make a move on it without one of us with you," Alexis said. "We don't know what kind of traps will be set, and I don't want any more *polizia* or civilians being hurt."

"You don't have to keep warning me. Gisela thanks you for your help in Sicily, by the way. She checked in this morning to say that they have arrested the Serpent members that you left tied up. Having their victims guard them was an interesting choice. You're lucky they didn't pull them to pieces." Marco frowned with disapproval.

Alexis gave a nonchalant shrug. "I didn't know who in the Sicilian police the Serpents had paid off. The women promised not to kill them and to wait for Gisela and her team. All I did was give them a chance to regain their power over their oppressors. That's necessary for anyone who has been a victim. I don't particularly care if they slapped the bastards around a bit. They deserve a lot worse than whatever was done to them."

"Remember the conversation we had about you working *with* us and not acting like a vigilante, Donato?" Marco said coolly.

"Do *you* remember the part where I said that I don't care?"

"Now, boys, play nice. We have enough enemies to fight without bickering with each other," Aelia purred as she came into the room. Marco jerked to his feet at once, and Aelia offered him her cheeks to kiss.

"*Mia Dia*, I'm relieved to see you unharmed after your adventures," he said warmly.

Aelia smiled at him. "You are too sweet, Inspector Dandolo."

"Aelia wanted to give the women guns. Aren't you glad I was there to stop her?" commented Alexis.

Marco frowned playfully at her. "*Bella*, you know you aren't allowed to give weapons to civilians even if they do know how to use them."

Aelia's violet eyes turned sultry. "I know, I know. You can put me in cuffs and punish me if you feel like it." Penelope choked on her biscotti as Marco's smile widened.

"Don't bother. Aelia knows how to get out of them." Phaidros's cool voice cut through the room. "We all know if you really want to punish her, all you need to do is ignore her."

"So you survived as well," Marco said, not bothering to hide his disappointment.

"Did you miss me too?" Phaidros imitated Aelia's sexy tone as he flopped into Marco's empty chair.

"Behave yourselves," Zo chided, appearing through the blue front door, balancing an armful of mail and a box. "Mail for you, Penelope. *Buongiorno*, Marco, have you made Phaidros cry yet?"

"Not yet, but I haven't been here long. How are you, Zo? Would you like a hand?" Marco moved to close the door and offered to take the box.

"*Grazie*. Perhaps you can teach these animals some manners," Zo said, pushing his sunglasses on top of his curly hair.

"Good luck. I've been trying for centuries," murmured Alexis.

"Looks like someone loves you," Marco said, passing Penelope the box.

"I doubt it," she said with a frown. There were stamps and forwarding address redirections on it from all over the world until she found one that looked familiar. "Tel Aviv! What are you sending me now, Tim?"

"Who's Tim?" Aelia asked suspiciously.

"An old uni buddy. He was working in Qumran in a new cave the last time I talked to him. It's one of our traditions to send each other kooky crap when we are on a dig," Penelope explained as she ripped the tape off the box. She took one look inside and burst out laughing. "You're such a wanker, Tim Sanders." She pulled out a plastic money box shaped like Jesus, his wounded hands stretched wide. "He knows I don't approve of creepy, white Catholic Jesus."

"The real Jesus certainly wasn't white," Alexis said, looking at the gift. "You have interesting friends, Penelope."

"Yeah, he's a weirdo. He used to date Carolyn before she got sick of his shit."

Penelope turned the money box over in her hands and heard something trapped inside. She twisted the plastic cap off the bottom, and a tightly rolled scroll fell out with a note written in a shaky script:

HAWKES, YOU HAVE TO HIDE IT. THEY ARE COMING FOR ME.

"What the hell, Tim?" Penelope reached for the ancient scroll. Before her fingers touched it, Alexis tackled her to the floor, and the room exploded with light and magic.

FIVE

"WHAT WAS *THAT?*" Penelope mumbled against Alexis's shoulder. Her ears were ringing as he eased off her and helped her to her feet. Zo had gotten Marco out of the way, and Phaidros was gripping Aelia tightly behind him, shielding her against the blast.

"It was nasty, whatever it was. Who did you say sent it to you?" Zo asked, leaning closer to examine the scroll. Alexis moved him out of the way, and a shield of blue light appeared, coating the length of the scroll.

"Tim's an archaeologist. There's no way he could have placed any magic on it," Penelope replied. She looked at the quality of the parchment, her unease growing.

"Is he into black market antiquities? Because that's an old scroll. Remarkable condition, but very old," Zo pointed out.

"We need to get it down to the Archives and see what it says," Penelope said.

Marco cleared his throat. "I need to get back to work. Tony Duilio's lawyer is due to fly in, and from our brief phone conversations, I don't think she's going to make wrapping up this case easy. Let's catch up later, Penelope. You look like you're going to have your hands full today. You're still wearing the pendant, right?" He raised a dark brow, and Penelope pulled the pendant of Saint Mark out of her shirt. "Good. I feel like you're going to need his protection today. *Ciao, Dottore.*"

She kissed his cheeks. "I'll be fine. *Ciao*, Marco."

"I'll show you out," Aelia insisted as she looped her arm around his.

Alexis was still frowning at the scroll. Penelope knelt down and picked up the scrap of paper from Tim.

"Why would he send me this? Tim is dedicated to his job and obsessed with the Dead Sea Scrolls. He would've had to have been really scared to smuggle anything off a dig site," she said. *Unless he didn't trust the people on the dig and wanted to protect it from them.*

"Let's get it downstairs and see if we can clear this curse that's on it. Maybe whatever is inside will tell us why it was worth the risk," Alexis suggested. He waved his hand over it, and the shield lifted the scroll into the air. "You come too, Zo. If it's from Qumran, you'll be able to give us extra insight."

"You lived at Qumran?" Penelope asked as they stepped into the elevator.

"Both Alexis and I were interested in Qumran, though I stayed with the Essenes more than once. We both have spent a lot of time in the Near East over the years," Zo said.

"What were you doing with the Essenes? I didn't peg either one of you as religious types, and they were next-level Orthodox." So much so that they had severed all ties to the Temple in Jerusalem, viewing it as corrupt, and had chosen to start a new community in the middle of the desert.

"We were interested in their magic, such as it was," Alexis answered as they walked through the stacks to Penelope's office.

"He was there for the magic; *I* was there for the poetry," said Zo with a dreamy smile. "One thing you need to learn about Alexis is that he's always investigating *something*. You should tell her the story of how you met them."

"Another time, perhaps. Let's focus on the scroll for now," Alexis insisted.

Reaching her office, Penelope turned on her lightbox and Alexis placed the scroll on top of it.

"What do you think of this curse, Zo? Anything you've seen before?" he asked.

Zo whispered something under his breath, and bright-orange symbols appeared around the scroll, glowing in intricate patterns.

"Oh yeah, this is definitely from Qumran. You know how crazy protective they were of their secrets and their writings," Zo said as he studied the symbols. "This must be one of their 'mad' curses I heard so much about. The kind that if you touch or read something without knowing how to disable the curse, it will literally drive you mad. You could know the secrets of the universe, but you'd be too crazy to be able to tell anyone. If you could, no one would believe you, anyway."

"If that's the case, how come none of the other works that have been found have had curses on them? They have been researching the Scrolls since they were first discovered in 1946," Penelope pointed out.

"Much of what has been found are scraps and old drafts," said Alexis. "The repository of information the Essenes really had was beyond anything that's been found to date. Where exactly would your friend have been digging to find such a thing?"

"I got an email back in February saying that they had found a new cave. It was still when I was unemployed, and Tim asked me to join the dig even though it's not my field. He needed someone experienced on the site and a lateral thinker, but I turned him down."

"Why?" Zo asked. "I thought this kind of mystery would really appeal to you."

"In a word? Carolyn. They had broken up a few months before-hand and even though we've all been friends since we were under-grads, I didn't want to run off to the desert with him. He's a good guy, but he can be...high-maintenance. They *both* can be. I didn't want to end up caught in the middle of their fights any more than what I already was."

The truth was, no matter how brilliant he was, Tim was obsessive-compulsive when he was on a dig, and Penelope would've spent her time babysitting him to make sure he ate and slept and didn't drink so much. They had once been on a dig in Greece for practical experience, and he'd gone missing in action entirely. They had gone out drinking one night, and Penelope had gotten a call four days later from him in Istanbul. He didn't know how he'd gotten there, but he'd had a great time doing it. Despite how much she loved him, Carolyn had broken up with him because her mental health couldn't handle him any longer.

"Ah! There it is," declared Zo, pointing to a symbol that glowed a little brighter than the others.

"That's the link?" Alexis asked.

"I'm sure of it. Want me to take the curse off?"

Alexis gently maneuvered Penelope behind him. "Go ahead."

The rosemary and leather smell of Zo's magic filled the air as he sung something low, in a language Penelope didn't know.

"What is that? Hebrew?" she whispered.

"Aramaic," Alexis replied.

The symbols glowed with golden light before they unraveled, like a thread in a weaving had been pulled, and the magic disappeared.

"It should be okay now," Zo said, and Alexis removed the shields around it. Penelope got a piece of weighted glass, and as Zo carefully unrolled the short scroll, she placed the glass over it, trapping the delicate papyrus beneath the light.

"Wow…" She exhaled, leaning closer. "What did you find this time, Tim?" It was written in Hebrew, and by the growing messiness of the writing, the scribe had been rushing to finish it. "What do you think, Alexis?"

He leaned down over her shoulder and studied it. "Can you read it, Penelope?"

"No…I…" Penelope's eyes went wide. "I can't read it! Why isn't the translation working?" She studied her hands: no glowing lights, no tingle of magic under her skin.

"Don't get too upset. I told you the Essenes had tricks for protecting their writing. Move aside." Zo moved them both out of the way. "I'll write you up a translation. I'm going to need a notebook and a pen." Penelope grabbed them off her desk, while Alexis pulled up a chair for Zo to sit on.

"It might take me a while," Zo warned. "My Second Temple period Hebrew isn't what it used to be."

Penelope sat down on her chaise lounge and put her head in her hands. "Bloody Tim. Why would he send me this? Why not report it or give it to the Shrine of the Book in Jerusalem? He can be a pain in the ass, but he believes in keeping antiquities in their own countries."

Alexis sat down beside her and placed a comforting arm around her shoulders. "He was scared, this much we know. Do you have a number for him that you could call? He could've sent it to you because he knew it would be safe with you if he was in trouble."

"That's the thing. Tim is nearly always in trouble, but never enough to smuggle antiquities."

"If the curse on the scroll passed to him, he might also be imagining threats that aren't there," Alexis said as gently as possible.

"God, he's going to have no idea what's happening to him." Penelope pulled her phone out of her back pocket, called Tim's number, and got his answering machine. "Pick up your freaking phone, Carter, it's important," she said before hanging up. "He can go off the grid when he's unstable. He usually takes his phone with him though, even if he leaves it off."

"What about Carolyn?" Zo asked from the other side of the room. "You might want to make sure he didn't send her anything either. If he has and it's from the same site, it could have a similar curse on it."

"Damn it. Tim is a dangerous subject with her." Penelope pressed her contacts list. "This is most definitely going to piss—hey, Caro! You got five minutes?"

"You don't call me for nearly two weeks, and you only want me for five minutes? You are such a cheapskate, Bryne," Carolyn answered.

"Yeah, sorry about that. I've been kind of busy."

"Getting busy with a hot Italian babe more like," Carolyn countered, loud enough for the others to hear. Zo snickered, while Alexis raised an eyebrow at Penelope. She quickly got up and headed out of her office.

"What I've been doing is working my ass off to be good at my new job. All that's irrelevant right now. Look, I hate to ask, but have you talked to Tim lately?"

Carolyn's warm tone vanished instantly. "No. Why would I? I'm too old and smart to keep burning a candle for that bastard. Why do you ask?"

"I received a present from him in the mail, and it was a bit odd."

"That's nothing new. You guys always send each other crap trinkets for laughs."

"I have a bad feeling, and I can't get through to him on his phone. He's a bastard, I know. I'm still worried about him."

"Wait…I'm going to need wine for this conversation," Carolyn said. There was a clatter of glasses and the pop of a cork.

"Isn't it a work night?"

"Don't lecture me, Bryne. Tim's MIA again? Is that what you're telling me?"

"Yeah, I think so. Do you have a number for the guys running the dig? An email maybe?"

"He might have left something with all of his other boxes of crap. I'll have to dig around for it. At least you cleaned your stuff out properly when you moved. Do you know how long ago the package was sent?"

"A couple of weeks ago from Tel Aviv," Penelope guessed. "Why? Is that important?"

"I got a bunch of calls from him around that time. I ignored them because I didn't want to have to deal with his bullshit. The messages he left were…well, I thought he was high on something. He kept babbling about something he'd found and the voices in his head. He thought he was being followed. I thought he was just shit-faced on a break, so I deleted them."

"He didn't sound scared?"

"Maybe a little? I honestly thought he was on a bad trip and he'd sleep it off," said Carolyn, edges of real concern creeping into her voice. "Oh shit, Pen, you don't think he's actually being followed? Who has he pissed off now?"

"I don't know anything for sure. I need to track Tim down to check he's okay. I'm sure it's my gut playing up and nothing serious."

"Let me find the numbers of the other dig members, make some calls, and I'll get back to you."

"Okay. Don't freak out just yet. I'm sure he's fine. You know, typical Tim shit," Penelope said, doing her best to sound upbeat.

"You're a bad liar. I'll be in touch."

Penelope hung up and stifled a groan. Carolyn was definitely going to be freaking out.

Alexis was waiting for Penelope by her office door. He held out a hand to her, and she slid easily into his embrace.

"How was she?" he asked, his fingers stroking her shoulder blades.

"Pissed. As predicted," Penelope replied. She breathed him in, enjoying the warm feeling of him pressed against her.

"Hopefully she'll be able to track him down, and we'll be able to find out what really happened at the site," Alexis said.

"Tim loves to party, and he's a happy drunk. He wouldn't do anything to warrant having people after him. The dig he was on had philanthropic funding. It was legitimate. Could the curse make him crazy enough to hallucinate people after him?"

Alexis brushed his hand gently through her curls. "I honestly don't know, *cara*. If it was strong enough, anything is possible."

"Hey, you two," Zo called from inside. "Stop mooning at each other. We have a problem."

"What is it?" Penelope asked as she hurried to join him.

"I don't want to alarm you, but I think I just found the followers of Thevetat in a prophecy, and maybe us, too," said Zo, rubbing his eyes.

"Damn it, not again," said Alexis with a sigh.

"What do you mean 'not again?' How many times have you been caught up in a prophecy?" asked Penelope.

"A few. You can't live as long as us and not get involved in at least one," Alexis replied vaguely.

"He's being modest. We've been in a lot of them, and they are a pain in the ass every time. The oracles at Delphi were the worst. They gave Phaidros such a hard time that he left Greece for three hundred years. I was caught up in one in Egypt that led to the Nile flooding. Aelia wiped out the Mayans on her own—"

"She gets the idea. You don't need to frighten her," said Alexis.

"I'm not frightened. A little surprised, that's all."

"Well, *bella*, you're not truly one of us until you get written into a prophecy," said Zo with a laugh.

"We will stop annoying you and leave you to it. We won't know what's happening with Tim until we do," said Alexis.

"Fine. Dismiss me. I'll come up when I'm ready." Zo gave Penelope a sly wink. "Welcome to the family, sister."

IT WAS nine o'clock when Zo left the Archives with a pile of notes. Deprived of his culinary expertise, Penelope and the other magicians had put together antipasto platters of whatever they found in the kitchen.

"Here, you look like you need this," Phaidros said, offering Zo a glass of wine. Zo took a mouthful and made a face.

"What is this swill? Are you trying to kill me after all the hard work I've been doing?" Zo demanded, before going to a wine rack and retrieving a different bottle. Penelope tried not to smile at his offended palate. To her, wine was wine.

"This is what happens when I try and do something nice," Phaidros said, sighing.

"The kitchen is not your place of strength, but you can give my aching shoulders a massage later if you want to help," said Zo.

"I don't feel like being *that* nice to you."

"How did it go?" Alexis asked once Zo had settled himself at the table.

"Two things: first, the scribe who wrote it was scared of being discovered, and second, I think the priests of Thevetat wiped out the Essenes."

From her first trip to the area with Tim, Penelope knew it was still one of the archaeological mysteries of the area. Being from a sect of pre-Rabbinic Judaism, the Essenes were a close community dedicated to purity, studying the mysteries and law of the Torah, as well as astronomy and other scholarly pursuits. They didn't have enemies eager to destroy them and weren't warmongers themselves, so the prevailing theory of their disappearance was a combination of famine and the strictness of the community. They had simply died away from lack of members.

"Why go after the Essenes, though? They were desert dwellers who just wanted to be left alone. They wouldn't have had anything that Abaddon would want," said Aelia.

"Except for their ability to produce accurate prophecies. It's a skill Abaddon was fascinated with even on Atlantis," Alexis replied thoughtfully.

"It gets better," Zo said as he passed Alexis his translation. Alexis skimmed it rapidly.

"Are you *sure*, Zotikos?" he demanded.

"Positive. I've been pouring over it for the last six hours to be sure."

Alexis passed the paper to Penelope.

"Read it out, Penelope. The suspense is killing me," Phaidros said in a bored tone as he poured more wine.

"'A vision has come to me of the hour when the Sons of Light, the sacred community, are defeated at the hands of the Prince of Darkness, Thevetat, brother demon to Belial. As perfect light, you have revealed yourself to me, to show me that the light will endure. The old ones shall come forth, those from the Ancient Priesthood, from the days before Melchizedek. Light ones and keepers of the mysteries, from them will come those who will defend the Light when the Prince of Darkness and the false priesthood will rise again. The ancient ones will use a gift from the hand of the Prince of Heaven, the seal of the King, who was blessed with the wisdom of all things, and the cursed one will be banished from this kingdom and back to his world of ash and death. You, O God, will reject every plan of this darkness, and your counsel alone shall stand, and the plan of your heart shall remain forever,'" Penelope read aloud. She sat back in her chair, hands shaking. "Holy crap. Tim found a prophecy."

"My thoughts exactly," said Zo. "It lacks their usual long, florid style, but you can tell by how quick and messy the writing is that the scribe didn't have time. Something or someone was attacking them. Hell of a time to get a vision of the future. We need to find out more about how your friend Tim got his hands on this."

Aelia sighed. "Sons of Light, ancient priesthoods, a king blessed with all wisdom? Which king? Sounds like typical cryptic prophecy drama bullshit to me."

"Just what we need right now," muttered Phaidros.

Penelope didn't care that it was a prophecy or a great archaeological find, all of her thoughts were on Tim. He was frightened, possibly cursed, and had people hunting him. *Who could he have pissed off this time?*

SIX

PENELOPE PACED THE halls of the palazzo, allowing them to stretch and move around her without paying much attention to where she was going. She kept checking her phone for messages from Carolyn, but it remained ominously silent.

Curses, illegal scrolls, and cryptic instructions swirled around her head, magnifying her worry for Tim. If he was under a madness curse, there was no way he would know it. They needed to find him—and fast—before he hurt himself or others.

"Would you like some company?" Alexis appeared from a hallway, his blue eyes filled with concern.

Penelope held out her hand to him, and he took it. "I'm sure I'm walking in circles. I can't sit still so I'm all about pacing."

"Talk to me."

"I can't help thinking that if I had been at the dig, Tim wouldn't have gotten himself into this epic mess. I've always been the most responsible of the three of us. I kept an eye out for Carolyn who's always been a bit off with the pixies, and Tim, who's always had a problem with substance abuse."

"As someone who has also been responsible for others, I know how you are feeling. I also know there is only so much control you can have over other people's actions."

"What if the scroll was right and Abaddon or one of his acolytes wiped out the Essenes? If they've been watching the Qumran digs, Tim could've been captured by them on top of having a madness curse." Penelope pushed a hand through her hair in frustration.

"If they have him, we will find them, kill them, and take him back," Alexis replied calmly. He drew her closer and kissed the top of her head. "We'll figure it out, Penelope. I promise you."

"I'm going to have to go to Israel to find him. I don't want to go without you, but I know you can't drop your leads from the Tony Duilio case to go and find my messed-up mate."

"Of course we will go with you if it comes to that. You're jumping too many steps ahead, Penelope. You can't decide anything until Carolyn gets back to you, so *breathe*." Alexis wrapped his arms around her. "You are not breathing."

Penelope took a big, exaggerated breath and burst out laughing when he tickled her side. "Stop that!"

"It stopped you worrying, didn't it?"

"Did not. You can continue to try and distract me if you want to," Penelope said as they began walking again.

"Tell me about the books you've been reading. I take it you decrypted my messages?"

They walked and talked, discussing everything from Da Vinci's lost diaries, the Citadel of Magicians on Atlantis, the bull pits of Knossos, and exactly how far the Phoenicians really went on their travels. The palazzo gently steered them back to the tower where Penelope first pulled out Nereus's astrolabe.

"I figured it out. You could've told me there was a sealing spell on it and saved me a lot of headaches," she said, placing the astrolabe into his hand.

"It wasn't my puzzle to solve," Alexis replied with a shrug. "Would you like to see what else it can do?"

"Moving forward, just assume I want to see everything involving magic," Penelope replied, following him to his workbench.

He put the astrolabe onto the wooden surface and opened it. Twisting the dials on one side, he opened each of the rings and, as they aligned, a shimmering projection of the world hovered over the device, surrounded by seven golden rings.

"They all converge on this one point," Alexis said, pointing to the glowing nexus of lines over Venice. "It's because we are all here. If the magicians were in different countries, their points would align over their locations."

"I wondered how she tracked them!" Penelope looked closer, running her fingers over the brilliant illusion. "Can you adjust it to track the magical tide as well?"

Alexis lowered the rings and flipped them to the other half of the astrolabe until only the glowing side of the Tide remained. Faint blue lines wrapped around the globe until it was covered in a pulsing web of light.

Penelope breathed an appreciative sigh. "It's so beautiful. I never knew there would be so many. It's like a network."

"That's a very good comparison," Alexis said.

"And when Atlantis sank, this was what was thrown out of whack?"

"Yes. As you read in that book a few weeks ago, the pyramids we built helped redistribute power so that magic could flow again and make up for the loss of Atlantis."

"And what does the high tide really mean? More magic?"

"So much magic that these current channels won't be enough to hold it, so new ones will be created. Like when a river bursts its banks and creates new streams. Magic will be found in places that it never has been before. When the tide goes down, the smaller streams will dry out again."

As Alexis went on about the magical energy and how it could be manipulated, Penelope rested her chin on her hand, enjoying the lecture. She didn't think she would ever tire of watching him, listening to his theories and stories, expressive hands dancing. A dull ache of emotion throbbed in her chest when she realized just how much she'd missed him; teacher, friend, lover.

"What are you smiling at?" Alexis asked, stopping midsentence.

"You. Just…you," she struggled to explain.

He ran his fingers up her forearm, tangling them in the tips of her hair. He leaned down to kiss her when her phone rang, making them both jerk in surprise.

Alexis sighed. "I think the universe is conspiring to keep me from kissing you tonight."

"Hold that thought," Penelope said as she answered her phone. "Carolyn, any luck?"

"I've been on the phone with a guy called Schaal, the professor overseeing Tim's dig. Tim's definitely missing in action. Schaal left him in the desert by himself—first mistake; you know what he's like when he's manic and left alone—and turns out Tim had a breakthrough. There was a hidden wall in Cave 12."

"You're joking! A hidden wall? Was anything left behind?"

"Bones. The scribe had buried himself alive. Tim left the remains where they were, but Schaal received a drunken message saying that he'd found a jar with the body. He flew back to Israel straightaway, but Tim was already gone. The remnants of the jar were still in his hotel room, but its contents were missing."

"Oh, God. Any idea where he's gone?"

Carolyn's gruff tone vanished as she burst into tears. "No! I don't know why I'm surprised, or even bloody crying. That man is such an asshole!"

"Yeah, he is. We still have to find him," Penelope said gently.

"Pen, you know I hate to get you involved in this, but I need your help."

"Tim involved me in this. We'll find him, I promise. Alexis knows some people and—"

"I'm going after him. Don't try and talk me out of it. I know how he thinks when he gets like this. I know where he hangs out and the type of trouble he likes to find. I don't want anyone else involved just yet. I don't want him getting into more trouble," Carolyn said, her voice steady once more.

"You're not doing it on your own. Come to Venice. We can travel to Israel together. I don't want you doing this by yourself, and I have friends here who can help us," Penelope insisted.

"I don't want to crash your life."

"Don't even start that shit with me, Carolyn Williams. Get your ass on a plane. I'll see you in thirty hours."

"Pen?" Carolyn sniffed. "I love you."

"I love you, too. Text me your flight details." Penelope hung up the phone and fought the urge to toss it out of the window and into the canal.

"How can I help?" Alexis asked, resting a hand on her back.

"Get ready for the emotional hell storm that Carolyn will be?" Penelope was only half-joking.

"Surely she's not that bad. You don't strike me as someone who would tolerate too many dramatics."

"You're right, but Carolyn is my one exception. I come from a family that taught you to keep your messy thoughts and emotions to yourself. When I met Carolyn, she was like this wonderful tangle of intensity. Her parents are hard-core hippies that believe you're entitled to all of your emotions, good and bad. I watched Carolyn cut a lecturer down to size on the extent of women's rights in Sparta, and I wanted to be her best friend from that moment onward. I wanted to learn how to be that openly passionate, to not be invisible." Penelope would never forget that day as long as she lived. Carolyn on a high was glorious and infectious; Carolyn on a low could make the sun cry.

"You don't need to learn how to be passionate, Penelope. I saw you on the night of the lecture on the Atlantis Tablet; your passion for it illuminated every part of you. It was mesmerizing. Never think for a moment you aren't a passionate person, *cara*." He held her face gently in his hands. "You're not invisible either. I see you, Penelope Bryne. It's looking away from you that I've always been unable to do."

Penelope stared up at him, his face the picture of calm as her own chest started to tighten. She didn't know how to respond, her ridiculous tongue too tied to even thank him, so she pulled him to her, resting her ear against the curve of his chest until she found the steady thrum of his heartbeat.

Alexis placed his arms loosely around her, not wanting to add to her panic by making her feel trapped. Penelope breathed, focusing only on his heartbeat until her own heart evened its pulse, matching his. Alexis ran his hands through her hair until she finally let out a sigh, the panic attack diffused.

"Better?" he asked.

"Just as long as we stay this way. Now for the next problem: how do we tell the magicians that Carolyn is coming?"

SEVEN

"**N**O," WAS LYCA'S firm opinion the next morning. Alexis watched Penelope narrow her eyes in a challenge few people had been brave enough to attempt over the centuries.

"She's already on her way," Penelope replied firmly, straightening her backbone. "You can't stop it."

"Oh, I can stop her," the assassin threatened.

"Lyca…" Alexis warned, and she turned accusing, silver eyes on him.

"Have you lost all of your reason, Defender? Another human? Look how well that turned out last time." Lyca looked pointedly at Penelope. "Penelope wants to keep us safe, granted. But we don't know this Carolyn will feel that way. There are dangers that come with knowing us, and Carolyn will have no idea what she is getting involved with."

"Don't forget Dandolo and his constant visits," muttered Phaidros.

"That's more people we've let get involved in our business than we've permitted in the last two hundred years," said Lyca.

Penelope groaned. "I don't know how many times I need to say it. Carolyn isn't going to dig about in your business. She doesn't need to know everything; she just needs to stay here a few days. All she knows is that I've come to work for Alexis to curate his collection. If you all behave yourselves and don't throw magic around in front of her, she's never going to know anything is off."

"What about the palazzo? Are you going to tell it to behave?" Aelia asked, inspecting her nails. "You know it does its own thing. How will you explain it to your friend when it decides to move her room? Or have a staircase appear out of nowhere in front of her?"

Penelope folded her arms stubbornly. "If it happens, I'll figure out what to tell her."

"Are you just going to say nothing, Alexis?" Phaidros asked.

"Penelope doesn't need my permission. She's one of us, so technically she doesn't need any of yours either. It is a courtesy that she feels the need to ask you at all," he replied calmly.

"Alexis is right," Zo said from the chair beside him. "Penelope's the Archivist, and she's not sharing any secrets. Her friend, her sister, needs help in her time of crisis and Penelope has offered it to her. Penelope is *familia* now; we look after our family. You have all made ridiculous mistakes over the years, so you can hardly judge. Keeping your magic in check for a day or two while Penelope makes a new plan with her friend won't hurt any of you."

"It could expose us and jeopardize this woman's safety. The Priests of Thevetat know where to find us. If they see her staying here, it's painting a target on her back," Lyca argued.

"If they've done the proper research on me—which of course they have—then Carolyn will already have a target on her back," Penelope said, matter-of-factly.

"She has a point," said Phaidros. "Tell me, are you going to show her the Archives?"

Penelope didn't hesitate for a second. "No! No one sees the Archives. No one knows what I'm really curating here. Besides, I'm sure the palazzo can make me a library aboveground to show Carolyn."

"No need. We have one," said Galenos before looking at Alexis. "You haven't shown her the library?"

"It's a rather underwhelming experience once you've seen the Archives," Alexis replied. Now that Galenos had pointed it out, it seemed like an egregious oversight on his behalf.

Penelope quickly came to his defense. "There hasn't been a lot of time, and I honestly didn't think to ask if there was another one."

Despite her words, she still had an ominous look in her hazel eyes. *An egregious oversight indeed*, he chastised himself. Perhaps if they had the opportunity for a traditional courtship, it would have given him the time to show her all the things he wanted to, inside and outside the palazzo.

She's not dead! Why do you think you won't have time to court her properly now? Nereus's voice said in his mind with uncanny clarity.

"Okay, I'm done arguing with you guys about this," Penelope said firmly. "Do you know why you can't find Abaddon and Kreios right now? Because they've got allies. They have friends and supporters to hide them and keep them safe. You have all shut yourselves off from trusting people, and now you have no one to help you. I'm going to see Marco. I'm sick of looking at all of you." Zo made to get to his feet, but she hissed at him. "Don't you dare try and follow me right now."

Zo quickly dropped back to the couch.

Penelope grabbed her coat as the palazzo opened the blue door for her, and she stepped out into the windy street.

"Hades help us, she sounds like Nereus," Phaidros muttered.

"I like her, too," said Galenos with an affectionate smile.

"And she's right," Aelia added.

Alexis stared at the door, fighting his instincts to go after her, fearing that she might not come back.

"You're just going to sit there and let her be angry at us?" Zo demanded.

Alexis turned away from the door, keeping his expression neutral despite the turmoil inside him. "She knows her way home."

PENELOPE MESSAGED Marco as she walked through the tight streets, carefully keeping out of the way of the locals going about their business. There was currently a pleasant lull between the Carnevale tourists leaving and Easter tourists arriving, and the streets were quiet with people moving at a more peaceful pace. Penelope tucked her cold hands in her pockets, breathed in the salty air, and did her best to push the arguing voices from her head.

Cagey, overprotective, distrustful magicians would be the death of her nerves at the rate they were going. Carolyn needed a place to stop over for a few days, and Penelope needed to see her to calm her own anxiety.

Penelope didn't have any siblings, and she'd always considered Carolyn and Tim the closest people to her. *They are* whanau, *the family you chose, so you have to love them even when they drive you crazy*, her mother, Kiri, would always say when Penelope would complain about their dramas. Chosen family were always extra special. *Extra special pain in my ass*, Penelope thought as she crossed over another bridge. Despite internal bickering, when one of them was in a crisis, they flocked together to sort it out. Alexis hadn't objected to Carolyn coming to Venice, and Penelope hoped that, in the end, his opinion would be enough to sway the others.

Walk and breathe, Pen, she prompted herself. The walk helped to clear her jittery tension, but it didn't stop her from ordering a glass of red wine when she reached her favorite bar at the Campo Santa Margarita. As a reasonable halfway point between the palazzo in Dorsoduro and the police station where Marco worked, they usually met there for wine and *Cicchetti* a few times a week. She was watching the terrifyingly large seagulls fighting over cuts near the fish market stalls when Marco appeared.

"Wine already? You are starting early today." He tossed his sunglasses on the table and ordered one for himself.

"It's almost lunchtime. You look about as cheerful as I do," Penelope commented. Marco's usual good humor seemed positively frayed.

"I met Duilio's lawyer, Francesca Garcia. My hunch about her making my life difficult is proving true. She's already given Adalfieri a hard time about how the investigation was documented, how the body was handled, where all of Duilio's assets are—everything."

"She might be able to help you find an additional property, something under a different name perhaps?"

"Anything is possible." Marco sipped his wine and frowned. "What's wrong? Did you solve the riddle of your scroll?" Penelope updated him on what it had said, Tim's disappearance, and Carolyn's understandable panic.

"She flies in tomorrow morning, and I have to find a way to get everyone to behave while she's here. That is, if Lyca will let her in the house without trying to stab her," said Penelope, poking at her food.

"If they want to be difficult about it, just bring her over to my place. The bookings are quiet at the moment, so we have space. Isabella will be overjoyed to look after you both."

"*Grazie*, Marco. I'm hoping it won't have to come to that. I'm sure Alexis will step in if he has to and knock their heads together."

"Of course he will. He won't want you to be away from him and the safety of the palazzo unnecessarily."

Penelope made a face. "You make it sound like he's my jailer."

"Not a jailer, but very protective. Zo wouldn't let you out of his sight while Alexis was away, even when you were with me. I think Alexis knows the minute he tries to lock you up he'd lose you, but you can tell he'd like to. He is…intense," Marco finished, as delicately as he could.

"He's got reason to be. To be honest, I've never had anyone really looking out for me before. I've always kept Carolyn and Tim on the straight and narrow and generally been the responsible one. Having someone being protective of me is a nice change."

Marco smiled mischievously. "He makes lovesick cow eyes at you."

"Really? Like the ones you make at Aelia when she walks all over you?"

"I don't mind, she has *piedi piccolo*," he said, pinching a small space between his thumb and finger.

"Phaidros doesn't have small feet, and he'll cheerfully stomp on you if you flirt with her too much," Penelope warned.

Marco shrugged. "He can try."

Penelope rolled her eyes. "Boys!"

"You don't need to worry about me, *Dottore*. I'm a forty-year-old man, a veteran of battles of the heart with high-maintenance women."

"Maybe you should find a normal girl to settle down with. Someone who doesn't have an ancient magician obsessed with her."

"Are you and Isabella in this together? What time do I have in my life to find this perfect woman you seem to think is out there? It would be unfair to bring a woman into my life at the moment, knowing the danger it would put her in."

Penelope ordered them both more wine. "You're a sweet guy, Marco. You deserve to have someone to come home to."

"I'm Italian. We *always* have someone to go home to. Isabella and her wife Guilia are trying to get pregnant, my home is never going to be quiet again."

Marco loved his sister, so Penelope knew his objections were bullshit. "Stop pretending you aren't going to love a tiny *bambino* running about."

"I only want it to be a boy so the pressure is off me to carry on the name," he joked.

AFTER LUNCH with Marco, Penelope walked a leisurely route back to the palazzo, not in any hurry to get back home and continue butting heads with Lyca.

Home… When did she start thinking of it as home? She had lived in her apartment in Melbourne for over a year before she'd bothered to unpack her boxes. She had an uncomfortable feeling under her ribs when she thought about what was different this time around.

Penelope paused at the end of the Calle dei Cerchieri as music swelled within her. She rubbed at her ears before she realized it was reverberating in her head. Her chest echoed with a deep bass scale, and she knew that wherever Alexis was, he was playing the cello.

The door of the palazzo opened for her, and she hurried inside. Drawn like a hapless sailor toward a siren's song, she pictured the tower, urging the palazzo to give her a quick way to the sound, to Alexis.

"Thank you," she whispered, running her hand on the wall as a door and staircase appeared. Taking the steps two at a time, Penelope quickly reached his rooms, and quietly opened the door.

Alexis sat by the windows with his back to her, dressed in a forest-green silk robe embroidered with the phases of the moon down his back in gold. She longed to trace her fingers over the exquisite design, but didn't want to risk disturbing him, so she tucked her hands into her pockets instead.

Unlike the first time she had heard him play, the soulful music was contained to the tower rooms, a faint glow of blue and silver in the air, the only sign that magic was being done at all. Penelope curled up in a reading nook of floor cushions to listen. She didn't recognize the song he was playing, but that didn't surprise her. He had told her that he liked to play his own compositions when he was thinking.

Penelope closed her eyes and let the music pull her under into a meditation. She focused on her breath, calming the insistent thrum of her heartbeat, and combating her rising anxiety for Tim's safety.

Suddenly she was standing in a back street behind a block of restaurants. The sticky, late-afternoon sun highlighted piles of rubbish waiting for collection, scraps of paper, and cardboard blowing in the high winds.

"Come out, little mouse, you can't hide in this city forever," a voice said from her mouth. Nothing answered, nothing moved... and then a man leaped from behind a metal dumpster, his filthy face twisted with fear and madness. Penelope would recognize that sandy hair and crooked nose anywhere.

Tim.

"Give me back what is mine, thief, and I'll end your suffering," the voice continued.

Run, Tim! Penelope tried to shout. Her head whipped around to the alley behind her, as if hearing her scream.

"*Penelope...*" the voice hissed, its cajoling tone gone, and only then did she recognize it. She knew it in a deeply familiar way from her nightmares and memories. *Thevetat.*

Penelope threw herself backward, recoiling, thrashing to wake herself up. Phantom hands grabbed at her throat, and she choked, clawing at them futilely.

"You interfering bitch! I should have drowned you in the sea when I had the chance," Thevetat snarled.

Heat filled her chest, and Penelope dropped her hands from her throat and reached for the lines that tied her to Alexis. She pulled hard and urgently. Finally, she tore free from the Vessel's head, flying away from the hissing demon, before slamming back into her body. Her eyes snapped open, and she heaved in a huge breath, her hands coming to her throat. Alexis crouched beside her, panic over every part of his face, his cello abandoned.

"Penelope, are you okay?" he asked, taking her face in his hands so he could check her eyes. "Where were you? You were just...gone."

"I saw him. I saw Tim," she said, panting, tears filling her eyes. "Thevetat's after him. I think I shared a head with him."

Through shaky breaths, she told him everything that had happened in the meditation. When she was done, Alexis pulled her into his lap, holding her tightly to him.

"You are going to be the death of me, I swear it," he said against her hair.

"How is it even possible?" Penelope turned so she could look up at him. "I found you in a meditation because of our connection, but Thevetat? Why? I didn't even know the person he was possessing."

"You are the only person I know who has survived being possessed by Thevetat without first being trained as a Vessel. It could be that it was a combination of your friendship with Tim, and an echo of Thevetat, that drew you to the moment they encountered each other."

Penelope looked down at the tattoos encircling her forearms and the shadows of scars underneath. She would never forget the look in Abaddon's eyes when he sketched them on her, the pain that had burned her.

"Help me find Aelia. We are going to do another cleansing. I'm not going to be sharing a body with that piece-of-shit demon again," Penelope said fiercely. As always, anger was more welcome than fear.

THIRTY MINUTES later, Penelope was neck-deep in a bath filled with herbs and whatever else Aelia deemed necessary to drive away a demon's presence. Penelope had climbed in without question, making sure her tattooed arms were under the cloudy water.

"None of Thevetat's influence was left in you, Penelope. I swear it on altars of all the gods," Aelia insisted from where she sat on the marble counter.

"I believe you. I still can't explain what I saw, but I *was* with Thevetat. I possessed his Vessel, the same way he'd possessed me. I wasn't quite in the body, maybe, because I didn't have permission to be there, while Thevetat did. It was more like I was in an antechamber." Penelope struggled to describe it. Like a dream, the smaller details were already fading.

"Thevetat has always been a sneaky bastard, but it sounds like whatever magic was involved in this, it came from you." Aelia tapped her nails on the counter as she thought. "Is the bath helping at all?"

"I guess? It doesn't feel like last time. I didn't know what else to do, though. I had to be sure." Penelope drew her knees protectively to her chest.

There was a gentle tap on the door, and Alexis stuck his head in. "Any changes?"

"Nothing. I'm bored, I'm going to find something else to do." Aelia jumped down and headed for the door. "You can keep an eye on her and let me know if something exciting happens."

"Thanks, Aelia. Sorry for the false alarm," said Penelope.

"It wasn't a false alarm. We just don't know what it is. Stay in the bath a while just to be sure."

"Do you want company?" Alexis asked Penelope.

"Sure I do."

Alexis pulled up a three-legged stool and placed it next to the tub. He held out a silver ring, a lapis lazuli stone glinting blue and gold in its center.

"Put this on. I refashioned one of my rings with grounding magic. It will make sure that your spirit doesn't go wandering off in any other dreams or meditations," he said, slipping it onto her wet index finger.

"Thank you, Alexis." Penelope kissed his hand before letting it go.

"I need to keep you where I can find you, *cara*. You scared me half to death tonight. I'm an old man, remember? You can't do that to me." Alexis rested his hand on the back of her neck and gently massaged at the knots that she always had there.

She groaned. "A fancy new ring and a massage? I should go astral projecting more often."

"Don't you even think about it. I'm half-tempted to shackle you to me and be done with it."

Penelope gave a mocking gasp. "You wouldn't dare. What if I needed to pee?"

"I'd look in the other direction." As she laughed, his smile turned devious. "I'm sure I could think of a few positives to the arrangement."

"I'm sure you could," Penelope agreed, her cheeks going red. "The answer is still no."

Alexis clucked his tongue sadly. "I'm going to have to work harder at convincing you, I think."

"You'd need to stay around long enough to do that," Penelope replied. She hated every minute of his absence, and it made her embarrassed of her own selfishness.

"We haven't had enough time alone in the last six weeks, have we?" he said, brushing her hair back from her face.

"Not nearly enough. There are too many people who need you. Carolyn will turn up tomorrow, and it will be someone else who needs attention," Penelope said with a sigh before summoning her courage. "This is really bad timing, but I need to say something before anything else happens to interrupt me."

Alexis leaned forward and rested his forearms on the edge of the bath. "What's on your mind, *cara*?"

Penelope had been practicing her speech for weeks, but now that the moment had come, every word in her head seemed to abandon her.

"The day I left, I didn't do it because I didn't want to stay. I was hurt and upset and…fuck, Alexis, you died in my arms! I was so freaked out by everything that had happened, I panicked. All I could think of was that if I stayed, I was going to get you killed again. You were only out at the Lido that night because you came after me. I thought Kreios was right; that I would compromise every battle you were in, that I'd be a liability to you. I couldn't be selfish enough to stay just because *I* wanted it. It wasn't worth the risk of losing you. Even if I were on the other side of the world and miserable, it would be worth it knowing the world still had you in it. I came back because I knew I wouldn't be a liability anymore. I could *help* you fight them," she said in one long breath.

She pushed her damp hair back from her face as she summoned the energy to say the hardest thing of all. "I don't want you to feel that because I came back that we have to keep doing…whatever *this* is that we are doing…if it's not something you want. I can be an adult about it. If it's different now because I've moved in, I'd understand. I don't want you to feel obligated because I'm the Archivist."

Alexis was so quiet she had to look up to make sure he hadn't used magic to disappear on her. He had the same look on his face that he usually wore when he was trying to figure out a puzzle or while reading a difficult manuscript. She tried not to shrink under the intensity of it.

"Penelope, do I look like someone who wouldn't be able to say no to something that I didn't want to do? If I've confused the situation by pulling back a little, it wasn't my intention. It is for the same reasons you've just stated. You came back, but it wasn't necessarily for me. I didn't want you to feel compelled to continue anything that you didn't want to. I would never deny you the Archives, even if you didn't want me anymore. I have centuries of baggage that should give anyone pause. I don't know what another war with Thevetat will unleash in me. You might not want to deal with the reality of that either."

Alexis twisted the rings about on his fingers, a nervous gesture that she'd never seen him do before. "If you do decide you are still willing to risk me, then I would like to court you properly, despite the constant interruptions. I should've shown better restraint in the beginning, but I didn't want you to leave Venice without being with you at least once. It was selfish, and I should've gone about it in a better way."

"And do I look like someone who wouldn't have been able to say no to something that I didn't want?" Penelope asked, unable to resist throwing his words back at him. "I think we both played a pretty strong part in that so-called selfishness, Alexis. You know I find you irresistible, right?"

A smile so bashful crossed his face that Penelope placed her hand over his. Alexis leaned over and rested his cheek on top of it.

"Does this mean I have permission to court you?" he asked.

"Only if it means I can court you," she said and then paused. "How *does* one court a magician from Atlantis?"

Alexis smiled against her skin. "You are very clever. I am sure you'll figure it out."

"I don't know if it's in the courtship rules, but I do want to sleep with you. Not necessarily having sex, but sleep. I'm not going to lie, I'm still not over you dying on me, and I'll have fewer nightmares if I can wake up and feel you close," Penelope said, trying not to sound awkward and ridiculous. *Not necessarily having sex? Idiot.*

"We both sleep better when we are together. You aren't the only one who dreams about that night. You have no idea what it did to me knowing that Kreios and Abaddon had you. Let us also not forget that you, too, almost died from a stab wound when I pulled you out of a canal. We both have scared each other too much in the past few months."

"Then sleeping and courting it is," she said. Penelope traced the stubble on his jawline and was bringing her mouth to his when a knock came at the door.

"Are you still in there, Alexis? Lyca needs you to test some blades, and Aelia and Zo are going to start cooking. Speak up if you have a preference, Penelope," Phaidros said from the other side of the door.

Penelope reached down the side of the bath, picked up her boot, and flung it hard at the door.

"Just fuck off and leave us alone for five bloody minutes, yeah?" she shouted.

There was a long silence from the other side of the door before Phaidros replied uncertainly, "Okay, Pen, I'll tell them you'll be down when you're ready."

Penelope turned back to Alexis with a smile of triumph. His wide-eyed look of surprise changed to devious delight. Penelope squealed in protest as he climbed into the bath, still fully clothed, and wrapped himself around her, kissing her until they were both breathless.

EIGHT

WHEN PENELOPE WOKE the following morning, it wasn't to another note, but with a tall magician wrapped around her. They both still smelled of salt and myrrh from the cleansing bath. By the time they'd finally climbed out, the water had gone cold. They spent the rest of the night talking about the city Penelope had seen in her vision, where Tim would most likely hide, and how the priests of Thevetat could have found out about the dig and his find. Penelope had fallen into her first deep sleep in weeks, her lips still on Alexis's, her body tucked warmly against him.

To Phaidros and the other magician's credit, they finally gave them some space to be alone and catch up. The tightness around Alexis's eyes that Penelope had noticed over the past few weeks had finally eased. Penelope reached out and touched his irresistible riot of black curls.

"You know they won't leave us alone forever," he murmured against the pillow.

"I wonder if the palazzo will make a maze for me to slow them down?" Penelope said thoughtfully. Alexis opened his eyes and gave her a smile that made her toes curl. He placed an arm over her, pulling her close.

"You're not making it easier to get up, you know," she said, resting her head in the crook of his shoulder. "I have to go and get Carolyn in another two hours, and then it will be chaos all over again. She can be a handful when she's emotional."

Alexis stroked slow circles over the soft fabric of her pajamas, his eyes already thoughtful. "I'll make sure the others know what's expected of them while Carolyn is here."

"It will only be for a day or two, then I'll go with her to Israel."

"Then *we* will go with her. We are meant to be hunting Thevetat, and we know he is hunting Tim. Lyca and Galenos will stay here and look after Venice." Alexis kissed the top of her head. "I'd best go and see Lyca about the blades she's finished if we don't want her stepping from a shadow to hurry us up."

"Do what you need to do. I'll go and get Carolyn and make sure she's calm. I don't want Phaidros getting excited over her nervous energy and being inappropriate." Penelope laughed at the thought of it.

"She's your friend, so I've no doubt that she can handle the likes of Phaidros."

TWO HOURS later, Penelope was standing in the arrivals lounge of the Marco Polo airport, waiting for Carolyn. It had been nearly two months since she'd seen her best friend, and despite what she had begun referring to as the "Tim Fiasco," Penelope was glad that she was coming.

It was easy to spot Carolyn who refused to wear black or any other neutral color. Dressed in a purple overcoat, her beach-blonde hair in a long braid over her shoulder, and a jaunty, yellow scarf around her throat, Carolyn cut a bright figure through the crowds. She spotted Penelope, and her tired face broke into a smile.

"Hey, Caro," Penelope managed as her friend caught her up in a too-tight hug.

"I'm so fucking glad to see you," Carolyn said, her Australian accent noticeably thick after months of Penelope listening only to Venetians. "Let me look at you." Carolyn held Penelope at arm's length. "Venice suits you, even if you still wear too much black."

"I'm Melbournian. I can't help it," Penelope said in an old defense, looking down at her black biker boots, jeans, and coat.

"Let's get out of here. I'm so sick of the smell of airports."

They left the terminal and headed toward the water where their boat was waiting. It was windy, and the sunshine was out for the first time in a week. Venice beamed across the water at them, and Penelope couldn't help smiling back at it. *Home.*

Carolyn sighed approvingly. "Look at that gorgeous city. You're looking good too, Pen. There is a bit of a glow around your cheeks I haven't seen in a long time. Is the sexy Italian showing you a good time?"

"We're courting," Penelope said, taking Carolyn's pink suitcase from her before looping her arm through hers.

"Courting? How very sweet and old-fashioned of you."

"He's a traditional sort of guy." Penelope smiled, mentally making a note to ask Phaidros about courting rituals they'd had in Atlantis.

"Just as long as he's not the traditional, misogynistic sort of guy who is going to be selfish in the sack and will try and make you raise his six Italian babies." Penelope instantly thought of the five magicians who frequently argued liked children and laughed.

"He's got enough to deal with."

"Uh-huh. We'll see."

"Don't you start getting overprotective and try to scare him away," Penelope warned.

Carolyn held her hands up in surrender. "Hey, you were the one who ran away to Venice and stayed here. He better be something magnificent—Sweet Jesus, who is that?"

Zo was waving at them, the combination of his huge smile and tight black shirt making women around them stop and stare.

"*Buongiorno,*" Zo greeted as he joined them and held his hand out for Carolyn's suitcase.

"Carolyn, this is Zo Dimakos," Penelope introduced. "He also works for Alexis."

"Hey, nice to meet you," Carolyn said. She mouthed, *what the fuck?* at Penelope as soon as Zo's back was turned. He put the suitcase into the boat and held out his hand to help Carolyn step on deck. She took it with a smile, but it quickly vanished.

"Wait. You're not Zotikos Dimakos…who wrote *The Voices of Delphi: The Feminine Superpower of Ancient Greece*?" Carolyn asked uncertainly.

"The one and the same. You know it?" Zo asked, in obvious surprise and delight.

"Oh, she knows it," Penelope said, as she hopped in after them. Carolyn hadn't shut up about it for months after it was published. It was the first time Penelope had seen Carolyn fangirl over something as hard as Jason Momoa.

"Shit," Carolyn said, sitting down heavily in a seat.

"What? What's wrong?" Zo asked as he turned on the boat.

"I'm going to sound like a jerk, but I thought you were a woman publishing under a guy's name," she admitted and shot daggers at Penelope who roared with laughter.

Zo just smiled widely at her. "Sorry to disappoint. Alas, I'm but a humble man who knows never to mess with the prophetesses of Greece."

Carolyn stared at Penelope again, her soft-brown eyes narrowing as she mouthed again, *What the fuck?* Penelope figured Carolyn wasn't too disappointed in the revelation as she took the opportunity to check out Zo's ass as soon as his back was turned.

"Why write about women oracles?" Carolyn asked, too curious to stay silent.

"Because women's roles have been grossly underrepresented and misinterpreted throughout Greek history. The Oracles were powerful and terrifying and definitely were *not* just another mouthpiece for a man, even if they were meant to have a direct line to Apollo. Their prophecies were their own, and they told the most powerful men in

Greek and Roman history that it was from Apollo so they would actually shut up and listen," replied Zo.

"Keep talking like that, and she's going to fall in love with you," warned Penelope, only half-joking.

"Too late," Carolyn said with a laugh.

"What is your area of study that you are so interested in my oracles?" Zo asked as he drove.

"Officially, it's esoteric religions. It has kind of evolved into women's roles within those religions specifically over the years," Carolyn replied. They kept up an easy conversation, Penelope momentarily ignored. She didn't mind, the more convinced Carolyn was that the house of magicians was a house of academics, the easier their cover would be.

The blue-and-gold door was already in the brick wall of the Calle dei Cerchieri by the time they docked the boat and made their way to it. With some relief, Penelope noticed that the palazzo had removed its usual glimmer and replaced it with something solid and a little weatherworn.

Thank you, she psychically whispered to the palazzo as she opened the door.

Carolyn let out a low whistle as she stepped over the threshold and took in the entrance foyer. "Damn, Penelope, no wonder you took this job! Is that a real Artemisia Gentileschi?"

"Most definitely. Try not to fall over your own jaw while you're here, and for the love of God, don't touch anything," warned Penelope with a grin.

"I thought I heard voices." Aelia breezed down a curved staircase Penelope had never seen before. "I love the color of your coat."

"Um, thanks?" Carolyn replied as Aelia beamed at her. Unlike the palazzo, Aelia didn't believe in dulling the intensity of her beauty. Even dressed casually in a fuchsia pink tunic and her usual leather leggings, she looked stunning.

"Carolyn, this is Aelia. She is Alexis's expert in ancient music and instruments." Penelope shot Aelia a pointed look.

"That's right, I'll have to give you a tour of my instrument room. Do you play anything?" said Aelia.

"Only a few songs on the piano, and all very badly. It's nice to meet you. Penelope speaks about you a lot. How many people live here?" Carolyn asked, her eyes unable to stop roving.

"There are seven of us, including Penelope. Alexis likes to keep his professionals close," said Phaidros. Poor Carolyn didn't know where to look as he took her hand and kissed it.

"You have my permission to ignore Phaidros when he tries to flirt with you, but otherwise he's an okay PlayStation partner when he doesn't cheat," Penelope told her.

"I never cheat!"

"As you can tell, he also lies."

"And your expertise would be?" asked Carolyn. Phaidros's eyes flared with amusement. Zo made a threatening gesture behind Carolyn's back which halted whatever suggestive thing he was about to say.

"I suppose the easiest answer is that I'm an expert in the ancient studies of energy and physical sciences. Sometimes there's a touch of alchemy as well," Phaidros said with a straight face.

"How fascinating. We'll have to chat about the Arabic alchemists. I've always been so intrigued by them."

"Bother me with questions whenever you like," Phaidros said.

"Alexis certainly has eclectic tastes to have such a wide variety of people in his employment," Carolyn said, gently removing her hand from Phaidros's grip.

"I certainly do," said Alexis as he came down the stairs.

Penelope tried and failed to keep the carnal thoughts from her mind as she took in his black suit and the jewel-blue shirt that made his eyes glow. He slipped his arm around Penelope's waist and held out his hand for Carolyn.

"It's a pleasure to meet you at last. Penelope has told me so much about you," he said, the charming playboy facade firmly in place.

Penelope took a small amount of female satisfaction in Carolyn's blushing cheeks as she shook Alexis's hand.

"Likewise," she croaked.

"You must be exhausted from your trip. We will give you ladies some time to catch up, and then if you like, Penelope, we can show Carolyn the scroll in the library," Alexis suggested.

"Sounds like a great idea. I'm interested to see what Tim thought was important enough to steal from a dig site and unbalance our lives over," said Carolyn, her frustration rising to the surface.

"I'll make sure there's good wine accompanying the tour of the library, shall I? Please tell me you drink red," Zo asked.

"Now you're talking my language. Nothing too sweet for me," Carolyn said.

"A lady after my own heart."

Penelope gave Alexis's side a reassuring squeeze as she let him go. "We won't take long."

"Take your time. The scroll and the library can wait."

Thankfully, the palazzo didn't move once as Penelope led Carolyn up the stairs, keeping her rooms firmly in her mind.

"And you said everything in this place is authentic?" Carolyn asked as she studied a pair of third-century *gladius* swords mounted on the wall. Aelia had told her they had once belonged to Emperor Diocletian, though Penelope could never tell when she was teasing when she said things like that.

"Yes, as far as I know," Penelope replied. "When your family has lived in Venice since its inception, you inherit relics apparently. Are you starting to see why I didn't turn down the job offer? This place is like the Louvre, Bodleian, and Aladdin's Cave combined."

Carolyn gave her a sly look. "Aladdin isn't half bad either, though I never knew you liked guys with beards."

"Then you weren't very observant."

"What I was observing was you never going out with anyone." Carolyn raised an eyebrow at her. "He has a very interesting...aura."

"Is that what the kids are calling it these days," Penelope said glibly.

"I'm not joking. It's the most vivid shade of indigo and gold I've ever seen. All of these academics shine so brightly I'm surprised even you can't see them. You and Aladdin seem very comfortable together even though it's been such a short period of time, Pen."

"That's a bad thing?" Penelope bristled. "And stop calling him Aladdin."

Don't measure this connection by normal human conventions. He makes your soul sing, Nereus's voice prompted from deep within her, just as her self-consciousness rose. Penelope took a calming breath and purposely avoided encouraging the auras conversation.

"I'm not saying it's a bad thing at all. It's just really unlike you to get attached to someone so quickly. Though I suppose now that I've seen Alexis in the flesh, it all makes sense." Carolyn gave her a dirty smile, and Penelope rolled her eyes.

"Shut up, I'm not that shallow."

"I know, but in this case, I wouldn't blame you if you chose any of them."

"You're such a dirty perv."

"I'm a woman in distress. You can hardly blame me for appreciating a handsome distraction."

Penelope was still laughing as she opened the doors to her room with a flourish. "These are my rooms. You can stay here for as long as you need and have my bed. I'll crash with Alexis."

"Old-fashioned courting, my ass." Carolyn took off her coat and flopped down on the bed. "Something is different about you, Pen. You seem calmer here. Happier."

"You've been here an hour, you can't make that kind of judgment call."

"An hour is enough. I *know* you. It's not like you to be so relaxed around so many people, but you are. It's like you finally found your tribe and can stop being so stressed all the time. Thousands of kilometers from your Dad probably helps too."

"He's still annoyed about me moving, though I've no idea why. Venice is definitely an interesting place to live, and these guys are good people," Penelope answered carefully.

"They are intimidating people. I'd constantly be worried about being the dumbest one here. How many more are hiding amongst the place?"

"Lyca is in charge of ancient weaponry, although I don't know if you'll get a chance to see her." Lyca hadn't argued about Carolyn after Penelope had stormed from the palazzo. All she had said when Penelope told her Carolyn's arrival time was, "I hope you don't live to regret this. Not everyone is built for our world. Don't forget that."

Carolyn made a face. "Ancient weapons, really? What does he need one of those for?"

"Dating and authenticating new pieces, things like that," answered Penelope, purposely vague. She didn't mention Lyca also forged sharp and glorious death-dealers for their daily use.

"I suppose if you have the cash, you hire the professionals," said Carolyn.

Penelope joined Carolyn on the bed and propped her head up with her hand. "Are you okay?"

"No. Yes…no. Fucking Tim. I can't believe I'm still running after him after everything that has happened," Carolyn said, staring up at the ceiling so her tears wouldn't fall.

"He's got no one else to worry about him. You know he hasn't talked to his Mom for at least ten years. In saying that, once we get him back, we are going to take turns kicking his ass. Have you heard anything else from him?"

Carolyn pulled out her phone. "This is the only message I have from the last two weeks, and I think he's on something strong this time because it is crazy. Not just Tim's regular, drunken, let's-talk-theology crazy, but lost-his-mind crazy." She tapped on the message and Tim's slurred voice echoed around them.

"Carolyn…Caro…I fucked up. Fucked up so bad. I found it. Found the secret door in the cave. And the guy. The guy, Caro. The poor fucking guy killed himself to hide the visions. Shouldn't have touched it. Shouldn't have been there. Now the demons are going to be summoned out of the planets and I don't know how to put them back. All of the Ancient Priesthood have gone, and I don't know what to do. The demons, they are coming. The brother. Belial—he's got a brother. I've never heard that before, but the guy saw it. Fuck, you gotta help me—"

The line went dead. Penelope took a shaky breath as Carolyn tossed the phone across the bed.

"That's all there is. Demons in the planets. Talking to dead guys. Sounds like the desert has broken the freak once and for all. Seriously, give me a flat-earther over another archaeologist any day," Carolyn said viciously.

Despite her anger, Penelope saw the worry eating away at her. Carolyn and Tim hadn't broken up because of a lack of love. If anything, it had been the opposite. The long separations while Tim was on digs and his hard-partying when he wasn't working had pushed Carolyn too far. She had cut him loose for her own sanity, and now she was getting dragged through his drama all over again.

Penelope took her hand and gave it a gentle squeeze. "Some of what Tim's ranting about actually makes sense. It was on the scroll he sent me. Zo and Alexis are analyzing it, but Zo's already done a translation."

Carolyn groaned. "Great! Another Dead Sea nut, just what I need. He's so cute, too. Such a waste."

"More like an ancient poetry nut who knows Hebrew and Aramaic and offered his skills," Penelope gently corrected.

"Oh, come on! It's hardly fair that he's an expert in feminine roles in Ancient Greece *and* into poetry *and* is a total babe. You're going to make me too nervous to talk to the guy," Carolyn complained, which was total bullshit because Penelope had seen Carolyn bring the toughest university chancellors to heel without a flicker of uncertainty.

Penelope rolled her eyes at her. "Just don't mention Ovid and you'll be fine."

NINE

*Z*O WAS GOOD to his word, and by the time Penelope and Carolyn made it back downstairs, he had two glasses of wine waiting for them.

"I think you'll both like this vintage. I got this wine from a vineyard in Pompeii. They made it with the original variants of grapes that grew before the volcanic explosion in AD 79. I like to think it's like drinking the past. It is quite extraordinary," explained Zo as he took his own glass and inhaled. Penelope wondered what memories the wine brought back for him when he smelled it and bit her lip to prevent herself from asking.

"A wine and history buff. I could get used to this kind of lesson every time I have a drink," Carolyn said before sipping and emitting a happy groan.

"I should warn you, Zo's choice in wine can be pretty potent," Penelope warned.

"She's a lightweight," Carolyn said, shooting Zo a quick wink.

"Tell me that tomorrow when you're nursing your hangover and Aelia tries to force one of her blended cures down your throat."

"We had better show her some books before she starts getting cranky. I'll take you to the library. I'm sure Alexis is already there," Zo offered, and Penelope sent him a grateful smile. She had no idea where the upstairs library was and wanted the palazzo moving about as little as possible when Carolyn was under its roof.

Penelope trailed behind Carolyn and Zo as they chatted and walked together like they had been friends for years. Zo had an uncanny knack of distracting Carolyn just as the palazzo's hallways changed, so she didn't notice doors and new rooms appearing around her.

"This place is a veritable labyrinth. I'll have to take a ball of string with me wherever I go and hope I don't find a minotaur," joked Carolyn.

"Don't worry, we haven't had a minotaur for quite some time," Zo said with a laugh.

Oh God, please tell me they never had a real minotaur, Penelope hoped silently.

"Seriously though, someone could get lost and not find their way back for days," commented Carolyn, not registering Penelope's concerned frown.

"It's happened more than once. Thankfully, I've never found a body," Zo said seriously. Penelope choked on her wine, but Carolyn just laughed again.

Zo opened a pair of gold-and-red painted double doors and Penelope carefully schooled her face. *Remember, Bryne, this is your workplace that you see every day and nothing is out of the ordinary at all.*

Alexis was leaning against a large, mahogany desk in the foyer of a three-leveled library. It was quite possibly the sexiest thing Penelope had ever seen. Wrought-iron staircases spiraled up to the higher levels, and handy step stools and ladders were placed near the higher bookcases. Warm oak paneled the walls while the shelves were crowned with carvings of leaves and mythological animals. Study desks and reading corners were spread out with couches next to fireplaces, and more priceless art hung on the walls. The phrase *Littera Scripta Manet* was carved into the marble floor. Penelope's magic translated the Latin quickly across her hand before she could cover it: The Written Word Endures.

"Welcome to my office," Penelope said when she found her voice.

"Fuck me," Carolyn whispered in awe, spinning slowly on her heel. "This reminds me of the Library of Trinity College...or like...

Hogwarts and Rivendell crossed together. And you didn't think to send me a photo of this! God, you are the worst friend ever."

"In Penelope's defense, I have kept her very busy since she's started," said Alexis.

"I bet you have." Carolyn snorted. Penelope pinched her hard in outrage as Zo laughed. Alexis shrugged unapologetically, making Penelope roll her eyes.

"Don't encourage her," she said as she joined him at the desk. Her laptop and supplies from her office downstairs had been set up, including a messy pile of Post-it Notes and a journal she was positive she had put in a locked drawer.

Alexis had sealed the scroll in between two sheets of glass and had placed it on a stand ready for her.

"Thank you, this is perfect," she said, kissing his cheek.

"*Prego*," Alexis replied, pulling her chair out for her. Pushing up the sleeves of her sweater, Penelope sat down and opened the file of Zo's translations. Carolyn was beside her in a second, her hand gripping Penelope's forearm.

"What the hell? Tattoos? When were you going to tell me about this?" she asked, inspecting them. "For years I try and get you to come with me to get something done, and you're in Venice for five minutes, and now you have matching forearm tats."

"Calm down. You're in no position to judge me for getting some ink."

Carolyn had a whole sleeve of tattoos under her pink top as well as a large tree of life backpiece. Penelope fought the urge to pull her sleeves back down. She refused to feel ashamed of the marks that meant she had survived Tony Duilio. Alexis's hand rested gently between her shoulder blades, and the bunching in them eased.

"It looks a lot like your Atlantis Tablet script to me." Carolyn's eyes narrowed as she looked up at Alexis. "Is this your influence?"

Alexis ran his long fingers over the dark-blue tattoos. "I wish I could take some credit for this beauty, but I had nothing to do with it.

Perhaps Penelope felt comfortable getting them done here, where others couldn't have an opinion on it." Alexis's mouth quirked in a smile to soften the barb.

"Perhaps Penelope would like to get back to the task at hand," she muttered.

"Yeah, yeah, don't start talking in the third person, I get the idea." Carolyn took the translations from the file and scanned through them.

"This scroll sounds just as crazy as Tim's voice mail," she complained when she finished.

"What voice mail?" Zo and Alexis asked together. Carolyn played it for them, and Penelope's stomach churned again. Sensing it, Alexis's fingers moved from her back to her neck to reassure her and help her avoid a panic attack.

"Tim's fixated on the Ancient Priesthood for a reason, but I don't know who it's referring to. My knowledge of Abrahamic traditions is sketchy. Wasn't Melchizedek the king that blessed Abraham? Like he was God's priesthood before Abraham took over? How much more ancient is the priesthood before him?" Carolyn asked, looking over the translations again.

"In the Essene tradition, Melchizedek can also be a reference to the Archangel Michael. I don't think Michael fits the overall message. The main issue here is that it claims that the followers of this demon Thevetat were the ones responsible for the annihilation of the Essenes. If this scroll can be authenticated, Tim has made one of the biggest discoveries ever," said Penelope.

"That is, if he isn't thrown in an Israeli prison for stealing artifacts or killed by black market smugglers," Carolyn added. "He sounds off his face, wherever he is."

"That brings us to the most pressing problem. The jar that this scroll was sealed in was booby-trapped," Zo explained as gently as he could.

"What do you mean booby-trapped?"

"Tim isn't high, he's poisoned. The Essenes were fiercely protective of certain knowledge, and they wanted to make sure that if they were ever looted, the culprits would be punished."

"I haven't heard of that from any of Tim's ranting, and believe me, over the years he hasn't shut up about the Scrolls." Carolyn folded her arms and looked to Penelope. "You believe this?"

"We tested the scroll, Caro. It contains trace amounts of the poison. We need to find Tim because even if a doctor gets ahold of him, they won't know what they are dealing with. If we can find him, we can treat him."

"Find him! He's probably in the middle of the desert screaming at the clouds for all we know."

"He must be in Tel Aviv. If the rest of his crew went there like Schaal said, then he could've gone to get them to prove his find and became sick on the way." Penelope showed her the plastic Jesus money box and the packaging it came in. "These stamps are from a post office in Tel Aviv too. We can start there and see if they recognize him, or maybe they'll have some footage of him on their security cameras."

"It's *April*, Penelope. You know what Easter and Passover are like in Israel. Everything is packed, including the hotels. We are just going to try wandering the streets with the hope we bump into him?"

"It's better than sitting here doing nothing and hoping he turns up in a hospital!" argued Penelope.

"I have a house in Florentin. We can set up a base there and avoid tourists," Zo said, referring to one of the more central suburbs of Tel Aviv.

"I'll talk to Galenos and see if we can find a trace on Tim's phone," Alexis suggested, before adding to Carolyn, "He's the tech and computer expert I collected."

"Of course! Because everyone has a live-in tech expert."

"Ignore her. She gets bitchy when she's jet-lagged," Penelope said, and then to Carolyn, "Cool it, Caro. We're going to get Tim like you wanted, so stop being such a pain in the ass about it."

Carolyn groaned. "I'm sorry, it's just…I thought I wouldn't have to worry about him once I gave him the boot."

"Maybe you shouldn't be so hard on yourself. It has been a very long day for you. Let Penelope and Alexis worry about flights and arrangements to Israel, and we can get you some more wine," Zo said, offering Carolyn his arm. She looked like she was about to burst into tears as she nodded and took it.

Penelope shot Zo a grateful smile behind Carolyn's back as he steered her out of the library. Penelope turned in her chair and rested her head against Alexis's stomach.

"Kill me now," she said, her voice muffled by his shirt.

"She's upset, *cara*. Zo will feed her, and she'll calm down."

"You say that because you don't know her. I forgot how much emotional work she can be when she's stressed." Alexis ran his hand over her braid, and she burrowed further into him.

"I've already booked us some flights for tomorrow so we'll find your friend soon enough. Carolyn likes Zo, so he and Aelia can look after her while we search with more magical means when we get there." Penelope put her arms around him, feeling grateful that he was shouldering some of the burdens of planning so that she didn't have to.

"Would you like a tour of the library?" he asked. Penelope let him go and got to her feet.

"Hell yes. It'll take my mind off how frustrating my friends are."

He leaned down and kissed her long enough that she began to wonder if the library door had a lock.

"That's a good start," she said when they broke apart. She took Alexis's hand and squeezed it. "Show me everything."

"It's still underwhelming compared to the Archives," he warned.

"Oh, I'm just so underwhelmed by all of the priceless manuscripts around me," Penelope said and then sighed dramatically, hand to her forehead. "You are such a jaded old man."

"You should've seen the library at the Citadel of Magicians in Atlas. Nobody knew how deep it really went underground. Nereus said that was where she kept the manuscripts of the darker times on Atlantis. Acolytes used to spread rumors that a chimera lived at the bottom. Every year they used to dare the new recruits to go as far as they could before they got too scared and came back up…" Alexis said, falling into memories as they walked between the beautifully carved shelves and Byzantine windows that opened out to the canals.

"And let me guess, you had to be the one to go the deepest," said Penelope.

"It wasn't like I was trying to test my bravery or impress the other apprentices."

"Of course not."

"It was about the chimera. I had never seen one before, and I wanted to. Nereus wouldn't tell me if there was one down there for sure. She told me she would feed me to it if I slacked off in my studies," said Alexis.

"Sounds like Nereus. Tell me, did you find it?"

"The chimera found me. I kept walking until I found the books from before the time of Poseidon. They had a dark energy, and I refused to touch them, knowing some history is best forgotten. The chimera stalked me and scared me almost to death. It was in the form of a lion, with magnificent wings, and turned out to be a delightful beast. She could shape shift too. Sometimes she was as big as a dog, and others the size of a bear."

"You're kidding me!"

"No, it's the truth, I swear it. She had been placed down there by Poseidon himself to guard and protect the Citadel if it was ever attacked."

"But what did she eat?"

"She fed off the magical energy of the Citadel itself. When I asked her if she ate people, she was most disgusted."

"I know I shouldn't be surprised that you made friends with a chimera, and yet here I am."

"I called her Antheia. She was lonely, so I visited her as much as I could."

"Alexis Donato, that may be one of the cutest things I've ever heard," Penelope said with a laugh, standing on tiptoes to kiss his cheek.

As they walked, Penelope breathed in the scents of wood and ancient leather and paper. Her frustration slowly melted away under the comfort of books and the warmth of Alexis's stories. By the time they made it back to the main doors, she had promised herself that if they got back from Israel in one piece, she was going to explore every inch of the library.

TEN

LATER THAT EVENING, once Penelope had taken Carolyn back upstairs after an incident-free dinner, Alexis went down to the Archives in search of Galenos and Lyca. She had finished constructing his new arm and leg, and Alexis was needed for the final piece of magic to hold.

Alexis found them in her workshop, Galenos already sitting on a wooden chair waiting, while Lyca ranted in harsh whispers about doing such strong magic when there were strangers in the palazzo. Galenos simply took her hand and kissed it, the simple gesture making her shoulders relax, her fire and heat tempered by his cool water. Alexis waited until Lyca had finished kissing Galenos before he made his presence known.

"Defender," Lyca greeted.

"You have done fine work on these, Lyca," Alexis complimented her. He picked up the heavy mechanical arm and turned it this way and that, inspecting the craftsmanship.

The magic Alexis felt pulsing through the work was astonishing. In every fold and layer, Lyca's protections had been hammered carefully into the metals. Galenos's magic could be felt in the smaller pieces, the animatronics that he had added so the muscles and fingers would move like real flesh. Alexis had never seen such a perfect synergy of science and magic.

"Are you ready to begin?" Alexis asked Galenos.

"Yes. I can't wait to be able to move about again," he said. "I've missed being down here. I can't remember when I've spent so much time above the lagoon."

Alexis placed the mechanical arm on the bench, sliding it up to where the stub of Galenos's arm remained. Lyca adjusted it, pulling the metal gently over his tight, black skin.

"You aren't going to mind having Penelope's changes about the place now that she's the Archivist?" asked Alexis carefully. They had *all* thought that Galenos was to be Nereus's heir, and he didn't think the shock of it not being him had completely worn off with the other magicians.

"My computer labs are still the same, and that's all that matters to me. Penelope is a good woman, Defender. She will do a far better job as Archivist than I ever would. Nereus knew that I wouldn't have paid enough attention to the books and artifacts. I believe she saw Penelope coming a long time before Penelope found your Tablet in the sea," Galenos replied, taking Alexis's hand and giving it a squeeze. "If nothing else, it will be nice to have someone so young around here to understand the technological changes I want to make."

"If you try and make me use a computer to search for things, I'll riot," Alexis teased.

"Can we get on with it? I'll need to know quickly if there are adjustments I have to do to make him more comfortable," Lyca said, interrupting. Her impatience and worry made her shorter-tempered than usual, but Alexis knew better than to call her out on it. He had enough to worry about without getting a dagger in his throat.

Alexis could feel the healing magic swirling in his veins as he placed one hand on the mechanical arm and the other on Galenos's flesh.

"Hold him, Lyca," he commanded, his magic building. Lyca placed her hands on Galenos's bare, muscled shoulders.

"I'm ready, Defender," Galenos assured him. Knowing what was about to happen wasn't the same as experiencing it, and Galenos bit down on a scream as Alexis's magic flew out of him and into Galenos's muscle, bone, and nerves.

Alexis barely heard Galenos's cries as he dropped deeply into his magic, seeing every connection he needed to mend and fuse in the other man's arm. Magical metals mended to his flesh, nerves connecting to wires until it was moving together, with Alexis checking every connection again before pulling back into himself. Galenos was covered in sweat and tears, Lyca cradling his head to her chest, whispering soothing words to him in the old tongue.

"It's done," Alexis said, his body feeling heavy and cumbersome.

Galenos looked down at the sleek, black metal, and the smooth, mechanical fingers twitched.

"Take it easy, my love. It will take some time for the pathways to recognize the right signals," Lyca said in the gentlest tone Alexis had ever heard from her. She passed him a bottle of water, and he gulped it down quickly.

"Now the leg," Galenos demanded. Alexis exchanged a look with Lyca, not wanting to push Galenos too hard in one night.

Galenos made a frustrated noise. "Don't look at each other like I'm some child who doesn't know what he's asking. It's my body, my pain. Alexis is going to Israel tomorrow—who knows when he'll be back? I don't want to wait any longer."

Alexis nodded, fitting the mechanical leg over the stump that remained. He wanted to work faster, to get Galenos's pain over quickly, but it was work that was intricate, and he didn't want to make any errors. He was pulled into that quiet place where there was only his magic and the puzzle of nerve and muscle and metal, unaware of how long he was at it.

When Alexis finally emerged from the trancelike state, Galenos had passed out, and Lyca was holding him up, singing an Atlantean lullaby. Alexis sighed before opening his eyes, giving her the chance to stop singing and school her face back into a warrior expression.

"Is it done?" Lyca asked.

Alexis rested his hand on the workbench and struggled to pull himself upright. "It's done. Let Galenos sleep for as long as he can. It'll give his body time to adjust."

With Lyca's help, they carried Galenos to a camp bed at the back of the workshop where Lyca usually slept when she was too engrossed in a project to leave.

"I owe you for this, Defender," Lyca said as she escorted Alexis out of the workshop.

"You owe me nothing, Lyca. He's my brother. You know that."

Lyca halted him, her strong hand gripping his bicep, her pale eyes fierce. "I *mean* it, Alexis."

Very carefully he rested his hand over hers. "If you want to do something for me, look after Venice in my absence and work with Marco Dandolo if he needs you. Reitia said that there's still darkness lingering in Cannaregio. Now that Galenos is healed, I need you to find it. Hunt down every follower of the demon that you can."

"It would be my absolute pleasure to serve you in this matter, Defender." Lyca let him go, a predatory gleam already in her eyes. "Look after Penelope. I feel that not everything is as it seems with her friend, Tim."

"I thought you didn't like her," Alexis said, mildly surprised.

"Of course I like her. Why do you think I get so angry when she wants to do stupid things that jeopardize us? Or run away to Israel where Thevetat is? The others know better; she does not. Her heart is a tender thing. She isn't like us."

"Maybe that's why Nereus chose her," Alexis said. Lyca's eyes narrowed even as she offered him a small smile.

"Maybe that's why *you* chose her."

AFTER LEAVING Lyca to attend to Galenos, Alexis pulled his phone from his pocket and rang Marco. He didn't know what time it was, but he doubted the police inspector would be asleep.

"*Signore* Donato, to what do I owe this late-night call?" Marco answered.

"We are leaving for Israel tomorrow."

"Penelope's friend still hasn't turned up, I take it?"

"No, and we can't do much from Venice. Carolyn is here, and we will all go to Tel Aviv in the morning," Alexis explained.

"Have you considered going to the police yet? I know it's hard for you to trust anyone, but if he's missing, then they will be able to help you find him sooner."

"Not yet. It's complicated. Thevetat's followers are already hunting him, and I don't want anyone else in their path unnecessarily."

"So what do you need, Alexis? I know you want something."

"I want you to keep in contact with Lyca while we are away. I've told her to assist you in your investigations and to protect you if Thevetat's followers should reappear."

There was a long silence at the other end of the line.

"Are you sure Lyca would be willing to help me? From my brief encounters with her, I don't think she likes me very much."

"Lyca doesn't like anyone very much. If you do find another residence in Cannaregio belonging to the followers of Thevetat, you aren't allowed to enter it without her. Do you understand me?"

"I understand, even though I hate it when you use your *generalissimo* voice on me."

"The house could be full of traps that will tear both your mind and body apart. Deal with the voice. I'm only trying to keep you alive. Galenos will be able to start doing a more thorough search on Duilio's resorts and assets for you in the next day or so. He'll be able to dig things up that the lawyer won't."

"Ah, the lawyer. I'm almost tempted to introduce her to Lyca just to see who would be the last one standing. I suppose I don't have to tell you to protect Penelope?"

"No, you don't."

"That's good. Happy travels, Alexis." Marco hung up the phone.

Alexis sighed, looking up at the floating lights in the cavern above him. His magic was drained, leaving his muscles aching and brain on fire. When he stepped through the portal and into his tower, Penelope was already there, lying backward across his bed and reading a book. He swayed, and she was off the bed and wrapping her arm around him to prop him up.

"What's wrong? Are you drunk?" she asked.

"Galenos's healing drained my magic. I'll be fine after a few hours' sleep," he reassured her. She was wearing a blue camisole, the lace and cotton outlining the curves of her breasts in a way that made him wish he hadn't drained all of his energy. With gentle hands, she pulled off his shoes and unbuttoned his shirt.

"You should've asked me to help if you knew that you would be this wrecked afterward," she muttered. Alexis wanted to tell her that he'd survived this long without anyone helping him, but he was enjoying her fussing over him too much. No one had ever done it before. She helped him out of his shirt, running her hands down his back in a gentle massage that made him groan.

"Don't get any ideas, magician. You're in no condition to satisfy me tonight," Penelope said, giving his shoulder a gentle bite.

"You know that, and still you torment me? Evil woman." He pulled her close, resting his head on her chest, the lace of her pajamas tickling his chin.

"Just go to sleep before you dig yourself too deep of a hole," she said, kissing his forehead, her hands stroking his hair. He summoned a final pulse of magic, and the lights went out around them.

ELEVEN

TEL AVIV WAS already hot by the time Penelope landed the following day. They had boarded during a misty Venetian morning, and now the dry heat of a Tel Aviv afternoon had her stripping off layers of clothing. She had spent the last four hours wedged between Alexis and Carolyn and had been ready to throttle her best friend by the end of the flight.

After sleeping in a decent bed, Carolyn's claws had retracted, so they had spent most of the flight talking pleasantly about their common areas of interest ranging from Sumerian mythology to recent films. It wasn't until the last half hour that Carolyn decided to stir up trouble.

"Tell me what you think of Penelope's Atlantis theory, Alexis," Carolyn asked sweetly.

"It's the most comprehensive and believable I've ever heard," he answered, wrapping his fingers around Penelope's hand.

"You know, whoever she's dated has always come second to her true love that is Atlantis, right? Is that going to be a problem for you?" Carolyn pressed. Penelope fought the urge to sink further back into her seat. Talking about her disastrous dating history was right next to pap smears on her least-favorite-things-to-do list. She was going to murder Carolyn.

Alexis pushed his aviators up so he could make clear eye contact with her soon-to-be ex-best friend.

"Penelope's obsessions and interests are just some of the many things I like about her. I'd never feel comfortable with a woman if she decided to give up all the things that are important to her just to wait on me. It would be an incredibly boring way to spend one's time, don't you agree?"

"Entirely," Carolyn said with a pleased smile.

"You're being a bitch," Penelope hissed at her.

"God, Pen. You can't blame me for wanting to be sure about him. Venice is a long way from Melbourne, if whatever arrangement you two have doesn't work out."

Arrangement. The word made Penelope's blood boil.

That's when it hit her: Carolyn was pissed that she had moved. Stuck in a plane wasn't the right place to have it out with her, so Penelope had remained quiet as they gathered their bags and headed out of the arrivals gate.

"This fucking city," Carolyn said with a sigh as they drove from the airport in the back of a sleek, black town car.

"You don't like Tel Aviv?" Zo asked from the front seat.

"It's not the city's fault. Every time I've come here with Tim, it's been a disaster. I don't think I've ever just…had fun."

"We are going to have to change that," Zo said with a decisive nod.

"We are caught up in more of Tim's bullshit, so I doubt it."

"You wouldn't be so angry if you didn't still care for him. Family is fucked that way." Then Zo told them about the time Phaidros had gone on a partying binge and set a fire that had nearly burned down Rome.

"Please tell me he's not talking about *the* Great Fire in AD 64?" Penelope whispered to Alexis.

"Unfortunately, yes. Between Phaidros and Aelia, I'm surprised Rome lasted as long as it did," Alexis replied, his expression amused. Thankfully, Carolyn thought Zo was exaggerating the scope of the fire and laughed until she cried.

"Okay, you win. That's definitely worse than anything Tim has done. He's more interested in damaging himself than destroying property when he's on one of his adventures."

Zo's property in Florentin was a three-story, white town house surrounded by lush gardens and a high, stone wall.

"Bedrooms are on the second and third floors, so take your pick. I asked the housekeepers to make sure the place was ready for us," Zo said as he opened the front door.

Penelope and Alexis claimed a room on the top floor that looked out over the flourishing gardens. Unlike the grandness of the Venetian palazzo, Zo's house felt more like a home with his choice of art and furniture and overall lack of magical sentience.

Once Penelope had dumped her suitcase in a corner, she kissed Alexis for courage and went to find Carolyn. Penelope managed to corner her in a room on the second floor, slamming the door behind her.

"All right, Caro, out with it," demanded Penelope.

"What? You're the one that's shitty all of a sudden," Carolyn said, throwing open her suitcase across the bed.

"Maybe I'm shitty because you grilled Alexis on the plane and dredged up my embarrassing dating history in front of him!"

"I wanted to take his measure, that's all."

"Isn't it enough that *I've* taken his measure? I've never needed your approval with guys I've dated before, so why do you care all of a sudden?"

"Because you never left me before, that's why!" shouted Carolyn, turning red.

"I've always been away on digs or traveling for work. Why does it matter now?"

"You always came back! You were only supposed to be in Venice for a few weeks, and then strangers turn up at our apartment to clean out all of your stuff, and you were just *gone*. No proper goodbye, nothing!"

"And me being in Venice means we can't be friends? Your reasoning is ridiculous."

"It's not that you've moved; it's these people, this lifestyle…how can a girl from a farm in Bendigo compete with it all?"

"You're not meant to compete! And you know I don't give a damn about 'lifestyles.' I'm not here because they are fucking wealthy, Caro! I stayed for the opportunity, the job, as well as Alexis." Penelope gave in and pulled Carolyn into a tight, angry hug. "I'm not replacing you, so stop acting like a psycho. We've been friends for ten years; these guys can't compete with you, not the other way around."

"I'm sorry. You know I've got the worst abandonment issues ever," sniffed Carolyn. "First Tim, then you. I don't like being left behind all the time."

"You aren't being left behind. We are just having different adventures for a while. You knew I wasn't going to settle down teaching kids at universities for the rest of my life."

"I don't want you giving up on your Atlantis dream for a comfortable job and a hot guy either," Carolyn said stubbornly.

"I'm not giving up on Atlantis! I'm using the job as an excuse to go through Alexis's library and files, using his connections. The books and manuscripts he has will help me find it."

Penelope wanted to tell her the truth; that she *had* found Atlantis, just not in the manner she'd expected. She loved Carolyn, but she was also beginning to experience a deeply protective streak when it came to the magicians and their secrets. *Have my loyalties changed already?*

Carolyn released her from the hug. "You're right. Alexis was crazy enough to ask you about magic at your Tablet lecture, so he's bound to know something right?"

"He's worse than me! He has an entire gallery full of Atlantis stuff. At least I stuck with the historical. He has everything, including whacky crystal power and all the new-age books and theories."

Carolyn managed a laugh. "Good to know he gets the obsession at least. And he gets *you*. That makes me happy, if a little jealous, that you're surrounded by a pack of good-looking men who adore you."

"Don't be silly. You can get anyone you want. You're just too damaged from Cyclone Tim to realize it," Penelope assured her.

"This is the last time I'm going to come to help him," Carolyn said quietly. "I can't do this anymore. Next time, he's on his own."

"I agree entirely. Time for that boy to grow up." Penelope took her hand and squeezed it. "Are we good?"

"Yeah, Bryne, we're good. Sorry for cornering Aladdin."

"I'm sorry I didn't come back to see you before I moved. There wasn't enough time."

"I know. It's selfish of me to have expected it from you. Hell, I know how much you hate moving so it makes sense you'd make your new employer organize other people to do it for you," Carolyn said.

"It definitely has its perks," Penelope admitted.

There was a friendly knock at the door, and then it opened, revealing Phaidros and Zo, both shirtless and sipping bright-yellow daiquiris.

"Are you two coming for a swim? Zo has a pool out the back, and this heat is already killing me," Phaidros said, with the smile that Penelope always thought of as the Golden Apollo.

"Yep. I like water…swimming, I mean," Carolyn stammered.

"Excellent. Drinks are ready in the kitchen, if Aelia hasn't gotten to them," Zo said, completely unaware of the effect their muscular torsos were having. Phaidros, who knew exactly what the view was doing to poor Carolyn, shared a mischievous look with Penelope. She ran a threatening finger across her throat in warning.

"We'll see you out there," he said, nudging Zo down the hall. Carolyn stuck her head out of the door to watch them go.

"Jesus, Penelope. How did you pick only one?" she whispered.

Penelope smiled widely. "Easily. I picked the best."

LATER THAT evening, Penelope made excuses for her and Alexis, and they slipped out of the garden gates and into the streets of Florentin. Carolyn was drunk by the pool and enjoying the other magicians' company, so after some good-natured ribbing about lovers needing time alone, she hadn't questioned them further or asked to tag along.

Florentin was alive with clubs and restaurants and people venturing out as the night cooled. Alexis laid Penelope's hand over his arm, and she drew close to him to keep out of the way of partying tourists.

"How are we meant to find Tim in all of this chaos?" lamented Penelope. She hadn't been able to recall any additional details from her meditation, and the back street she had seen had been too generic to be useful.

"I could try and trace the magic that was left on the scroll because it had such a unique signature to the power used. The problem with doing that is if there are priests of Thevetat still in the city, they may be able to sense me doing it."

"Wouldn't Thevetat be able to track Tim the same way?"

"Not without having handled the scroll first to know what he was searching for. That doesn't mean they won't be able to search for him by other means. If they have been trying to find him in the past three weeks and they haven't, then your friend is very resourceful." Penelope didn't think it was Tim's resourcefulness, but pure dumb luck which had always been his friend.

"Tim might be hiding with people that he knows. He's always kept contacts with people trading antiquities in case something authentic came up. I've never approved of getting involved with such dodgy people even if he's never had any trouble with them. He might've convinced them to stash him somewhere." Although Penelope wasn't sure if that was better or worse. Tim's black-market connections were something they had always fought vehemently over, even when Tim assured her that what they usually traded were knockoffs.

"We'll start tomorrow at the post office where he sent the package and go from there," Alexis said, moving her out of the way of a group of drunk men. A few checked her out, but one glare from Alexis soon had them looking in the other direction.

"I haven't sensed any other magic yet," Alexis continued when the drunks were out of earshot. "I'm not stretching my magical feelers out in a way that would attract attention, but I'll feel the ghost of the magic if Tim has been nearby."

"Thank you, Alexis," said Penelope, squeezing his arm. She didn't want to put him at risk more than she had to. If they didn't find Tim soon, the curse would eat his mind until it turned to Swiss cheese, and she wouldn't be able to keep Carolyn from going to the police for long.

"It's the least I can do, *cara*. Besides, it's a nice night for a walk with a lovely woman." He kissed her hand.

"Is that so? If I didn't know any better, I'd say you're just trying to get into my pants."

"Is it working?" He was giving her a smile that made her mind go places that were dangerous in public. Penelope quickly looked away.

"Most definitely."

"Excellent. I like this courting we have decided on."

"I'm just happy you still want to court me after getting grilled for the last two days by Carolyn," said Penelope as they reached the promenade at Alma Beach. It was windy and warm, the streetlights along the concrete paths reflecting out over the ocean. Alexis drew her into a kiss.

"It would take a lot more than the likes of Carolyn Williams and a few snide comments to stop me from courting you," he assured her. She went to kiss him again, but he paused, head tilting, listening to a sound she couldn't make out.

"What's wrong?" she asked. Penelope looked around, searching for a face in the crowd that she might recognize, looking for a threat.

Alexis began to walk, following whatever had caught his attention. He headed away from the beach toward a strip of waterfront hotels and turned down a side street. Penelope's heart raced as she realized she was standing in the street from her meditation, the sickly yellow florescent lights turning the street murky with shadows. Alexis closed his eyes and placed a hand on the side of a building.

"He was here."

TWELVE

THE POST OFFICE at Gane'i Sharona was packed with people, its service staff eying Penelope and Carolyn warily as they came in. Penelope showed them the stamps ripped from her package as well as Tim's photo. They refused her help until Zo came to her aid, using his charming smile and fluent Hebrew to flatter his way into a cramped back office to review security footage on a tiny, black-and-white TV.

"What did you do? Convince them you're police or something?" Carolyn asked suspiciously.

"I'd never imitate the authorities!" Zo protested.

"Maybe not in Israel," Penelope whispered to Alexis who struggled to hide a smile. She wasn't about to forget that he'd somehow gained access to the piece of the Atlantis Tablet she'd found long enough to not only replace the original with a fake but also get the real piece out of Greece. Zo was charming, but not that charming. Somehow Penelope doubted a jail cell would hold him for long.

"There he is!" Carolyn said, pointing at the grainy footage.

"He looks like shit," Penelope replied, bending closer at the frozen frame. Tim had a black eye and looked like he hadn't slept or eaten in days. When they let the footage play, they watched Tim pay for the postage, talk in a friendly manner to the service staff, and disappear out of the door again.

"I remember him now," the manager said after Penelope had asked for the service woman's name. "He was talking about partying too hard. We see it often in the tourists. A group of his friends came searching for him about ten minutes later. They said they lost him at one of the clubs. They made everyone uncomfortable."

"What friends?" Penelope asked, and Zo fiddled with the controller to speed the footage up.

"Stop! That is them," the manager said. Two men and a woman were asking questions and looking around them. "They were high on something. I know that for sure. Everyone was calmer once they had gone."

Alexis leaned forward and took a photo of the screens with his phone.

"Do you know them?" the manager asked.

"No. But I'm going to," said Alexis, the strong hint of a threat in his voice. "Let's see if Phaidros has seen them before."

ACROSS THE other side of the city, Aelia and Phaidros followed the walkways along Alma Beach and the hotel strip searching for any signs of Tim and the priests of Thevetat. It was a beautiful, spring day, and Phaidros would've preferred to be lying on the beach with a drink, Aelia lounging in a skimpy bikini beside him, than searching a day's old trail.

"Can you feel it yet? The signature that Alexis was talking about?" Aelia asked beside him. She wore a bright-green sundress that showed off too much of her distractingly lovely limbs and made it hard for Phaidros to concentrate whenever he looked at her.

"I can, but it's very faint," he replied with a frown. All magic was energy, and Phaidros could trace the trail of it even better than Alexis. He pushed aside two metal bins and found a bundle of clothes. The magic from the scroll coated them and the wall behind it. "Penelope's friend must've been hiding here for maybe a day before Thevetat flushed him out."

"I want to know how the bastards got onto him at all. They would've had to have someone feeding them information about the digs in the area to learn of the discovery so quickly," said Aelia. Her sunglasses hid the uneasiness in her eyes, but not from her voice. Phaidros didn't want to risk losing any body parts, so he didn't reach out to comfort her.

"We'll find them, Aelia," he assured her as he straightened. She rewarded him with a small smile. It wasn't the too-dazzling one she turned on when she wanted her own way, but something quieter and more genuine.

"What?" he asked, hating that she still made his heart beat faster whenever she looked at him.

"You said, '*We'll* find them.' I like that. I appreciate you letting me come with you, and that you aren't trying to force me to stay behind," she admitted.

"Now that I've seen you in action, I wouldn't dream of leaving you behind, princess. I need someone to protect me."

Phaidros had only told Alexis what had happened the night that the priests of Thevetat had attacked Venice. He had gone with Aelia to the Malamocco inlet to protect the MOSE gates and to stop anyone from sabotaging them. While Alexis had been nearly drowned at the Lido, Phaidros had watched slack-jawed as Aelia tore through a group of Thevetat's thugs on her own. She used her voice to harness her powerful magic, and she had sung to their enemies to render them helpless before using that potent gift to explode their hearts. Then she had calmly beheaded every single one with her *gladius* to ensure that Thevetat couldn't resurrect any of them.

Phaidros had known Aelia's weakness for powerful generals and warriors over the centuries. He hadn't realized until that moment that she had been learning from them. When he'd asked her if she could use a bow, she had laughed and simply said, "Attila said I was the best marksman he'd ever seen from the back of a horse. He was a good teacher, so really he was praising himself." And had left it at that.

Now Phaidros was kept up at night thinking not of all the other men who had loved her, but what all those other men had taught her. No one could cloud his judgment like Aelia, and for the first time, he'd been able to see how much he'd overlooked as he dwelled on his own hurt feelings. To not be fighting with her was new and made him happier and more uneasy than he'd felt in years.

Phaidros's phone buzzed with Alexis's ringtone, ruining the moment. A black-and-white picture of three figures looked back at him.

"What is it?" Aelia asked, leaning into him so she could see the screen.

"They were following Tim. They must be Vessels or acolytes of the demon."

Aelia looked away from the screen and back to the pile of Tim's clothes on the ground. "We need to keep searching. If they find him first, I'd hate to see what that will do to Penelope."

"She was their captive, too. She knows the stakes and what we are most likely to find if we fail," Phaidros said firmly. It was Carolyn he was worried about. She seemed too kind and clueless to be caught up in such a mess.

He touched the clothes, absorbing the energy of the curse as well as Tim himself. He shut his eyes and let the sensations flood him. He could feel the terror and the madness vibrating from each article of clothing. The intensity nearly overwhelmed him, pulling him down, down, down into darkness.

A small hand rested on the back of his neck, gently kneading. "Come back, Phaidros," Aelia whispered in his ear. The only thing strong enough to rattle him harder than a two-thousand-year-old curse was the feeling of Aelia's soft hands on his too-hot skin. He shuddered all over and opened his eyes. She was leaning over him, her hand still at his nape.

"I thought I'd lost you there for a moment," she said uneasily, pushing a golden curl back from his forehead. He was still too dumbfounded to find her touching him to form a proper sentence. He closed his eyes again and tried to steady his breathing.

"It was a necessary risk. Now that I've absorbed the magic, I'll be able to follow it much easier."

Aelia let him go and stepped back. "Please tell me next time you plan on doing that. You scared me. I was talking to you, and you couldn't hear me. You were completely vacant."

"I'm sorry, I didn't expect it to be so strong. Lucky I have you watching my back," he said, standing up again. He didn't want to look at her and see concern for him. He didn't like the idea that she cared. It unnerved him and left him with too many questions that he didn't want to know the answers to.

"He went this way." Phaidros pointed, as he let the sensation of the energy pull him in the right direction. Aelia merely nodded her head and followed, not questioning his abilities for a moment.

The sun was going down as they reached the slums of Neve Sha'anan. Phaidros drew fractionally closer to Aelia, too aware of the hungry eyes of the men who passed by her. The energy signature had led them to an old office building full of squatters, piles of rubbish clogging up the walkways in front of it. They found a place to stand across the road where they could keep an eye on people coming in and out of the front doors.

"We can't just go in. If Tim is there, he might think we are priests hunting him. He'll spook and run again," said Aelia.

Phaidros rang Alexis. "We think we found him. We are going to need Penelope and Carolyn."

"Where are you?" asked Alexis.

"Neve Sha'anan. I'll send you the coordinates," Phaidros answered before hanging up and sending him a link.

"Do you really think he's going to bring Penelope with him?" asked Aelia, knowing full well that Alexis would cringe at the thought of letting Penelope enter such a place.

"Penelope isn't going to give him a choice. He'll just have to protect her as she does as she wishes. If the priests are there, she'll just have to see that side of him as well."

"She already has, and it still wasn't enough to scare her away."

"And what of Carolyn? You can bet that she'll arrive with Penelope." Phaidros and the others had been very careful around the far too perceptive Carolyn. She was a pretty woman and had a lovely, warm energy that made her easy company. Unfortunately, she could see auras almost as clearly as he could, and it made the magicians even more wary of her.

"From what Carolyn has told me, I doubt this is the worst place she's been while hunting for her illusive ex-boyfriend in the past. He must be something special to have both her and Penelope so concerned," said Aelia with a sniff of disapproval.

"If he's not, I'm sure you'll tell them," Phaidros replied with a grin.

"I would never tell them who to care about. I'm not above telling *him* to pull himself together for their sakes."

"Under pain of death?"

"Death would be the least of his worries," Aelia said with a small laugh. Phaidros had the overwhelming desire to kiss her like he always did whenever she smiled. He contented himself to letting his magic ever so slightly touch her aura. It was vibrant and intoxicating, and he knew he would kick himself for doing it in a few hours' time.

Fifteen minutes later, a black SUV pulled up at the sidewalk and Alexis, Penelope, Carolyn, and Zo climbed out.

"Thank you so much for your help," Penelope whispered to Phaidros, squeezing his hand gently before Carolyn joined them.

"How do you know he is here?" she asked, looking up at the building with skeptical eyes.

"I have some less-than-savory contacts that told me a story of a raving Australian who's been scaring locals in the neighborhood. Not an easy task in this part of the city," Phaidros told her, the lie believable enough that Carolyn didn't ask further questions.

"Let's get it over with," Penelope said, crossing the road before anyone could grab her. Alexis hurried after her, ignoring the cars that slammed on the brakes and horns that blared.

"She's going to give him a heart attack one of these days," said Zo before following. Alexis was speaking to Penelope, his hand resting lightly on her arm to stop her from going in.

"Let me go first, *cara,*" he was saying. "Phaidros and Carolyn can come next, and Aelia and Zo can watch our backs. We do this safely, yes?"

"Fine," Penelope said with a sigh. She waited for him to disappear into the filthy hallway before following.

"I've never seen Penelope let a man take charge before," Carolyn said disapprovingly to Phaidros.

"She knows it's for the best."

"Oh yes? And what does a rich boy know that she doesn't? She's done enough self-defense over the years to not be caught off guard."

"Alexis has many skills. Stay close to me," Phaidros instructed. Everyone was carefully sheltering Carolyn, always ensuring one of them was close to either side of her, whether she realized it or not. He'd forgotten how complicated it was to have humans around. Penelope had plunged headfirst into their world, absorbing and accepting it so quickly that he'd never worried about pretending to be anything other than what he was.

Inside, the building smelled like despairing humanity. People were crammed tightly into too-hot rooms: junkies laid on mattresses of filthy clothes and blankets, a refugee family stood protectively around a gaggle of children, whores cooed as they passed, and hard-eyed men glared. Phaidros shot a glance over his shoulder at Zo, but he hadn't needed to ask; Zo was already subtlety moving Aelia closer between them to shield her.

Alexis was a looming figure in the sketchy light, Penelope poking her head into every room and knocking on doors. People hid their faces from Alexis, but Penelope coaxed them with gentle words, showing them pictures of Tim.

"She's going about this the wrong way, and I don't want to be here all night," Aelia said before she reached into her bag and pulled out a handful of money.

"I have a hundred euros for anyone who can give me information about a blond male tourist talking about demons," she shouted in Hebrew, the power of her voice carrying through the dilapidated building.

"Are you trying to get us killed?" hissed Zo.

"Just wait..." Aelia insisted.

Phaidros reached for the dagger in his pocket just as a door opened beside them. A girl no older than ten stared at them, her little body frail, but her black eyes sharp.

"A hundred and twenty and I'll take you to him," she said shrewdly. Aelia's smile widened.

"You'll get the money when I can confirm it's him," she said. The girl nodded solemnly, the bargain struck.

"This way," she said. "He's a few floors up from us."

Alexis looked worried as Aelia took the girl's grubby hand and let her pull her along the hall to a set of stairs. Phaidros felt the tension in Zo rise even further as they filed into the narrow stairwell. They would be trapped like rats if they were attacked. Thankfully, the girl pushed open another fire escape door after only two floors, and they were in another dark hallway. A wall of dirty glass windows looked out over the street. It seemed likely the floor had previously been used for conference rooms.

"Other people were up here. They were too afraid of his screaming to stay." She stopped and pointed to a tiny office with a dark bundle cowering on the floor.

"Tim?" Penelope approached the broken door and shoved it open. "Tim, is that you?"

The stinking figure unwrapped himself. His dirty blond hair ensnared his face, falling into bloodshot, blue eyes that burned with madness. Phaidros's skin shuddered at the curse that had its claws deep into the man. It covered him in faint layers of orange light that were slowly draining the life from him.

"Hey, Tim? It's Pen. I got your package. I'm here to help."

"I won't be tricked by you again, demon!" He lunged for her, a shard of metal in his hand. Phaidros reached for Penelope just as Tim hit a bubble of air in front of her and was flung back, scrambling and suspended in the air. Alexis was standing between Tim and Penelope, shimmering blue light racing under his skin.

"What…the fuck?" Carolyn squeaked just as Phaidros grabbed her hand and she sagged to the ground.

"Well, hasn't this gotten interesting," Aelia said with an amused laugh. "Nice save, Defender."

"I could've handled him," Penelope insisted.

"You couldn't have handled the curse that he was about to pass onto you," replied Alexis, still staring at the man clawing at the air. "Phaidros? Knock him out. We need to get him back to the house to try and remove whatever this is." Phaidros passed a sleeping Carolyn to Zo before stepping forward to Alexis.

"I'm sorry I was too late to grab Pen—" Phaidros began.

Alexis silenced his apology with a look. "She wasn't hurt, that's what matters."

"Oh, but Penelope's gonna be," Tim said. "Thevetat wants her. He whispers about her on the wind. Penelope, Penelope of the soft skin and delicious mind." Tim cackled. "He's going to release the demons from the sky, and they will take the earth back. Seals of Kings, ones wielded by emperors and conquerors will do nothing to stop him. Trinkets! Sleeping for centuries with no one to know it, to wield it, to use it."

"Crazy people," Phaidros said and then sighed before placing a hand on the bubble that held him, and Tim slumped, a puppet with cut strings.

THIRTEEN

ACK AT THE house in Florentin, Penelope watched as Alexis carefully wiped Tim's face with a wet cloth in an effort to find the man she knew under the dirt and grime. He didn't want her touching Tim while the curse was still active, but he held no fear of it transferring to himself.

"It's because he's already mad, *bella*. It would be like trying to catch the flu while you already had it," Phaidros had said. "It's a shame to cure him really; magicians love mad people."

"Not when the madness is killing him," snapped Alexis. "And the reason I can touch him is because of the warding, not because I'm mad. Get out of here, Phaidros. I don't have the patience to deal with your ridiculousness right now."

Phaidros had gone but not before shooting Penelope a glance that said, *I told you he is mad.*

Carolyn was sleeping in the room beside them, whatever magic Phaidros had used keeping her solidly knocked out. Penelope sat down on the floor next to Alexis's chair and rested her back against the wall.

"Are you okay?" he asked, not taking his eyes off his patient.

"He didn't recognize me. Not really. Do you think Thevetat planted the thought to kill me?" she asked, drawing her knees up to her chest.

"If he had Tim, he wouldn't have risked letting him go. The Vessel could've mentioned you when he was close enough to hear. Tim could've heard Thevetat ranting. I've never seen this kind of curse before, so I can't be sure."

"Zo will know how to break it, right?"

"Perhaps. If Zo can't, there is one other we know who definitely can. I'm reluctant to go to him unless the circumstances are dire."

"More dire than this?" Penelope pointed at her unconscious friend.

"He's still alive, Penelope. He had enough sense to hide where no one could find him. He's not entirely lost to us if those instincts are still there."

"And what about Carolyn? You know she saw him just hanging there frozen. You can't keep her knocked out forever. How are we going to explain it to her? What can I tell her? She won't believe there were drugs in the air or any other nonsense excuse."

Carolyn never forgot a damn thing. It was one of the reasons she'd gotten through her PhD in half the usual time. She would ask questions.

At least we aren't in Venice where she could demand to see the Archives. A fierce protectiveness rose in her again, her own magic shimmering under her bare forearms as it flicked with the words ἀγάπη, agapē, love. Love, yes. She loved the Archives and their secrets fiercely and selflessly. For a moment, she wondered if it was the remnants of Nereus's magic inside her that made her feel that way, or if it was from herself. Still, she loved Carolyn, too, and would hate lying to her.

Alexis rested a hand on her curly head. "You are starting to understand one of the greatest challenges of our world, Penelope. You will always be torn between your loyalties. You'll always have to lie to the people in your life in some way."

"May I tell her a very small amount?"

"You're asking my permission?" Alexis's deep-blue eyes widened in surprise.

"You are our leader now, whether you like it or not. In some regards, and despite how much it may irritate me, you have the final say on what I can and can't share when it comes to the family."

Alexis clasped her chin gently. "I will *never* be the leader of you. At times I might be bossy in my need to protect you, but you'll never answer to me like they do. Our relationship would never have balance, and I *need* you to be my equal, always. Do you understand?"

Penelope placed her hand over his and kissed his palm. "Thank you, Alexis. I promise not to abuse it, and I'll only tell her a very small bit. If she freaks out, I expect you to do the Atlantis mind wipe on her."

"I wish you'd find a better name for it, but I'll agree to do it, if it's what you want." He kissed her forehead.

Carolyn stumbled into Tim's room minutes later, clutching her head with one hand. "Is he still alive?"

"He's okay, Caro. Just sleeping," Penelope said.

"What the hell did you do to him?" Carolyn turned on Alexis, her face flushed with anger.

"What do you think I have done?" he responded, calmly getting to his feet.

"You did something! Tim went for Penelope, and you…he was in the freaking air, just hanging there! How did you do that?" she demanded.

Penelope stepped between them and gently pushed Carolyn down into the wooden chair Alexis had just vacated.

"I'll go and get you some water," said Alexis and left the room without looking back.

"What's going on, Penelope? What *is* he? I'm not crazy—I know what I saw!"

"Calm down, you are getting worked up unnecessarily," Penelope said. Dealing with upset women wasn't her strongest area of expertise.

"Just tell me! Whatever it is, I can take it."

"He's a magician! Okay? Happy now?"

Carolyn went from furious to calm within seconds. "Now you sound like the crazy one."

"Yeah, I felt that way too when I first found out. He's saved my life more than once, Caro. You saw what he can do."

"You are going to have to do better than that. That was no magic trick." Carolyn crossed her arms. Penelope's mind raced, searching for a story to tell her.

"The short version? I came to Venice to find what the writing at the crime scene meant. Alexis is descended from the survivors of the fall of Atlantis, and with the help of his friend Nereus, we figured out what the writing meant, and we stopped the guy who was killing people. He was part of a cult, also from Atlantis, and they are the ones after Tim." Claiming Alexis was a descendant seemed a lot more believable than claiming he was over nine thousand years old.

Carolyn exploded with harsh laughter. "You are such a fucking liar!"

"Do you really think I would take a job in Venice for anything *other* than Atlantis, my only true love, as you were so willing to point out on the plane?"

The laughter died on Carolyn's lips. "He has evidence of where it is?"

"Yes, lots of it. It was passed down through Alexis's family, and I have looked through it. It's legit."

"And the reason why they haven't shared this amazing discovery with the rest of the world is…?"

"The cult that's after them wants to wipe them out. The cult is powerful, and they are fanatics. They are connected through crime families. Alexis had to keep Atlantis quiet to stay safe from them."

"You believe he can actually do magic? *You*, the cynic? That is the wackiest part of this whole thing."

"You *saw* it, Caro. He held Tim in the air so he wouldn't hurt himself or me. Tim's not ill, he's cursed, and Alexis believes that it can be passed on by touch."

Carolyn slumped back in her chair with a long sigh. "But they can help him, right?"

"I believe so. Alexis is smart about this kind of thing."

"That's why he asked you about magic that night of your talk? Because he thought you might be like him?"

Penelope shook her head. "No, it was because of the Tablet. Alexis knew it was from Atlantis and could read the dialect because of what he was taught. He knew it was a petition to Poseidon. You know, I really thought out of everyone in my life, you would believe me about this. You've been putting crystals under moonlight and smudging your apartment weekly since I met you. You see real magic for the first time, and you have a go at the guy!"

"I hate to admit it, but it sort of makes sense. You really haven't let go of Atlantis. You found a descendant. It's no wonder you fall all over yourself whenever he's around," Carolyn replied. Her eyes narrowed. "So do you know where Atlantis was at least?"

Penelope couldn't stop the smile that spread over her face. "Cyclades Plateau."

"No. Fucking. Way. You were right?" Carolyn demanded, almost screeching with excitement. She reached out to grab Penelope's shoulders tightly.

"I was right, Caro."

"Goddamn. Everyone thought you were so full of shit with your theories. I remember the arguments you had about people claiming it was in the Atlantic Ocean because of the name. You swore until you were black and blue that they had it wrong. You were the only one looking in the right spot." Carolyn pulled her down for a hug. "I'm so happy for you. Why haven't you said anything if you know where to dig now? You should be writing a paper or a book or something."

"I can't. Not without exposing Alexis and those like him. Knowing that I was right, and that it was there, is enough for me."

Carolyn quickly let her go. "What do you mean others like him? You don't mean...the crew of experts? Oh my God...*Zo*?"

Penelope rubbed at the back of her neck. "Yeah, they are descendants, too."

"I knew Phaidros had knocked me out!" Carolyn said as she sat back down. "Okay, so magic is real. What do we do now?"

"We are going to help Tim and keep him away from the assholes chasing him." Penelope took Carolyn's shoulders and squeezed them. "You can't tell anyone about this, Caro. It's a life-or-death secret. You do understand that, right?"

"Who would believe me, Pen? As you said, I'm pretty open, and even I wouldn't have believed you if I hadn't seen what Alexis did."

"I need to hear you say the words. *Promise* me, Carolyn."

"I promise, Pen. You don't have to worry about me."

"That's good to hear," Alexis said from the doorway. He held out a glass of water to her, and she took it.

"Um…I'm sorry I yelled at you," Carolyn apologized.

"It's fine," he said, waving her concern away.

"How goes our patient?" Phaidros asked, sticking his head into the crowded room.

Carolyn glared at him. "If you ever hoodoo me like that again, Goldie, I'll knock your pretty teeth out."

"You told her about us? Lyca is going to kill you. I've always wondered who would win in a proper fight between her and Alexis. I guess now we will finally find out." He looked far too smug, and Penelope was about to tell him so, when an alarm sounded through the house.

"Penelope, go and grab your bag and passport. Nothing else. Meet me downstairs in the garage," said Alexis.

"But—" Carolyn began, but Penelope was already moving, dragging Carolyn behind her. Phaidros followed them as a precaution, holding knives.

"What's happening?" Carolyn asked as she grabbed her purse.

"I believe we are about to be attacked," Phaidros said calmly. Penelope slung her black satchel over her shoulder after making sure the scroll and her laptop were inside.

"Don't ask questions, Caro. Just do as they say for your own safety."

"I'm glad to see you're finally learning," said Phaidros.

"Just be ready to protect me if Thevetat jumps through the window, okay, smart-ass?" Penelope risked looking out of the large win-

dows in the hallway. Figures in black were standing on top of the high
brick walls.

"That's not half cliché for a cult," she muttered.

"Least they aren't in ceremonial robes with like…glitter and stars,"
said Carolyn nervously. They both snickered, trying to hide their fear
with humor. Phaidros quickly pulled them away.

"Stay down and beside me. I don't know how good Zo's warding
is on this place," he said.

"I heard that, asshole!" Zo called from the stairs.

"Where's Aelia?" Phaidros demanded.

"In the garden with Alexis. Come on, ladies, we need to get you
to the car."

"Wait, what about Tim?" Carolyn asked.

"Alexis stashed him in the back of the car already. He's fine for the
moment," said Zo. The ground underneath them shuddered, and Zo
grabbed Penelope, sheltering her under his body.

"Go!" Phaidros shouted, and they ran to the stairs as the priests on
the wall opened fire on the house.

"Looks like they aren't stupid enough to use magic," said Zo as
they crouched behind a thick brick wall.

"Or they don't have any because Thevetat isn't with them,"
Penelope added. Carolyn was white and shaking, so Penelope grabbed
her hand.

"Wait for it…" Phaidros held up a finger. The shooting stopped as
the screaming started, interspersed with chords of Aelia's stunning voice.

"I do believe she's serenading them as she's killing them. I love
that woman," Zo said with a chuckle.

"Me too," Phaidros added.

"Are you people insane? How can you laugh about that?" Carolyn demanded.

"Lots of practice. Save your weeping for later. We are going to
have to make a run for the garage," Phaidros said, passing one of his
knives to Penelope. "Just in case. You know what to do with it."

"Fingers crossed this one will do more damage to Kreios if I get a chance to sink it into him again." Penelope took it and slipped it into the front pocket of her satchel, resting her hand on the hilt for easy access. Carolyn was looking at her like she'd never seen her before. Explanations would have to wait.

"Ready?" Zo asked.

Penelope nodded and pulled Carolyn closer. More gunshots sounded, but farther away, not aimed at them anymore. Penelope tried to shut down any worry she was feeling for Alexis, knowing he had done this a hundred times before. They stopped by the garage door, and Zo went out first. There was a yelp and a meaty thump before he appeared again.

"Mind your feet," he said, kicking a body out of the way.

"I think I'm going to puke," Carolyn said as Penelope opened the passenger door of the SUV and hurried her inside. Tim was still unconscious in the cargo space behind the back seats, a blanket tucked around him. Zo got behind the wheel, and Phaidros climbed into the back, wedging Penelope in the middle.

"Hurry up, Zo," he hissed as he let down the electric window, a gun ready in his hands.

"Don't tell me how to drive," Zo snapped.

The garage door opened and he reversed fast, taking down two more figures in black. He slammed on the brakes as they reached the gate to the property and Alexis appeared through the trees, looking like a vengeful god, blood-splattered, with sword in hand. He made the weapon disappear as he climbed into the front seat. There was a loud bang on the roof rack, and Aelia slid gracefully through Phaidros's window and onto his lap.

"Go!" she urged, and Zo floored it.

"Out of the city, Zo. They are going to be following us in moments," Alexis instructed. He gave Penelope a quick once-over, and she gently squeezed his shoulder.

"I'm fine," she assured him. He nodded and took a handgun out of the glove box.

"Where are we headed?" asked Zo as he wove through the tight streets.

"Toward Ein Karim."

Zo swore foully. "You know we can't just turn up on his—"

"Just drive," Alexis said coldly, shutting him down. "Phaidros and Aelia, get ready. We are already being tailed."

"I haven't had this much fun in years," said Aelia happily as she reached her arms behind Phaidros and pulled out another gun from the back of his jeans. "Try not to get an erection and distract me."

"Just don't get me shot," he replied, ignoring her quip and looping an arm around her waist to steady her. She leaned out the window and fired off a few rounds at the sedans behind them.

"Get down," Penelope said, pushing Carolyn's head between her knees. Penelope leaned over her to shelter her friend and try and keep Carolyn calm.

"Is living with them always like this?" asked Carolyn in a muffled voice. She jerked hard as bullets hit the back of the car.

"Pretty much," Penelope replied, holding her close. "Don't worry, they will get us out of this." Lights flashed in the corner of her eye as a car drew close. She looked up just in time to see the man in the passenger seat pointing a gun at her.

"Zo! Beside us!" she shouted. Without being told, Alexis took the wheel as Zo turned in his seat and shot first. The attacker's windshield shattered, and the sedan crashed into a row of parked cars. Alexis let go of the wheel again as Zo took over. They hit the highway, and Penelope risked looking around again.

"These two aren't giving up so easily," Aelia said, as she slid a fresh clip into her handgun.

"They've either got bulletproofing on their windows, or you're a bad shot," said Phaidros and then yelped as Aelia shifted hard on his groin.

"Oh, sorry! The car jerked me," she said sweetly.

"Gods, Alexis, are you waiting for an invitation or what?" Phaidros snapped angrily.

"Not until there's room," said Alexis.

Zo overtook more cars, shifting in between tight spaces and out again so quickly that Penelope wanted to shut her eyes. "We have a good stretch coming up," he said as they cleared the traffic.

Alexis lowered his window, looking in the rearview mirror as their two pursuers closed in. Penelope shivered as the scent of firecrackers and cinnamon filled the car. Alexis reached out of the window, and a stream of magic flowed out of him, hitting the cars behind them. One flipped over onto the other before both of them rolled over the concrete guardrails and crashed down into the brushland beneath the overpass.

Aelia let out a wild whoop into the wind, and Penelope allowed Carolyn to sit up. Carolyn stared at their grinning faces and laughter, wide-eyed with horror.

"You are all mental," she squeaked. The *you* definitely included Penelope.

"It's going to be okay, Carolyn. We are going somewhere safe—right, Alexis?" said Penelope.

"I wouldn't be so sure. It'll depend on whether the Cursebreaker wants company," Phaidros replied. Penelope prodded him hard in the shoulder. "There won't be any priests of Thevetat there, if that's what you mean," Phaidros added, pulling his seat belt out enough to fit around Aelia and clipping it in despite her squirming.

"If we bring Thevetat to his door, I swear by the gods, Alexis, I *will* kill you," Zo threatened in a tone Penelope had never heard him use before.

"We aren't being followed," replied Alexis.

Fifty minutes later, they pulled up in front of an electric gate and Zo punched a code into a keypad.

"Where are we?" Carolyn asked as they drove through a long driveway lined with trees.

"A house in Ein Karem where we can get help for Tim," said Alexis.

Zo drove slowly up a tree-lined, gravel road for a few minutes before parking in front of a stunning house made of white stone. With gardens hanging from window boxes and warm lights illuminating inside, it certainly didn't look like the kind of house belonging to someone called the Cursebreaker.

Once they were free of the car, Penelope moved to Alexis's side, taking his hand.

"Are you okay?" she whispered.

"I'm fine, none of this blood is mine," he replied. Penelope stared at him, flushed with magic and victory, and she desperately wanted to push him up against the car and kiss him with relief. His eyes flared as if reading her thoughts. *There is a time and place, Penelope,* she reminded herself.

Zo looked uncharacteristically nervous as he rang the doorbell. There was a shuffle behind the door, and a tall man opened it. He was in pajamas and a robe, his glasses pushed up on his curly, salt-and-pepper hair. He studied the bloody, bedraggled group, and despite Zo's protests, he didn't look remotely surprised to see them.

"I'm sorry, I wouldn't have come if it wasn't—" Zo began.

The older man pulled Zo into a hug. "Forget it. It's been too long, Father."

PART TWO

MAGGID

Hebrew, noun:
"Storyteller and preacher."

FOURTEEN

"WHAT DOES HE mean by 'father?'" whispered Penelope to Alexis.

"Zo's adopted son. It's a long story," he said. As Zo let the man go, the stranger's eyes came to rest on Penelope.

"Doctor Bryne! How in all the worlds did you come to fall in with this rabble?" he asked.

"Penelope, this is my son Elazar," Zo said. Elazar gently pushed him out of the way so he could take Penelope's hands in his.

"I'm surprised you know who I am. It's nice to meet more of Zo's family," said Penelope awkwardly.

"You are the leading scholar of Atlantis, and my father is Atlantean. Of course I know who you are, even if I hadn't listened to dear Alexis rant about you for years." Elazar's eyes sparkled as Alexis made a choking sound.

"I look forward to hearing those stories later," said Penelope, eyebrows raised.

Alexis hugged Elazar. "Don't you dare tell her anything."

"What if she asks nicely? You know I can't deny a beautiful woman anything. Speaking of which, where is my auntie?"

Aelia shoved Alexis out of the way so she could gather Elazar in her arms and kiss his face all over.

"My little bird, it's been too long since we sang together. Will you tell me a story while we are here?" Aelia asked affectionately.

"Any that you wish. Why is it that you become lovelier as you get older and I get uglier?" he complained.

"It's because you read too many books," said Phaidros.

"You're caught up in all of this too, Uncle? It must be serious if it's pulled you away from your Florence."

"You know when the Defender calls, everyone must come running."

"Lucky for you, he calls so rarely. What have you brought me this time, Alexis?" asked Elazar.

Alexis smiled warmly. "A madman from the desert."

"They are my favorite! I'm surprised you remembered," said Elazar with a laugh.

Alexis opened the rear door of the SUV to reveal Tim lying in a mound of blankets and Carolyn watching over him anxiously from the back seat. Elazar's eyes were wide as he studied the bedraggled man.

"Alexis, what in heavens have you done to Timothy Sanders?"

"How do you know him?" asked Carolyn suspiciously.

"I keep an eye on the archaeological activity at the Dead Sea. I knew he was overly ambitious. It looks like he finally dug too deep and found something he didn't expect," Elazar said, expression worried.

"Can you help him?" asked Penelope.

"I won't make any promises. Get Tim inside, and I'll see what I can do."

Phaidros gave Elazar an encouraging pat on the back. "Don't be bashful, nephew. They don't call you Elazar the Cursebreaker for nothing."

"Only you call me that, and I'm sure it's just to get on my nerves," Elazar pointed out.

Penelope kept Carolyn out of the way as Zo and Alexis carried Tim into the house. She saw flashes of bookshelves, pages of illuminated manuscripts hanging on the walls, artifacts in display cases, and had to look away before becoming too distracted. She didn't have time to admire the décor, only to get Tim cured. Elazar led them down a set of carpeted stairs to a basement flat with bedrooms and a small kitchenette.

"Put him through there on one of the beds," Elazar instructed before giving Penelope and Carolyn an apologetic look. "You might not want to be here for this. Your friend will be angry and disoriented once Alexis wakes him up."

Penelope took Carolyn's clammy hand as a sign of solidarity. "We aren't going anywhere."

"Also, this is hardly the first time we have seen Tim angry and disoriented," Carolyn said.

"Would any of you like to tell me how this happened?" asked Elazar.

Penelope showed him the photos on her phone of the scroll Tim had sent her, telling him quickly of everything that had happened since. Zo explained the curse that was on the scroll in details that went over Penelope's head, but Elazar followed carefully.

"The emperor. The emperor," murmured Tim. "Purple and gold and laurel leaves."

"That's new. He's been ranting about demons in the sky, but not emperors," said Penelope uncertainly.

"Sounds Roman. Weird," agreed Carolyn.

"Why is that stranger than demons in the sky?" asked Alexis.

"Tim hated Roman history and avoided it when he could. Most of what he knows in detail is isolated to Near Eastern politics, so it's weird that he's dreaming about Rome."

"He is going mad. Who knows what he's dreaming?" said Zo.

"Purple and gold and laurel leaves. City of stone. Temple of twelve. I see, I see. Empty tombs," Tim said, moaning.

Elazar read through the scroll again, his frown deepening. "We will have to discuss this find in greater detail. The symbology alone will take time to process, not to mention its prophetic nature. For now, we'd best look to the curse. We are going to need Tim sane and lucid to get to the truth of things."

"As sane as he can be after he's carried the curse for so many weeks," pointed out Phaidros. Penelope gave him a sharp look over her shoulder. She didn't need Carolyn even more upset.

"I'll keep an eye on them in case the curse tries to jump," Zo said to reassure both Elazar and Alexis.

Elazar took a copper bowl engraved with prayers from one of the cupboards and filled it with dried ingredients.

"What's all that?" asked Carolyn.

"It's an old Second Temple period incense made from myrrh, onycha, galbanum, and frankincense," explained Zo in a whisper. "It will help cleanse the room from negative influences. The Essenes were sticklers to Torah, so it's highly likely that they used the same recipe in their exorcism rites."

Once the contents of the bowl were smoking, Elazar waved it over Tim. He jerked hard but didn't waken from the sleep magic Phaidros had used on him.

The hair on Penelope's arms rose as Elazar started to sing in Hebrew. Aelia had magic in her voice, but Elazar's was something else; authoritative, full of light and power. Despite the modern surroundings, Penelope had the disorienting feeling of witnessing something far older, of being connected at that moment to something no average archaeologist would experience or understand.

Carolyn was shaking so violently beside her that Zo took her other hand.

"It's going to be okay, trust me. Elazar is the best," he whispered.

Through the smoke, the same glowing, golden symbols that Penelope had seen on the scroll were now wrapping themselves around Tim's body.

"Magic," whispered Carolyn in wonder.

Unlike Zo who had to move to search the glyphs on the curse, Elazar reached out to touch the bands and spun through them like a combination lock.

"I would have liked to meet the scribe who created this. Even for an Essene, it's something else," said Elazar as he searched.

"It's very complex and very, very good," agreed Alexis.

"But not good enough to stop *me*." Elazar grinned, and Penelope saw Zo's likeness in the expression. He might've been adopted, but Elazar had all of Zo's mannerisms and a healthy dose of his cockiness, too.

With three more turns of the ringed script, the symbols glowed bright and hot before they unraveled entirely.

"Well done, my boy," beamed Zo, letting go of Carolyn so he could grab his son around the shoulders in a congratulatory hug.

"I suppose we should wake him and see what kind of state he's in," said Elazar thoughtfully.

"Zo, please be ready if he decides to run or attack," Alexis instructed.

Zo moved between Tim and his son, blocking the doorway that Penelope and Carolyn stood anxiously outside of. Penelope didn't see what Alexis did as the room glowed with faint, blue light. Tim woke with a cry and started thrashing violently.

"Get the fuck away from me!" he shrieked, scrambling up the bed and slamming into the headboard. He covered his face with his hands. "Not real. Not real. Not real." Carolyn shoved Zo out of the way.

"You're okay, Tim. Calm the fuck down and let us help you," she said in a teacher tone that she used on her rowdy tutorial students. Tim froze.

"Caro? What…what are you doing here?" he asked, peeking at her between his dirty fingers.

"I've been dragged here to rescue your sorry ass, as usual."

"Thanks for making us worry about you, Carter," Penelope added. Tim looked from one woman to the other and promptly burst into tears.

"We can take it from here, guys," Penelope said to Zo and Alexis.

"I'll find him something to wear," Elazar replied, giving her an encouraging pat on the shoulder.

"Thank you. All of you."

Alexis ran his hand down her arm on his way out. "Let me know if he needs anything. There is a bathroom through that door. Maybe keep an eye on her. She can berate him when he's recovered." He looked pointedly at Carolyn who was watching Tim as if she was torn between wanting to hug or strangle him. Penelope gave Alexis a quick kiss before he followed Zo up the stairs.

"I got your package. Plastic Jesus? Even when you're mad, you give the worst gifts," Penelope joked.

"I'm so sorry, Hawkes," Tim managed to say, rubbing the tears from his cheeks.

"We'll kick your ass later about it. For now, I think a shower is in order," said Carolyn, no-nonsense once more. They assisted him off the bed and into the bathroom, Penelope retreating to the door as Carolyn helped him out of his reeking clothes. He sat down in the bathtub and Carolyn turned the shower on above him, closing the curtain until they could see only his face.

"You sure know how to make me worry, Timothy," said Carolyn, sitting down on the closed toilet.

"I didn't mean for any of this to happen. Especially not to you guys," said Tim. He picked up a bar of soap, staring at it like he was unsure what it was for before running it slowly down his arms.

Penelope left Carolyn and him to talk while she met Zo in the hall.

"These will fit him okay," Zo said, passing her a bundle of clothes. "Elazar is putting together some tea that will help settle his stomach and some food when he's ready for it."

Suddenly overwhelmed by the day, Penelope collapsed into Zo's arms and hugged him tightly. "Thank you, Zo. I know what you've risked to let us come here. I won't forget it."

"Think nothing of it, little sister. We are family now, remember?" he said, rubbing her back. "We'll always be here if you need us."

"Thanks." She sniffed as he let her go.

"Go be with your friends. We'll look after the rest."

Tim was climbing out of the shower just as Penelope passed the clothes through the door. When he finally emerged, he looked like a thin, tired version of the man she'd known for the last ten years.

"You look like crap," Penelope said, giving him a grin.

"Whatever, Hawkes. Come here and hug me."

The three of them ended up side by side on the bed. Penelope and Carolyn held Tim's hands as he lay between them.

"What happened? How did you find me?" asked Tim softly.

Penelope told him everything, starting from when she first received the money box in the mail to how they'd found him hiding in a squatters' building. Tim had started crying again, and both women carefully avoided commenting on it.

"I didn't know what was real and what wasn't," Tim said finally.

"You probably won't ever be sure of that," said Penelope as gently as she could.

"Don't push yourself," Carolyn added. "Rest, and we can help you sort through it tomorrow."

Penelope propped herself up on an elbow. "You know, you might have found the greatest scrolls discovery since the forties. That's something to focus on right now. Few days of crazy seems almost worth it."

"You don't understand. The people who were after me, after the scroll, they aren't going to stop," he said urgently.

"Tim, look at me," Penelope commanded. His blue eyes were bloodshot from crying as he turned his face toward her. "I know who they are. They aren't going to get anywhere near you or the scroll ever again. You hear me?"

"How do you know that?"

"I promise to tell you in the morning, but only if you go to sleep now."

Tim let out a small laugh. "That won't work on me. I'm not a ten year old, Hawkes."

"Stop acting like it then," said Carolyn.

"Don't tell me what to do, you're not my real mum."

"Only because your dad was frigid," Penelope added, and the three of them laughed, easing the worry between them.

When Alexis came in with a tray of food and tea twenty minutes later, Tim and Carolyn were both asleep. Penelope looked up and smiled at him as he placed the tray down on the bedside table. His hair was damp from a shower, and he looked refreshed. She smelled like three different types of sweat and a trip to a squat house.

"Hey," she whispered.

"Are they okay?" he asked, looking down at Tim and Carolyn tangled together.

"As good as they can be," Penelope replied. Careful not to disturb them, she edged slowly off her side of the bed and pulled a blanket over them.

"Do you want to stay with them tonight?" Alexis asked.

Penelope reached for him. "No, take me somewhere quiet where I can breathe."

Without a word, Alexis wrapped his arms around her and portaled her outside into the gardens. The sun was starting to rise over the mountains, the valley beneath them still in shadow. There was a white building on the next hill over with a tall tower catching the light.

"What's that over there?" asked Penelope.

"That's Saint John the Baptist Church," said Alexis, before adding, "The Catholic one, not the Eastern Orthodox one."

"This is some spot." She sighed, looking around her. The house had been built to match the shape of the mountain, with tall poles holding the large balcony over the gardens.

"Zo's had this land since...forever, I suppose. He built the house, and Elazar insisted on the trees and gardens," said Alexis as they walked through them. Penelope was hopeless when it came to plants, only recognizing the pine, olive, and almond trees, and the blasts of colorful poppies and chrysanthemums, amidst the other species.

"This is my corner of the property," Alexis said as they followed a path to a small bungalow hidden amongst the greenery.

"You really do insist on your space, don't you?" teased Penelope as he opened the door.

"I like my privacy, something you know the others have trouble respecting at the best of times. When they are all in the same house, there is constant noise and bickering. They never shut up, and after a day of them, I need to be alone. It's either that or using magic to steal all of their voices."

Penelope laughed. "You would not."

"Not since 1827. Nereus gave me such an ear-bashing lecture afterward, I've never done it since."

The bungalow was decorated in a style Penelope instantly associated with Alexis: Persian carpets, over-stacked bookshelves, art on the walls, and a cello in the corner for whenever he needed it.

"I'm stealing a shirt. I need something to sleep in, and these clothes are gross," she said before raiding Alexis's wardrobe.

"You'll find what you need in the bathroom. My visits here are sporadic so there should be emergency packets of toothbrushes and soap in the cupboards," Alexis said.

Penelope lathered herself over twice with the sandalwood soap, desperate to get the sweat and grime off herself. By the time she had finished her shower, the last of her energy was waning. She buttoned up a green shirt and went in search of a bed. Alexis was still up, reading in a mound of maroon sheets. He looked up and smiled as he watched her walk to her side of the bed.

"What are you reading to make you smirk like that?" she asked.

"It's not the book. I like you in my clothes," Alexis admitted.

"Is that so? What a shame you insist on courting, or I'd be using your body shamelessly right now to deal with my brush with death," Penelope said. His surprised look was priceless as she slid under the blankets. A warm hand looped around her and dragged her closer to him so he could spoon her with his long body.

"I'm sorry you were shot at tonight," he said, sighing against her hair.

"I'll add it to the things you can make up for later."

"You're making a list? What else is on there?"

"Oh, lots of things," she lied, enjoying stirring him up. Alexis ran a hand up her bare leg, and her whole body broke out into goose bumps.

"This is because I didn't show you the upstairs library, isn't?"

"That one's going on a whole different list."

"How many of the infernal things are there?" he demanded. Penelope rolled on her side, still biting her lip to keep from laughing. He made an exasperated sound before kissing her.

"Go to sleep and stop teasing me," he said when they broke apart.

"I don't know what you're talking about, I'm far too tired to tease you," Penelope replied, shutting her eyes. She rested her head on his shoulder and draped a leg comfortably over him.

Above her head, Alexis whispered something that sounded like a prayer or a curse, and Penelope smiled against his skin, the world temporarily a good place again.

FIFTEEN

MARCO SAT AT his desk ignoring the pile of paperwork in front of him while he combed through everything they still had on Tony Duilio. He had collated most of it, he *knew* what was in the files intimately, but the feeling that he was missing something refused to go away. He had requested Duilio's full real estate portfolio from Duilio's lawyer, though he doubted he would get it from her.

Francesca Garcia wasn't a woman to give him what he wanted because he'd asked her nicely. In fact, quite the opposite. She'd been making his life difficult since she walked through the door of the precinct. She had won the argument about cremating Tony Duilio's body, and now she was doing everything she could to salvage the bastard's name and reputation.

The press loved her, and so did Tony Duilio's hard-core fans who thought the police had convicted and shot the wrong man. It didn't matter to them that Duilio had died in a firefight with the police after being discovered as Venice's bomber. The truth had no clout when scandals sold more papers.

When Marco had asked Francesca why she was so hell-bent on trying to protect the memory of a monster, she had tossed her shiny, black curls and replied, "Someone has to protect his investors. They aren't dead, and the business is sound, no matter what you accuse Tony of." When Marco had asked who "they" were, she'd smiled and walked away.

Marco shut the file and pulled up his map of Cannaregio. He was sectioning it off and would start investigating the districts one at a time with Lyca, even though the warrior magician terrified him. He'd promised not to attempt anything without her, so he'd have to get over it. At least Lyca looked like she could take on an army. That reassured him.

After the night at the Lido, Marco knew he was underqualified to deal with the priests of Thevetat. Working with the magicians as they investigated privately on their own went against nearly all of his instincts and training as a police officer, and yet he was doing it, knowing they would be the ones who would stop the killing. *Duilio was one man and look at the damage he's done.*

It had been two days since Penelope and the other magicians had left, and Marco felt slightly off-kilter without them. In the past eight weeks, they had been tangled up in each other's lives, and it was odd not having them in Venice. Now that he'd had a brush with magic and true evil, he felt better knowing they were around to keep the city safe. Marco had sworn to help them where he could because it was the right thing to do, even if it was in direct conflict with the law.

The sharp tapping of heels on the polished floors had Marco minimizing the map of Cannaregio on his screen and replacing it with the latest results of a football match.

"Inspector Dandolo, you're working hard, I see," a smooth, feminine voice said behind him. He tried not to cringe as he swiveled in his chair. Everything about Francesca Garcia was smooth, from her cultured Spanish accent to the beige, overpriced heels on her feet. Marco liked beautiful women, but for all of her good looks, there was something about her that put him on edge.

"Ah, *Signora* Garcia, have you come to bring me the information I requested from you?" he asked in as pleasant a voice as he could muster.

She smiled at him indulgently. "In an attempt to keep fostering our good working relationship, I made a few calls, and I have this for you." She opened the sleek, leather portfolio she carried and passed him a single piece of paper. "This is all of the properties listed under my client's name. I don't know why you are so interested in them. Aside from the apartment that was bombed, none of them are in Italy. You don't have the jurisdiction to search any of them."

"I already have irrefutable proof that Duilio was guilty of the murders he committed. He is dead, justice is served. I'm more concerned about his associates now," said Marco, sliding the piece of paper into his desk drawer and closing it before she could take it back.

Francesca's laugh was all feminine charm. "His associates? He was a billionaire. If you plan on investigating every one of his business partners or friends, you'll die from old age before you are done."

"I'm not interested in all of them. Only a few have been flagged as suspicious, and once I rule out their involvement in his crimes, I'll close his case for good."

Francesca's pretty, red lips curved as she ran her eyes over him, appraising. "You don't class *me* as suspicious do you, Inspector?"

Yes, yes I do, Marco thought. When he didn't answer, she let out a small, wounded sigh.

"Here I thought we were becoming friends now that most of the ugliness and misunderstandings had been put behind us."

"Is that so?"

"I have to admit, I've never waited so long for a man to ask me out for a drink before."

Marco tried not to laugh. She could wait until Judgment Day. "You want to have a drink with me? Really?"

"A drink would be a good start. Where things go after that, I suppose we'll have to wait and see," purred Francesca.

"I'm sorry, *Signora,* you aren't my type," Marco said politely.

Far from looking wounded by the rejection, Francesca leaned over Marco to write a phone number on his notebook. Her too-sweet perfume forced him to hold his breath.

"In case you change your mind, you know where to find me." She winked at him before straightening and, ignoring the looks of the officers, glided out of the building.

Marco pulled the page out of the book, scrunched it up, and dropped it into the bin beside his desk. He didn't like this sudden change in her mood, or that he was now the object of her particularly aggressive brand of attention. He didn't have long to contemplate it before his phone rang.

"*Dottore*, how is Israel?" he answered.

"In full spring and warm," Penelope replied.

"Has your search been fruitful or are you calling to finally take my advice and get the police involved?"

"No need, we found him." Penelope gave Marco a brief update on the discovery of her friend in Tel Aviv, as well as the unexpected guests who visited with guns. She was careful in her description on the phone, and he knew there was much she wasn't saying. He got the message clearly though; they had been attacked by Thevetat's followers and confirmed that their numbers stretched beyond the three that had nearly sunk Venice on their own.

"How is the house hunting going?" she asked him.

"Slowly. I have a list of properties that are owned under Duilio's name, and none of them are helpful."

"The lawyer came through, then? That's a surprise."

"She's a piece of work. The list is useless. I'm going to stick to my other plan and do a section per evening with Lyca to see if she can sense something I can't."

"Date nights with Lyca. You are a sucker for punishment. It might be the only way to find it though. If he did his worship there or made his bombs, he would've been careful with it. Duilio wasn't worried about burning his identity, so if he did have a property there, it wouldn't be affiliated or tied to him in any way. Kreios and Abaddon could've used it as somewhere to hide when they got to Venice, too," Penelope said.

Marco could just about hear her mind ticking over the problem. In another life, she would've made a good police officer.

"If it's there, we'll find it. You did say this source of yours was reliable, yes? She didn't just pick Cannaregio off the top of her head?" he asked.

"I wouldn't even think about questioning her. Maybe we are looking at this in too logical of a way. Searching for records and what not. That can all be faked."

"What do you suggest?"

"It might be a long shot, but after seeing Thevetat's cronies last night, I've been thinking. Duilio, Abaddon, and Kreios, the priests, they all have something in common. They are creepy guys. If Duilio were using a house as well as the apartment, he would've had to go there late at night when no one could recognize him. The Serpents didn't look or act like upstanding members of society. They were dodgy, and they would've been noticed. Maybe you should look into complaints, in case someone reported something suspicious. I'm sure Cannaregio would have its share of nosy residents keeping an eye out on their neighborhood."

"You're right. I feel like an idiot for not thinking of it myself," said Marco as he logged back into the police systems.

"I'm glad I can help. I want to dislodge these bastards anyway I can from my city."

"Your city? It didn't take long for Venezia to earn your loyalty," teased Marco.

"Just take care of her for me, and yourself. Don't do anything stupid without Lyca there to protect you."

"You are starting to sound too much like Alexis. When will you be back?"

"I'm not sure. Tim and Carolyn are both really shaken up by everything. There are some leads here we need to look into as well. Zo's son is going to help us."

"We'll have to raid his wine cellar when you return, and you can tell me all about it," Marco said.

"It's a deal," Penelope promised before they said their goodbyes.

Marco's stomach grumbled angrily, but instead of going to get lunch, he brought up every complaint listed in Cannaregio for the last two months and started reading.

SIXTEEN

PENELOPE HAD DOZED off after her phone call with Marco. Alexis was gone, and she was starting to wonder if he ever slept more than four hours a night.

When she woke again, it was to a cat sitting on Alexis's side of the bed. Its pale-green eyes were studying her in a bored way before it started licking its silky, brown paws.

"How did you get in here?" Penelope grumbled, giving its ears a scratch while she checked the time. Two o'clock. With a sigh, she sat up and noticed someone had left her clean black jeans and underwear.

"Someone's been doing laundry," she said to the bored cat. There was no shirt, so she took it as permission to take another of Alexis's before heading to the shower.

By the time she got out, the cat was sitting by the door, waiting for her. It mewed plaintively and scratched at it.

"Yeah, I'm coming," Penelope said irritably. "You know, if you hadn't wandered in here uninvited, you wouldn't be in this predicament."

She opened the door, and the cat scampered along the path in front of her. The day was sunny and warm, and despite her urgent need for coffee, Penelope took her time wandering back to the main house.

The house felt different in the daylight and, unlike during their rushed arrival, Penelope now had time to study all the treasures Elazar had on display. He seemed to have inherited Zo's fondness for poetry, with a whole bookcase dedicated to classical and modern poets with prints of verse by William Blake and Milton on the wall beside it. On another wall hung a large, colorful depiction of the ten emanations of the Kabbalah's *Sefirot*. A painting of the Tree of Life hung on another, the geometric Flower of Life pattern illuminated in golden paint.

Drawn always to the books, Penelope found copies of *The Book of Raziel, Zohar, The Hermetic Corpus, Sefer Yetzirah*, and other Jewish texts.

Penelope was studying a photo of an older-looking Zo and a child of about eight years old at the beach when a throat politely cleared behind her.

"That was in Caesarea in the seventies," said Elazar.

"Zo looks older there than he does now."

"That's because he asked Nereus to do some aging magic on him so no one would ask questions as I aged and he didn't."

"That was clever."

"No, what was clever was when he turned up at his own funeral as a distant nephew. He shamelessly consoled all the women and got drunker than I've ever seen him."

Penelope burst out laughing. "What an asshole."

"He loved it."

"I hope you don't mind me looking at your collection. What's your field of research?" asked Penelope. His book tastes went beyond a simple interest or a hobby. The house felt like one giant academic office.

"My area of interest is huge. Mostly it's traditional Jewish mysticism and magic."

"I thought the magicians would've had that covered."

"There are only six of them, and they don't have time to look into all the magic that's around, even if they had the inclination. I have a special fascination for the Second Temple period and the influence of Babylonian culture on traditions. There were once many variations of Judaism as opposed to the one rabbinical religion that survives today. It's one of the reasons I keep a watch on Qumran and what they find. I don't believe they have found half of what was originally there."

"Can't Zo help point you in the right direction? He was there after all."

"My father could talk your ears off about the structure and imagery of their poetry, but he was never initiated into their mysteries," Elazar said with a chuckle. "Alexis has a better understanding. He stayed with them for a few months after they found him wandering the desert, half dead."

"What?" Penelope started. "He never told me that."

Elazar's dark eyes twinkled. "Ask him. It's a good story."

"I wonder how long it was before Abaddon found them. If he and the priests of Thevetat destroyed the Essenes, they could have also taken the library's sacred documents and left everything else that they felt had no value," said Penelope thoughtfully.

"I've often wondered if they had a *genizah* underground that has yet to be discovered." Elazar's eyes glowed at the very thought of it.

"*Genizah*?" Penelope drew a blank.

"A *genizah* is a storage area, usually in synagogues, but in the past, they have been built underground, or caves have been used. They are for manuscripts that are worn out or no longer in need. Or, as in the Essenes' case, manuscripts that need to be hidden and protected."

"If anything like that exists, I hope you're there when they discover it. If the Essenes used curses like the one on Tim, they will need you to make sure they don't end up dead or worse. Speaking of my friends, have either of them woken up yet?"

"No, and I've forbidden anyone from disturbing them. Curses like that take their toll on a body, and Carolyn's worry has exhausted her. They are better left to sleep it off."

"It's a good idea. She's always stressed over him far too much."

"Love will do that to a person. One day I will have to tell you how much you worried Alexis before he ever said a word to you."

Penelope tried and failed to hide the smile that sprang to her lips. "He was going to kill me! He can't have been that worried."

"You might struggle to believe me when I say this, but I will always be grateful that you worried him so intensely. Alexis has always had a complicated heart and a reserved nature. He'd withdrawn so far that I was starting to worry he would try and destroy himself. The next time I saw him, he was an equal mix of furious and excited that you had found his stone tablet before him. I knew at that moment that he would become entangled in your life one way or another; he wouldn't be able to help himself."

Penelope's chest grew hot. She had seen Alexis when he was onto something; enthusiasm and energy radiated from him, making him irresistible. That he'd become like that over her made her ache with joy.

"He makes me very happy," she said, struggling to articulate the emotions surging through her.

"And the Archives?"

Penelope laughed. "The Archives are the love of my life. I regret not having more time to know Nereus, to learn everything I needed to about protecting such knowledge and figuring out what I am meant to do with it all. I want to know everything in it, and I have no idea where to start."

"She was the best of grandmothers," Elazar said with a sigh, holding his hand to his chest, his face filled with repressed grief.

"I can't imagine what it was like growing up with them all. I've barely been with them two months, and I'm overwhelmed at least once a day."

"My childhood was filled with wonder and love, and that is the very best way to live. Unfortunately, having such an upbringing meant there was much about 'normal' life I found incredibly disappointing and mediocre."

"I bet it was. Is that why you chose to keep studying the history of magic?"

"Partly. As I said before, the Atlanteans can't do everything. Alexis is the only one who has continued to be fascinated by different forms of magic when it pops up around the world. He's spent most of his long life seeking out stories of those with magical abilities and finding the truth of them."

"Why? I mean, there's the Archives. He was taught by Nereus, so what could a human magician teach him?"

"A lot of things. Including how they access and use magic, which is different across cultures. He would collect accounts and information for Nereus and the Archives. Go for a walk through it sometime and look for them. There are thousands, all written by him. Alexis's true purpose for searching is deeper than that. Even though he will probably deny it, he's still searching for other survivors or evidence that it wasn't just them."

"And when he finally did find survivors, it was the two biggest assholes in the whole of Atlantis," said Penelope sadly.

"Indeed. I don't believe Alexis will ever stop searching for survivors. He's also endlessly fascinated that despite the best efforts of realists, atheists, scientists, and skeptics, mankind still seeks the supernatural, the mystery of magic. I've seen and experienced more than most, and I'm exactly the same. Science, for all its discovery and wonder, is a cold comfort. It is why even though we know what elements and conditions go into making the rain, we still can't let go of our stories of thunder gods."

Penelope smiled wider the more he talked. He had so many mannerisms that were identical to Zo's, but when he discussed magic, he was like another Alexis.

"Elazar, I have a feeling you and I are going to be great friends," she said.

"I hope so. You are already a part of the family, and that is a very good sign."

"Speaking of family, how did you come to be adopted by Zo?"

"The short version is that he saved my life. I was barely two years old when Golan Heights became a war zone in 1967. Zo had come to check on his vineyard, which is where my parents worked. They died when a bomb fell. He found me wandering a field, right before he found his wife who'd also been killed. When he couldn't find a family to place me with, he adopted me. He stayed and raised me in Israel, even though he was grieving for his wife. He has been the best of fathers."

"It's easy to be a good father when you've been blessed with such a son," said Zo, hooking him into a hug. "I was starting to wonder where you had disappeared to."

"I've been playing host to the lovely Doctor."

"I should've known! Penelope, have you been raiding Alexis's clothes?" asked Zo with a smile as he looked at the pale-blue, button-up shirt she was wearing.

"I couldn't walk around topless, could I?" she pointed out.

"I wouldn't have stopped you," teased Zo.

Elazar shook his head in disapproval. "Don't let Uncle Alexis hear you talk to Penelope like that, Abba, or you'll really be in trouble."

"Where is he, anyway?" asked Penelope.

"He's on the balcony talking to the cats and waiting for you to find him." Zo pointed her in the right direction, stealing Elazar to help him in the kitchen.

Still beaming from her talk with Elazar, Penelope opened the doors to the balcony and found her magician surrounded by females.

Alexis was reclining on a white, wicker chair with three cats demanding his attention. The small, brown one that had woken her was perched on his lap, and he was deep in conversation with her.

"I thought Zo was joking when he said you were talking to the cats," Penelope teased. He looked like he was about to say something, but as he stared at the shirt she was wearing, he paused. Blue light flickered under his skin and behind his eyes, making heat flare at the base of her spine.

Someone really loves me in their clothes. The longer Alexis stared, the hotter and more flustered she became.

"That cat woke me up," she said, needing to say something—anything—to change the subject of the conversation they weren't having with words.

"Sasha was curious to meet you. I've never brought anyone outside the family here before," Alexis said, refocusing his attention on the cat. "She also says you've been awake for an hour and you were talking on the phone."

"Sounds like she's a dirty spy for you. I can't believe I gave her a scratch," Penelope said, eyeing the cat. "Marco says hello, by the way."

Sasha jumped lightly onto Alexis's shoulder and rubbed her face against his ear.

"Oh? Is that so?" Alexis crooned at the feline.

"What now?" asked Penelope.

"She said you're in heat," Alexis said wickedly.

"I always knew I was a dog person for a reason."

"Don't listen to her, Sasha, she's just embarrassed. Do you think she should come and give me a kiss good morning?" Sasha, the traitor, meowed in response before hopping down to his lap again and curling up into a ball.

"I'm certain that means yes," Alexis interpreted.

"You know, I'm never going to believe you can actually talk to cats," said Penelope, leaning down to kiss him. As he stroked his thumbs along her cheek and down to her neck, she had to admit that Sasha was right: she was definitely in heat.

"But I *can* talk to cats," he said when they broke apart.

"And don't get between him and Sasha, whatever you do," warned Elazar as he came out of the house with a platter of fruit and a cup of coffee for Penelope.

"Is she yours?" Penelope asked.

"Cats aren't really anyone's," said Alexis vaguely.

"Alexis used magic to save that stray from dying in 1976, and now it refuses to die or move house," Elazar explained. "All of these other cats around the place are descendants of her babies. I won't see her for months, and as soon as Alexis arrives, she turns up within hours. Sometimes she'll arrive the day before he does. She always knows." Elazar gave Sasha a pat before heading back to the kitchen.

As soon as Penelope sat down, a tabby cat sauntered over and leaped into her lap. Sighing at the hair already on her clean jeans, she gave in to the inevitable and started stroking its head.

"Elazar was telling me about how he came to be adopted by Zo. It's quite the story. I can't imagine what it would've been like to be raised by a magician," said Penelope.

Alexis's smile was tender as he said, "You should have seen Zo when he bought Elazar home. He was such a tiny, brown bean, full of energy. Zo hadn't had a child in a long time, and he was completely overwhelmed and terribly in love already. Elazar refused to leave his side for the first six months, he was like an adorable, tiny shadow. Naturally, we all doted on him."

"He's definitely turned out well. I'm kind of surprised he doesn't have a spouse. He's a lovely man." Penelope knew how hard it was to maintain a relationship and an all-consuming academic passion. She had all but resigned to be single until Alexis had changed her mind.

"Elazar had an incredible wife. Rada knew about us, loved us, was a true part of the family, and Elazar adored her."

"What happened? I didn't see any wedding photos or anything in the house."

"No, you wouldn't. She died about seven years ago. A bus crashed into her car in Jerusalem, and she was killed. It has taken Elazar a long time to recover. There are no photos of Rada because it hurts him too much."

Penelope cuddled the cat on her lap closer, trying not to imagine that sickening, gut-wrenching feeling of loss. She'd felt it for only a few minutes at the Lido. To have endured it for seven years was unimaginable.

She was halfway through her lunch when Aelia and Phaidros arrived, arms laden with shopping bags.

"I wondered why it was so quiet in the house. It didn't take you long to need a shopping fix," Penelope said.

"I couldn't have you wearing Alexis's clothes for the rest of the trip."

"I don't mind," replied Alexis.

Phaidros looked between him and Penelope and his smile widened. Penelope scowled at him, hating when he read her aura. Between him and the cats, she wouldn't be able to keep anything secret.

Aelia handed Penelope two large bags. "Don't look so worried. I knew better than to deviate from your usual black, khaki green, and when you're feeling daring, maroon."

"Thanks, Aelia," said Penelope. She looked in the bag and noticed with some relief that there were no things that sparkled or were bright enough to be seen from space.

"Any sign of priests in the area?" asked Alexis, moving into general mode.

"No, not a glimmer of their magic either. We've lost them for the time being," said Phaidros. He sat down next to Penelope and helped himself to the fresh hummus and dipping bread Zo had made.

"Once Tim wakes up, we will try and get a straight story out of him about what happened at Qumran. It might give us a time frame on how quickly the priests were notified of the find," Alexis replied.

"I want to talk to him about the scroll itself and the visions he had while the curse was on him," said Elazar from the other side of the table.

"Could you trust them?" Penelope asked. "They could be a result of the madness. He was ranting about a Roman emperor, that's how nuts he was."

"Mad people often see the hidden more clearly than the sane. He could have insight into the prophecy that we need."

"What do you mean?"

Elazar poured himself some mint tea, his brows drawn together. "Despite the brilliant way the magic was constructed over him, I sensed something off. I don't know how to explain it. Like a note of discord within the symphony? I'm interested in what he has to say. There might be more to the magic than we guessed."

"You think he's become a prophet?" asked Zo.

Penelope choked on the grape she was chewing. "Tim Sanders, a fucking prophet? No amount of magic could make that happen. Despite his love of Qumran, he doesn't even believe in God."

"That's not always a requirement for a prophet," replied Elazar thoughtfully. "Besides, I'm only speculating. This kind of magic is hard to predict, and to be honest, I don't know enough about it. He might go back to being completely normal, or the experience might change him in different ways. He's brushed against something old and powerful, and it's unlikely that he'll emerge unscathed."

"Awesome. What are we going to tell Tim? That he has Jerusalem Syndrome and hope that he doesn't end up in a psych ward?" muttered Penelope.

"Easy, Penelope. None of these side effects may occur. Elazar is only trying to prepare you in case it does," soothed Alexis. She felt him touch the *moíra desmós* inside her chest, reassuring her.

"Looking on the bright side, if he's a prophet, he'll be able to tell us what the scroll means," Aelia said.

Penelope seriously doubted it.

SEVENTEEN

THE SUN WAS setting when Tim and Carolyn finally joined them. Penelope was up in an instant to provide hugs and get them settled at the large table. Alexis was still unsure of the dynamic of the three as they talked together. He'd assumed Penelope would be more relaxed with them all together, and the exact opposite was proving to be true. Penelope was tense, and she fussed, pouring tea and forcing plates of food on them.

"I suppose I should formally introduce you. Everyone, this is Tim, Tim this—" Penelope began.

"Wow, you're Elazar Adir, aren't you?" Tim interrupted, smoothing his sandy blond hair back from his face.

"It is nice to meet you, Doctor Sanders. I've followed your recent articles closely," Elazar said with a polite smile. "Please, eat and relax. There is a lot I want to ask you about your recent find."

Before Tim could reply, Penelope quickly introduced him to the other magicians, arriving at Alexis last. She rested her hands on his shoulders. "And this is Alexis, who I've told you about, and if you tell him any of my secrets, I'll destroy you."

Alexis shook Tim's hand, quickly assessing whether any traces of magic were left on his skin. His energy told him other things, too; that he was nervous, curious, and feeling jealously protective of Penelope. *Excellent. Someone else to disapprove of me.* Alexis could hardly blame

Tim or Carolyn for feeling protective of their friend. He just hoped they didn't view her as a prize to fight him over.

"It's nice to finally meet you. When Pen told me she'd shacked up with a guy in Venice, I could barely believe it," said Tim, releasing Alexis's hand.

"What's hard to believe about that? Any man would do his best to keep a woman like Penelope. I hope this isn't going to be another 'Penelope will never love you more than Atlantis' lecture," Alexis replied with a smile.

"I'm sure Carolyn would have covered that with you already," Tim teased. "I'm just pleased Pen's finally realized men exist in the world."

"Whatever, asshole. Maybe I would've noticed them more if you hadn't tried to set me up with every one of your football buddies," retorted Penelope with a scowl.

"Alexis has a huge library," said Carolyn with a laugh. "All other men can't compete."

"Now it's all starting to make sense." Tim winked at Penelope.

"Alexis is more than his library," Penelope defended playfully. Alexis doubted anyone else picked up on the undercurrent of annoyance in her tone. He gave the hand on his shoulder a kiss.

"Thank you, *cara*," he said.

"You don't even know the best bit," Carolyn said with a gleam in her eye. "Tim...*this* is Magic Guy."

Tim looked from Penelope to Alexis and back again before he broke out in hysterical laughter.

"Magic Guy?" asked Phaidros, one golden eyebrow raised. Carolyn and Tim quickly related the lecture night when Alexis and Penelope had first butted heads over Atlantis. Penelope looked like she was going to throttle them.

"She was livid. I've never seen someone get under Penelope's skin so badly that weeks later she was still furious and ranting about him," said Tim.

"I'm glad I made such a strong impression," Alexis replied with a smile.

"And here we are." Penelope kissed him, ignoring the snickers as she slid comfortably onto his lap.

"Disgustingly loved up," commented Carolyn. Penelope tensed, her hands clenching where they rested on his thighs.

"It was worth it," she said.

Alexis tightened his arms around her, knowing she had drawn a line in the sand and that she had chosen him again in front of the two people she cared about most.

"Enough about Alexis and Penelope. They are perfect, we know," Zo cut in, reading the heightening tension around the table. "Tim, I want you to tell us about your dig at the Dead Sea. I thought they had found everything out there already."

"I doubt we've gotten half of what's buried there. What happened at my dig is going to sound pretty unbelievable," Tim replied, shifting uncomfortably.

"Try us. We are all academics who believe in impossible things," said Elazar.

"You'll receive no judgment in this circle. We are all friends here," assured Aelia with an encouraging smile.

"For now," Penelope whispered to Alexis. She was smiling, but there was still annoyance in her eyes. He knew what she had chosen to give up when she had walked back into the palazzo to be the Archivist; Penelope was only starting to realize. Her life had changed irrevocably, and even those closest to her weren't going to understand.

Despite their shots about her never noticing men, Alexis was starting to doubt they would've been inclined to share her with anyone even if she had dated. They kept looking at her and quickly glancing away, puzzled by what was different. Carolyn must have had some idea, having seen magic performed the previous night. Yet Penelope hadn't shared the fact that she, too, had magic coursing in her own veins, and that interested him.

"Last February, I was at the Shrine of the Book researching for a new paper I was working on, when Professor Schaal called me," Tim began. "A cave had been found. It was like it had just appeared out of nowhere, and it had the entire community in an excited uproar. Archaeologists have been researching the Scrolls for years and had no idea that Cave 12 was right in front of them. I tried to get Penelope to come along, but she was too bummed out and crying over Atlantis."

"I like to think I was waiting for my breakthrough," Penelope quipped.

"A year waiting could've been a year of hanging out with me, Hawkes. Just saying. Anyway, a couple weeks ago, the other academics and Schaal cleared out for holidays. I decided to stay and work without any interference. Cave 12 had only produced some fragments of scrolls and carnelian beads, and there was a pickax head that we assumed had been left by a looter in the fifties. The cave appeared to be empty. Despite that, there was something about it that I couldn't let go of."

"Ah, obsession, you bitch of a mistress," said Phaidros.

Tim laughed. "Yeah, that's a really good way to put it. With the site empty, I thought I'd camp for the night and not head back into Kalia. It was an uneventful day. I had a few beers and went to sleep under the stars. Nothing excessive," he added to Carolyn, knowing she would disapprove. "It would've been about midnight when things started to get weird."

Alexis listened as Tim told them how he'd tried to rescue a trapped man, only to break through a wall and find nothing but bones and a clay jar.

"I knew I should've waited and documented the site properly," Tim said, noticing the horror on Penelope's face. "As soon as I touched that jar, it was like I lost my mind. I couldn't put it down or let it out of my sight for a second. I texted Schaal—he was still in Spain, so I knew it would be hours before he'd wake up and try and get a flight. I couldn't wait for him or a proper lab, so I opened the jar."

"What was the seal like? Was there any blood?" asked Elazar.

"Yeah, there was. How did you know?"

"I've read that the scribes sometimes mixed blood into the clay to seal certain jars," Elazar replied vaguely.

"I've been studying the Dead Sea Scrolls for the past fifteen years, and I've never read anything like that," argued Tim.

"We'll discuss it later, Doctor Sanders, when we won't bore our friends. Please continue," Elazar said politely. Alexis saw uneasiness and suspicion drape over Tim like a veil. They wouldn't be able to fool such a person for long, and Tim wasn't going to leave Elazar alone until he got answers. *So that's the reason he and Penelope get along*, Alexis thought. They were both bloodhounds when it came to mysteries.

After a moment, Tim continued. "I found the scroll inside the jar. When I read it, I couldn't believe it. Pairing it with the vision I'd had of the scribe, I think he composed it while the attack on the Essenes was happening. In all my research, I've never read of Belial having a brother called Thevetat, let alone a priesthood dedicated to such a demon god in the Second Temple period. Or a priesthood that predates Melchizedek for that matter. Then I started getting messages from Schaal, saying that he was making arrangements to return to Israel and that he had ordered some of the team back from Tel Aviv to help me start cataloging the find. It wasn't Schaal's team that arrived first, though. These guys—" Tim broke off, searching for the right words.

"They had all these black shadows hanging off them. I took one look at them, grabbed the scroll, and bolted through my bathroom window before they made it to my hotel room. They were already checking out my Jeep, so I climbed into the baggage hold of a tour bus. I couldn't let them get it. It was almost like...like the scroll was making me protect it.

"Then when I got to Tel Aviv, shit started to get really weird. I started seeing stuff. Carolyn had talked about auras before, so I knew what the colors were. I didn't know what to do when I started to see other things, like whether someone had yelled at their kids that morning, or if they had been cheating on their spouse. It got worse, to the point where I thought I was walking through different time periods, the whole world changing around me. When I did get sleep, I had nightmares of events I've never even heard of. The guys with the shadows kept finding me, I don't know how. I only knew I had to keep the scroll safe and I couldn't keep outrunning them, so I sent it to Penelope. I don't remember much after that, only hiding and the shadows always finding me. It's going to sound strange, but do you think that the shadow guys might have been followers of Belial's brother? Like they could still be operating? I know it's a long shot. It was probably the sleep deprivation…I thought I heard one of them talking about Thevetat like he was someone giving them orders."

There was a long, tense silence before Elazar said, "I believe that's very likely, Doctor Sanders."

"Really? Because I thought you guys were going to straight up laugh at me for thinking a demon cult from the Second Temple period was after me."

Alexis fought an internal struggle on whether or not to tell Tim the truth about their connection to the prophecy, and Penelope's words came back to him. *We need allies, not enemies.*

"Why would we laugh at you, Tim?" he said finally. "We *are* the Ancient Priesthood."

"Ha-ha, sure."

Alexis only stared at him. Tim looked to Penelope. "Is he serious right now? You guys are what, another cult?"

"Absolutely not," said Phaidros.

"Not a cult. The Ancient Priesthood is what the people of this area called our predecessors," explained Alexis, wanting to maintain the story Penelope had already established with Carolyn.

"And why would they do that? Were they like the Zadokites or something, attached to the Temple?" Tim asked, referring to the traditional bloodline of the Jewish high priests.

"No. They were Atlanteans who survived the destruction of the earthquakes and volcanoes that destroyed it forever," answered Alexis. Tim let out a nervous laugh and looked to Penelope again for help.

"It's true, Carter. Why do you think I decided to take a job half-way around the world? I found my proof," Penelope said.

"Did you ever stop to think they could be lying?" Tim asked. "No offense, guys. I'm sure you believe it."

"I've seen the proof. You think I'm dumb enough to take their word on it?"

"I saw it, too. They can use magic," said Carolyn.

"Uh-huh. And say I believe you, what does this have to do with the Essenes? They aren't involved in any of the Atlantis theories. Pen would've told me."

"It's possible that this scribe saw the descendants of the Atlanteans in his vision and didn't know how else to describe them. Their own magic was very different—" Elazar began.

"What are you talking about? The Essenes didn't use magic! They were obsessed with Torah and would've condemned any form of witchcraft, just like it says in Leviticus."

"Confuse magic and witchcraft at your peril," warned Aelia.

"Elazar, please rescue him," said Alexis.

"The Essenes practiced a form of magic, though they didn't view it as such," began Elazar. "You know how they actively practiced exorcisms, healings, casting of lots, yes?"

"Of course. There's written proof of that, but I wouldn't call that magic," said Tim.

"Then there was *pesher*, a form of deep interpretation of holy texts to discover the inner meanings and mysteries hidden there. In the *Zohar*, the Kabbalists take this practice one step further with their four levels of interpretation of Torah: Peshat, the simple or surface interpretation; Remez, the allegorical meaning; Derash, the rabbinical meaning that can use similar words or verses as comparisons; and Sod, the secret or metaphysical meaning…"

"And your point is? We aren't arguing about Kabbala," said Tim.

"We are discussing communication and access to divine power. The Essenes dedicated their lives to prophecy and interpretations, the secrets of God, and the angels whom they communed with and asked for assistance. They believed they were chosen, special, and they had their own form of what we would call magic that they saw as a gift from God, as a reward for their devotion. Not all of them were inducted to use it; only the holiest was even considered for the training. The scroll you found had such magic on it. They used blessings and protections on their most valued writings. You have heard the theory that what has been found in the caves at Qumran was their old drafts? I believe that is the case."

"Okay, if that's true, then where is the rest of it?" asked Tim, grasping onto the one part he was willing to consider seriously.

"I believe it's still hidden, protected perhaps in a *genizah* deep underground. Not all of the community would have known where it was and those who were initiated into the mysteries would've died horribly before revealing its location. It's probably why the priests of Thevetat killed them all."

"The priests of Thevetat that are mentioned in the scroll I found? You know about them too?" asked Tim nervously.

"Yes. Our bloodlines have passed down the knowledge of them, and they are still active in the world today. But you already know that though, don't you?" Alexis guessed.

Tim fiddled with the glass of wine in his hand. "Yeah, I think so. As I said, when I was in Tel Aviv, a few times the guys chasing me got close enough that I heard them talking about Thevetat a lot. I'm having a bit of trouble wrapping my head around all of this, to be honest."

"That's understandable," said Penelope, taking his hand. "You've been through a lot, and it might take you a bit of time to gain a clear head again. You were under a pretty old curse, after all."

"An Essene magical curse. Fuck me. If you know all of this, Elazar, why haven't you published anything? Why not get funding and go out and search for their hidden storehouse of secret knowledge?" demanded Tim.

"Because the world isn't ready to know. You know how much of an uproar the Dead Sea Scrolls had when they were first discovered. There are a million theories out there about who the Essenes really were. There is still too much war, and Qumran is already a contested historical site. You really think adding magic to that mix is a good idea?" said Elazar.

Tim pushed his hands through his hair. "There has to be a way. People deserve to know about it, who the Essenes really were."

"They already know. The Essenes were a highly devout people who wrote many books of scriptures and apocryphal texts. That is who they were. They wanted their secrets to stay that way, and who are we to argue otherwise? They would've ensured that no one find their *genizah* anyway. We don't have the abilities to find it, so we have to satisfy ourselves with the theory of it," Elazar explained.

Alexis saw Tim nod to appease Elazar, but there was still a fire burning in his eyes. He shared a look with Penelope and Alexis saw an understanding there. Tim wasn't going to let this go. They would need to find a way to recruit Tim Sanders or convince him to keep his mouth shut. Otherwise he was going to bring a world of trouble down on their heads.

IT WAS late when Penelope and Alexis made their way back to the bungalow. Sitting on a soft couch and looking out over the night-time gardens, Penelope gained a whole new appreciation and gratitude for Alexis insisting on his space. She curled up next to him, tossing her legs over his, and resting her head in the crook of his shoulder.

"I suppose that went about as well as it could," she said finally.

"Tim didn't like finding out that what he knew about the Essenes was incomplete," Alexis said.

"That's a diplomatic way of putting it. The poor guy has had an awakening, and he's not going to enjoy it one bit."

"I've never understood why some academics become so married to an idea that they refuse new evidence."

"When you devote yourself to something so entirely, it hurts when someone comes along and tells you that you spent all that time searching in the wrong direction. Tim will get over it. It's once he's absorbed all of this new knowledge that worries me."

"Why?"

"He won't let go of the idea of a *genizah* of magical texts still hidden in Qumran. I know what he's like. Elazar will have him on his doorstep wanting to learn from him. He's never going to be satisfied to keep going the way he had been and not trying to find it."

"That will be up to Elazar and him to sort out. You can't be responsible for everything, Penelope."

"I know. Tell me a story?"

Alexis shifted her closer and made them more comfortable. "Any requests?"

"Elazar said to make you tell me the story about how you met the Essenes. It seems like the night for it."

"Elazar is as bad as his father for not knowing when to keep quiet, it seems."

Penelope elbowed him gently. "You can't only tell me stories that make you look good."

"Why not? Everything I tell you should reinforce your decision to stay with me."

"I hear a lot of arguing and not a lot of storytelling."

"You are going to get the short version. Otherwise, we will be here all night," Alexis said with a defeated sigh. "I can't quite remember the year. I believe it might have been in AD 1 or 2. There was a Herod on the throne, and the Romans were still occupying Judea after Pompey invaded it sixty-three years earlier. I had enough of the world. It has happened more than once, to all of us. When Atlantis was destroyed, the blast of magic changed us in ways that we've never been able to understand. I don't believe we are true immortals, as proven by Nereus's death. We can die from a mortal wound, or we can find a way to drain our magic and, hopefully, age faster and die. The truth is, there is no real way of knowing how long we will take to age, and that very thought has often been unbearable.

"I was at an extremely low point when I decided to leave Jericho, where I was living at the time, and venture into the desert to put the idea of immortality to the test."

Penelope gripped him a little tighter, hating the very thought of him hurting himself, angry that no one tried to stop him. "And then what happened?"

"I wandered the barren land during the day, and at night I released my magic. I was careful not to do anything too out of the ordinary that would draw attention, so I went with lightning."

"Lightning?"

"I created storms and cast huge bolts of lightning to drain my magic as quickly as possible. I didn't realize that from the caves at Qumran, the Essene astrologers and brontologists were taking note of the unusual activity."

"You probably made them think Judgment Day was upon them."

"Not as dramatic as all that. The Essenes sent a man to deal with the mad sorcerer in the desert who was upsetting the weather so much." Alexis chuckled softly.

"And they convinced you to stop?"

"Not for a few days. His name was Yeshayah and was perhaps one of the most patient men I've ever met. He made a camp not far from me and waited for me to stop my nightly tantrum before approaching. I was a twisted horror, blistered and burnt from the sun. He wasn't afraid of a ranting, naked man throwing lightning into the sky."

"I would've taken one look at you and left you be," admitted Penelope.

"I told him to do the same. He wouldn't leave. He was fascinated by the magic I was using, and we eventually got to talking. After four days, I passed out from exhaustion and dehydration, and when I woke, Yeshayah had dragged me back to their settlement on a makeshift stretcher. The bastard had waited me out until I couldn't fight him."

"Very clever of him."

"He saved my life, even if I was a gentile magician. I stayed with them for nearly a year before Zo found me. He quickly became enamored of their writing, and I spent time learning about their magic even if I was never allowed to practice or be initiated myself. They pieced my mind back together, but Zo has never let me forget the time I was mad and naked in the desert." Penelope could feel Alexis's laughter as a soft rumble in his chest.

"Zo is just trying to keep you on the same level as us poor saps. I wonder how long it was before Abaddon found out about them?" Penelope asked.

"It would've had to have been after our visit with them." Alexis paused for a long moment.

Penelope glanced up at him. "You don't think they heard you and Zo were there?"

"It is possible. I never considered it. If Abaddon had heard of a sorcerer, they may have gotten curious and found the Essenes instead. I suppose it depends how closely Abaddon has been keeping tabs on us over the years," said Alexis, his face clouded with worry.

Penelope touched his cheek. "Either way, we will get justice for what they did to the Essenes."

Alexis's eyes refocused on her, and he smiled gently. "We will. Come, Doctor Bryne, we should sleep. I have a feeling tomorrow is going to be another hard day."

EIGHTEEN

SITTING IN A sunny corner of Elazar's office the following morning, Penelope felt the smallest part of normality creeping back into her life. Alexis had given her a new journal bound in leather, one of the many spares he seemed to have, and she had started writing notes about the scroll, the prophecy, Tim's visions, and the curse. She always did her best processing with a pen in her hand. This was an area she was comfortable in, not being on the receiving end of the intense emotions of the past week.

Tim had taken the information about the magicians about as well as Carolyn had, and even though they had spent so many hours of the previous evening explaining, she could still sense their unease. Tim had thought that Alexis holding him in the air using magic had been a part of his mania, and now he would probably be even more nervous around him.

Tim had taken the knowledge that he'd been under a curse with an intense academic curiosity about the hidden mysteries of the Essenes and with hardly any concern for the impacts on his own health. He only ever had a one-track mind, and that track led to the Dead Sea. That magic was real in the world, and that descendants of Atlantis existed, was always going to be a secondary wonder to the thought of a hidden *genizah* of Essene magical history. Alexis had been surprised by his reaction; Penelope and Carolyn hadn't. Tim would do just about anything to know more about the Essenes.

An uneasy feeling had settled over Penelope the previous evening as she'd watched the two halves of her world collide. She hadn't told Tim and Carolyn the whole truth and knew that she never could. That she had begun to withhold secrets from the two people in the world she had always shared everything with was a strange sensation and one she didn't like, no matter how necessary it was.

Penelope had slept poorly after her story with Alexis and had crept back to the main house at dawn with her laptop and journal. She had found a window chair to nestle in, hidden amongst bookshelves, and made herself comfortable. She studied the scroll again before writing up a copy of Zo's translation into her journal. Even with the curse on it neutralized, the translation magic in her was useless, refusing to work on it. She had located a book on Jewish signs and semiotics on Elazar's shelf and started to work her way through it. Thankfully, her magic worked on it; otherwise, she would've been tripping over the Hebrew for hours.

"Can't sleep either?" Tim asked softly, so as not to startle her.

"Nope, not with a new mystery to solve. Where's Caro hiding?"

"Still asleep."

"Still in your bed downstairs?" Penelope cocked an eyebrow.

"Yes. Sadly, it is only platonic sleeping."

"You couldn't handle anything more exciting at the moment."

"Shut up, Hawkes. Carolyn is really spooked."

"You disappeared and went mad. Of course she's spooked."

"I've gone missing in action before. It was different this time, but still the same deal. You're who's spooking Carolyn. You and the rest of these guys you're living with."

"Me? What did I do?" Penelope knew the magicians could be hard to take with their overabundance of personality, but the thought that she scared Carolyn was something else entirely.

"She told me about the attack on the house in Tel Aviv and that you weren't even scared, like it was something that happened every day. She didn't think you were reacting normally to the threat, and that people died and you were happy about it. Is it true you stabbed a guy called Kreios?"

Penelope tried to think of the best way to explain without revealing too much. "I was kidnapped twice in Venice."

Tim's expression fell. "What? You never told me that."

"I didn't tell anyone. I thought you would all freak out."

"Yes, we would have because *you were kidnapped.* It's not like you had a bad one-night stand."

"I survived them both. I saw people die in front of me. I've felt what it's like to be truly bound and helpless in a fight. The people who attacked the other night were also the ones who hurt and kidnapped me. But this time I was free, and I was going to fight to stay that way. Yes, we killed them, but only in self-defense. The last few months have changed me, and I don't know how to make Carolyn less spooked about it."

Tim rubbed his face. "If they were trying to kill you, then I guess I understand why you weren't upset when they died. Don't worry about Caro. You know what she's like. She just needs a day or so to figure it out in her own head. We can worry about other things until then."

"Like this. It's a great find, Tim," Penelope said, passing him the scroll, still held securely between the glass plates. His face seemed to relax as soon as he held it, and Penelope wondered if the magic still lingered inside him. Elazar had warned her that the curse would leave him changed, both mentally and physically. She hoped that if he did crack, they would be there to hold him together as best they could.

"Thank you for looking after it." Tim exhaled, holding it as gently as a newborn. "And for everything afterward. I didn't want to drag you into this; I just didn't see another way to hide the scroll."

"I'm glad I *could* help. If you'd found it any sooner, we all would've been screwed. It was lucky Alexis knew what to do."

"Ah yes, the prince. Interesting guy," Tim said, sitting down at the other end of the window seat.

"I guess that's an upgrade from calling him Aladdin. Am I going to have to give you the talk I gave Carolyn about me being a grown-ass woman who can make her own choices? Because I'm really not in the mood to be questioned about who I hook up with." Penelope shut her notebook with a snap.

"No, nothing like that. He's an okay guy, and I'm surprised you didn't leave Melbourne years ago. Carolyn has trouble letting go, you know that. Melbourne is her security blanket, she can't even fathom anyone wanting to leave it because she won't ever give it up. The only thing that Carolyn and I agree on is that you shouldn't stop trying to prove your theory about Atlantis to the world because he doesn't want his own secrets getting out."

"I haven't stopped," huffed Penelope.

"I know what you're going through, Penelope. I had so many people tell me that Cave 12 was a bust, that there couldn't be anything left. When I found that jar, I felt like...like my whole world and every sacrifice and minute I dedicated to the Dead Sea was worth it. I know you would've felt the same when you saw your Atlantis Tablet together for the first time. I don't want you giving up your discoveries for the sake of the charming smile of Alexis Donato."

Penelope pinched the bridge of her nose. How was she ever going to get them to understand that she'd found proof, so much glorious proof that she could never share with anyone except Alexis? That magic was tied so closely to Atlantis that she didn't know how to prove one existed without exposing the other?

"I haven't given anything up. I'm not like you, Tim. I never did it for the publications or a chance to throw it in the face of all the people that ever doubted me. And before you get shitty at me for saying it, there's nothing wrong with wanting a bit of glory and praise for your hard work. You like the publishing side of it, I only published because I wanted funding and now I don't need it. It's enough for me to know that it existed."

Tim shook his head. "It might be enough for you, but not for me. That poor scribe gave up his life to write down that they had been attacked. Take all the mysticism out of it, and that's what it comes down to historically. A rival religious group killed their entire community. People deserve to know the truth about what happened to the Essenes. Don't people deserve to know that Atlantis really existed? You aren't the only one out there obsessed with it, Pen. I don't know what gives you the right to keep it secret from them."

"Because I have to," she replied, her chest tightening.

Tim looked down at the tattoos across her forearms. "When I look at them, I see things. I see you screaming in a crypt, I see you pulling Alexis from the sea. I see things when I look at your new friends too. Colors and flashes of memories that aren't my own. Maybe I have lost my fucking mind after all. I don't know if any of it's true. And if it is, I don't know why you would keep so much from us."

Penelope swallowed hard, hating that he knew she hadn't told them the whole truth. "I have my reasons. A lot of them are to protect you and Carolyn. I don't want you a part of what's coming. I will always tell you what I can."

"I understand. I think. You saved me, Pen. I'm here for anything you need. Any way I can help. I can't imagine what it's like for you, knowing about…all this…and keeping it to yourself. I know you're holding back, and that's okay too."

Penelope reached out for his hand and squeezed it. "Thanks, Tim. You're taking this a lot better than Caro did."

Tim gave an affectionate chuckle. "Yes, for all her talk about auras and whatnot, she seems to be in shock now that she discovered something real. She's a bit jealous too. Try not to hold it against her."

"It's because she saw the library I get to work in. I'm sure she'll get over it."

"I don't think I'm ever going to get over the fact that I'm staying in Elazar Adir's house right now. Do you know how hard I've tried to meet this guy over the years? He's cagey and elusive even for an academic.

I suppose now I know why. The Essenes actively practiced magic, and he has proof. That would blow the roof off the whole archaeological world if he actually published a fraction of what he knows." There was a longing in his voice that Penelope understood, even though it made her uneasy. If Tim tried to start excavating Qumran for a storehouse of magical knowledge, he could release a whole world of curses like the one he suffered.

"Elazar will publish something when he feels the time is right. Maybe he's doing it out of the sheer love of it. If you had the opportunity to study alone, wouldn't you do it? It's not even my field of research, and I'm freaking out over his collection."

"I see you've already found something that piques your interest. Signs and semiotics, eh?" Tim was looking at her books. "What's brought this on?"

"I want to figure out the prophecy in the scroll, of course."

"You believe the prophecy could actually be real?"

Penelope almost slipped off her cushions in surprise. "You don't?"

"I don't know. Even with everything that I've seen, prophecy is tricky. Just because the prince says they're in one doesn't make it so. You know me, I'm skeptical of everything. If I believe in one prophecy from the Dead Sea, I'm going to have to start believing all of them. You can see my hesitation."

"I know you weren't awake for the attack on us in Tel Aviv, but the priests of Thevetat are very real. They are extremists. They've killed a lot of people, Tim. The serial killer in Venice was one of theirs, and what he did to those people will give me nightmares for the rest of my life. I can't make you believe in a prophecy. I can't prove to you that it's true. Let me tell you what I know for sure: the priests of Thevetat need to be stopped. If they think you've got something they need, they won't stop until they have it and you're dead."

"They were the ones that did this to you?" Tim stroked the tattoos on her forearms, tracing the sigil of the scars underneath.

"Yes."

"Was it because you sided with Alexis and his Ancient Priesthood?"

"Partly. You might not believe him about the prophecy, but the priests of Thevetat sure as hell do. Why else would they go after you like that if they weren't worried you had found something that was a threat to them?"

Tim moved his hand away from her. "Okay. So what do you need?"

Penelope smiled with relief. Tim could be a selfish pain in the ass at times. When it counted, he had always believed her and helped out when she needed it.

"I need you to help me break down this prophecy. Figure out what this seal is that it's talking about and if it can be used to stop the priests of Thevetat," she said. Another thought occurred to her. "When the curse was on you, you were ranting about an emperor. Do you know which one it was?"

Tim frowned, looking down at the scroll in his hands and back to her. "I saw a lot of weird shit, Pen. I...I still am."

"Do me a favor? Start writing down whatever you can remember. It doesn't matter how strange it is. It could be important to understanding what the scribe's magic did to you." Penelope passed him her laptop. "Create a file. It might even help you process what happened."

"Okay, shove over, and I'll get started," he said, moving her feet to one side before he curled up next to her and began to write.

PENELOPE STARTED to feel her concentration crashing later that afternoon. Elazar only smiled when he saw her surrounded by books and moved a small table to give her space to spread out. Alexis had come by a few times to bring her coffee and to plant a kiss at the base of her neck that she could still feel hours later, but by four o'clock, her brain was numb. Tim was in a deep discussion with Elazar and Zo, so she decided to take Alexis up on his offer to walk the two kilometers to the medieval church of Saint John the Baptist.

"The tour buses should be gone for the day so we might have a chance of getting the place to ourselves," Alexis said as they walked hand in hand in the warm, spring sunshine. One of the things Penelope liked about Alexis was that both of them could enjoy being silent in each other's company. It didn't tax her to be around him, and he never got offended if she was less than chatty with what was going on inside her head.

There had been good rainfall in the past few weeks, and the hills were alive with freshly washed pine, wild flowers, and green vegetation. Penelope breathed it all in, trying to let go of her constant worry, and reminding herself, again, that they were all safe.

The church of Saint John the Baptist was built of pale-brown stone with well-maintained gardens and views of the green hills around them. Alexis, acting as a tour guide, explained that the building had been constructed in AD 1113 and was now maintained by the Franciscan order.

Penelope sighed as they stepped into the cool quiet of the church, taking the time to appreciate the complex, tiled patterns of the mosaics and the colorful stained-glass windows. The few people who lingered were quiet and observant, and Penelope let the hush soothe her. She wished she could bottle the quiet and take it with her wherever she went.

Like any other tourist couple, they walked slowly with each other, admiring the artwork, the imposing altar, and the architectural design of the cupola, before making their way to the cave shrine that was believed to be the birthplace of the Baptizer himself. The hair on Penelope's arms rose as they stood in the sacred space.

"What is it?" asked Alexis.

"I just had a really weird feeling. Like the earth shifted even though I know it didn't. Everything that's happened in the past two weeks; the scroll, the prophecy, coming to *this* place... I spent the day reading the history of the Dead Sea, and I failed to even consider that we ended up *here*."

"In the town that John the Baptist was born, a man who, for most of his life, had a ministry at the Dead Sea and who has an intimate connection with Venice," said Alexis, catching instantly to her train of thought. "I'm an idiot for not realizing the significance sooner."

"Even I know the theories about John being the Teacher of Righteousness that the scrolls focused on. Tim will rant long and hard against the theory if you mention it to him, but even he can't rule out how much time John spent at the Dead Sea. He would have undoubtedly known of the Essenes, if not had direct contact with them," said Penelope as they headed out of the cave. She rubbed at her chest, the uneasiness in her refusing to dislodge. "I feel like, on the one hand, the fact we are here is pure coincidence, and on the other hand, we are getting our strings yanked."

"And this is precisely why I hate being in a prophecy. I find the easiest way to deal with it is to let it happen. Even if you try and fight, it'll end up working around you and happen anyway." Alexis placed a comforting arm around her shoulders as they reached the main part of the church once more.

"Can we sit for a bit? I don't want to go back just yet," Penelope said before choosing a wooden pew.

Alexis sat beside her. "What's bothering you, *cara?*"

"You mean, apart from prophecies and psychotic demon priests?"

Alexis gave her a slow and patient smile. "I saw how well you acted the night of the attack. Psychotic priests don't trigger your anxiety. You were clearheaded and focused, even in the heat of things."

Penelope twisted the rings nervously on her index fingers, the Phaistos Disc on one and the silver ring Alexis had given her with the lapis lazuli stone held between a laurel crown on the other. One from her old life, and the other gifted to her in her new. She was seeing symbols even on her hands, and it made her cringe.

"I don't know what to do. It is like there's two Penelopes now. One who's Carolyn and Tim's best friend, that stubborn, searching academic, the steady friend who was always there for them, who stayed at home while they went on a crazy adventure and took risks. Then there is this new Penelope. The one who's hunted serial killers, found the rest of the Atlantis Tablet, and is a part of this crazy magical world." *And who's so in love with you, she can barely stand to look at you without admitting it,* she didn't have the courage to add.

"The new Penelope can't—won't—go back to being who she was then. The person who constantly dropped her life to be there for them. I can't do it, but this new Penelope I'm becoming has to lie to her friends. Even though it's to protect them, it's still lying. I don't know how to merge both sides of myself. I don't know how to be like I used to be with them and still be me. I'm still that person, and I'm not. I think I'm having an existential crisis." She let out a tired laugh.

"Do you need to talk out your thoughts or are you asking for my opinion?" asked Alexis, too polite to assume she needed or wanted his advice.

"Give me your opinion because I don't know what to do or how to process it, and if I can't figure it out soon, I'm going to end up snapping and hurting everyone, *or* I'm going to end up as mad as Tim."

"When you first came to Venice and were stabbed, I had to bring you to the palazzo so that Nereus could heal you. Seeing you in my home, I was torn between relief and terror. I made a deal with Nereus and wiped your memory because I knew if you stayed, you'd eventually find yourself in the position you are in now. I wanted you to stay, but I had to send you back as a final chance to avoid you being dragged into this life.

"The hard truth is that you will never be able to go back or be who you once were for them. It's not their fault, they don't understand what's changed, only that it has, and so they are reacting the way they have been. They want you to fit into this safe, ideal vision of you they have in their heads, and it's not who you are anymore. You should never have to force yourself to be something that you're not just to make other people more comfortable. If they are your true friends, they will never ask that of you. They will accept the person you are becoming, secrets and all, or they will not.

"Everyone has secrets, Penelope, things they hide from other people. Don't let them make you feel like you are lying to them because there are things you can't share with them. They keep things from you, too. Those hidden parts of ourselves are what make us who we are, and you should never, ever, have to apologize for being you."

Overwhelmed and unable to think of how to respond, Penelope glanced around at the empty church before taking his face in her hands and kissing him soundly.

"You are making me think inappropriate thoughts while in a house of God," Alexis chastised, heat and longing in his eyes.

"I'm sure it's fine. I'm pretty sure it was a John who said, 'God is love,'" joked Penelope as she wrapped her hand over Alexis's long fingers. "Thank you, Alexis."

"They love you, *cara mia*. You shouldn't have to fight so hard to make anyone comfortable at the cost of your own peace of mind. Give them the chance to adjust. They will choose to stay with you or they won't."

NINETEEN

W HEN PENELOPE FOUND Elazar the next morning, he was flipping through a book and muttering to himself.

"What has you so worked up this early in the morning?" she asked curiously.

Elazar tossed his glasses across the desk. "Your friend is argumentative and perhaps not in his right mind, but he's good at making me think in new directions. They were still drinking with Aelia, Phaidros, and my father when I woke up at 4:00 a.m. with phrases burning in my brain, and now I need to find the books to silence the noise."

"Tim will do that. Let me guess, he told you he doesn't believe in the prophecy?"

"Amongst other ridiculous notions. The books I need aren't here. Would you like to come down to the *genizah* with me?"

"You have a *genizah*? How am I only learning about this now?"

"It's what I call it, when in fact, it's just another library. Come along, I'll take you before the intrepid Tim Sanders wakes up and wants to come snooping." Elazar led her to his private study before pulling back a bookcase to reveal a locked door.

"Smuggler's house!" Penelope said with a gasp. "I love it."

"I can only imagine your reaction when you first saw the Archives," Elazar said, chuckling. He opened the door and switched on some lights, illuminating a spiral staircase.

"I'll have you know I was very calm and collected."

"She wasn't," said Alexis behind them. "I knew it would only be a matter of time before you tried to woo my woman with your collection."

"I'm a simple man, made of flesh," said Elazar unapologetically. "Are you coming?"

"You need a chaperone," insisted Alexis.

"Now I *am* intrigued," said Penelope, following Elazar down the stairs. The temperature dropped, and Penelope shivered. "Are you keeping them refrigerated?"

"No, fire-protected. If the house burns down, at least I know my books would be safe."

At the bottom of the stairs, Elazar opened a thick, iron door, and Penelope found herself in an underground library filled with books and scrolls.

"This is where he keeps all the interesting things," said Alexis, smiling at Penelope's astonishment.

"Are these original?" she squeaked, studying the labels tied to clay jars that identified their contents.

"Most of them. You can see why I didn't want Tim to know about them. If I ever got him out of here, I'd still have to check all of his pockets."

"He would never steal from you!" defended Penelope.

"Like he would never take anything from a dig site? Men, when they are desperate, do stupid things; academics do unethical ones. I didn't mean to offend you, Penelope. I don't know the man, even though I like him immensely. The only reason I'm showing you is because Nereus vetted you and made you Archivist, not because you are Alexis's lover."

"Your collection, your rules," said Penelope. "I just don't want you to think Tim is a thief."

"Not a thief. An academic. I'm not going to subject myself to any of his lectures about how I need to give my personal collection to a museum and share my knowledge with the world. He did enough of that last night when I was telling him about my interest in Essene magic."

"You blew the mind of an academic in a field of study he's devoted his life to. How did you expect him to react?"

"Like the Archives, what Elazar has here is too eclectic and dangerous to be entrusted to humans," explained Alexis.

"Okay, so what are we looking for? What questions have had you up since 4:00 a.m.?" asked Penelope, her eyes incapable of staying still with so much to take in.

"Phrases and titles and gifts," murmured Elazar as he moved amongst the shelves. "There are two phrases from the scroll that are bothering me in particular. The first is, 'The ancient ones will use a gift from the hand of the Prince of Heaven.'"

"It sounds messianic. Isn't Jesus referred to as the Prince of Heaven? The right hand of the king and all that?" said Penelope.

"Yes, but the Essenes wouldn't have been referring to him. They would've known about his ministry, as they did John's, but they expressed no interest in it from what I can tell. Judea was a small place that almost had more Greek and Roman citizens than Jewish. The Essenes might have even gone to investigate John and Jesus for themselves. In any case, that another group of Jews had condemned the Temple in Jerusalem for being corrupt wouldn't have surprised the Essenes, but they wouldn't have considered either in a messianic light. To answer your question, the Prince of Heaven, in Essene tradition, always relates to the Archangel Michael." Elazar pulled down a scroll and placed it on a long table.

"If you already know it's referring to Michael, what's brought on your agitation?" asked Alexis.

"I need a list of the gifts Michael has given throughout history and references from all the texts; Jewish, Christian, Muslim, Gnostic, and apocryphal. No stone unturned must be our policy. If we know what he's given to whom, it'll help narrow down our search. From there we can worry about how to find it in the here and now, and perhaps find any accounts relating to Rome that would help explain Tim's vision of an emperor."

"Wow, you really have been thinking of this since 4:00 a.m. Okay, I'm at your disposal, Professor Adir. Point me in the right direction," insisted Penelope. Alexis placed his journal and pen down on the table.

"I'll help, too. My ancient Arabic is better than yours, and it will make scanning texts easier."

Elazar's Arabic sounded very fluent as he sent a long list of profanities in Alexis's direction. The magician only laughed harder and disappeared into the stacks.

"I swear, that man would be insufferable if he weren't so lovable at the same time," Elazar added in English.

"If it makes you feel better, I was going to stab him with an oyster knife once," admitted Penelope.

Elazar's dark eyes twinkled with amusement. "He probably would've let you."

"It didn't get that far. Nereus saved the day."

"As was her way. I miss her," Elazar said, sighing. "She would've known what to do about Abaddon and his nest of vipers. She would've known what to say to help your friend understand the magnitude of what he's found and convince him to keep quiet about it."

"You're really worried about him, aren't you?" Penelope could the see the tension in Elazar whenever he mentioned Tim.

"Don't misunderstand me, Penelope, he's a good person with a strong heart. I don't believe there's any intentional maliciousness in him."

"I'm sensing a but…"

"But he's ambitious, and that may very well be his undoing. You have seen this life." Elazar gestured at the treasures around him. "You've seen these wonders and more, and as much as you'd like to talk about them, you know it's better that some knowledge is kept hidden to stay out of corrupt hands. People like Tim want to expose every secret and mystery in the world, thinking that what they do will provide illumination and understanding, but in truth, it will bring only darkness. No matter how much Tim loves you, he loves the scroll more. Don't forget that."

"You don't think the curse is still in him? That some of it has been left behind?"

"No, whatever the curse was, it is gone, I assure you. But you have to understand, for better or worse, it's changed Tim, just like your own experiences have changed you. Do you believe he'll be able to keep it to himself forever?"

And to that, Penelope didn't dare answer.

TWO HOURS and a pile of books later, Penelope sat across from Alexis at the table, both jotting notes into their journals and asking Elazar questions. Penelope couldn't help but enjoy spending time researching with Alexis. Bouncing ideas and relaying theories with him was akin to foreplay. She recalled how Aelia had once said that her vision of Penelope and Alexis's relationship would be them both getting lost in the Archives for days, only to come together for passionate sex and to tell the other person everything they had learned before disappearing into the Archives once more. As it was then, the visual was delightfully accurate, and Penelope smiled down at her manuscript without really reading it.

"I believe you're blushing, Penelope Bryne," said Alexis, without glancing up from his book. "Is there anything you would like to share with me?"

"Nope," she replied cheekily.

"If I didn't know better, I'd say you are having lascivious thoughts, and I happen to know *The Hypostasis of the Archons* isn't that sort of exciting read."

"Sounds to me like you are the one having lascivious thoughts and are projecting them onto me."

"Is that so? I'd be far more obvious about my intentions."

"Not that I've noticed. You never did tell me how to court a magician from Atlantis," said Penelope. "I suppose I'll have to keep all my lasciviousness to my thoughts for a while longer."

"If you two are done flirting with each other, I have a list of books I need you to find, Penelope," said Elazar, placing a fresh stack down in front of her.

Alexis set his pen down, and Penelope thought she could detect the smell of firecrackers and cinnamon over the leather and paper of the library.

"I'd better go and see Zo so that he can distract the others and keep them from looking for us. I know Carolyn and Aelia were talking about going on another shopping trip to Jerusalem," said Alexis.

"Excellent idea. That means I'll get out of having to do it," Penelope agreed.

"Carolyn's going to catch on that you are avoiding her. Aelia can't distract her forever," Elazar cautioned Penelope before turning to Alexis. "Don't dawdle upstairs either, Uncle, I need you."

Penelope kept reading. Later, when she went to make another note, a strange line of script had appeared on the page. It was that curious cross between Arabic and Atlantean that Alexis favored.

"Firecrackers," she whispered.

"Pardon?" Elazar asked.

"Sorry, just thinking aloud." The magic inside Penelope began to dance, and as she studied the script, the symbols and strokes began to rearrange themselves.

Even though you are across from me, every part of me yearns for you until I can't read or think from longing…

Penelope read the line twice, heart pounding so hard that her vision swam.

"Why don't you ever play fair, Alexis Donato?" she murmured.

"It's because he plays to win. Always." Elazar gave her a pointed look over the top of his glasses before going for more books.

"Well, two can play at that game," Penelope said primly, reaching for Alexis's journal. The relentless want of him that she'd felt for weeks peaked as she focused on the part of herself that was the Living Language.

Holding her intentions within her mind, Penelope picked up her pen, selected the next blank page of his journal, and began to write. Her hand flew from right to left, a perfect mimic of Alexis's code. She described, in graphic detail, exactly what torment he'd put her through the past few weeks with his languid kisses and sly caresses, both of which had left her frustrated and unfulfilled. She had filled half a page before Elazar cleared his throat, his dark eyes concerned.

"Alexis doesn't let anyone touch his journals, and he might not appreciate you doing…whatever it is you are doing." Elazar's concern turned to curiosity as Penelope lifted her pen. "Are you writing in his cipher?"

"I suppose I am. Just a little reminder for him," she said, returning the journal to its original page and position.

"I can't believe he taught it to you," said Elazar, looking at her like she'd grown two heads.

"He didn't. It's a side effect." Penelope quickly explained how she touched the Atlantis Tablet and the Living Language that transferred to reside under her skin.

"And this gift was in addition to Nereus's magic?"

"Yes. It's been invaluable, considering so many of the books in the Archives are written in dead languages."

"Can you show me how it works?" Elazar asked keenly. Penelope spent the next thirty minutes with light and letters over her skin as Elazar placed everything from Ancient Greek to Sumerian in front of her. While they experimented, she told him of the times the magic had tried to warn her, like an additional sense.

"What an incredible gift, and a perfect one considering you were destined to become the Archivist. Nereus would've been overjoyed."

"If her 'being overjoyed' was telling me not to worry about it, then yes."

"Never doubt for a second that she knew exactly what you were the moment she saw you. I wonder what Poseidon's magic will bring out in you," he said thoughtfully as Penelope choked.

"What now about Poseidon?"

"Nereus was Poseidon's heir, and…and you don't know anything about it, do you?" Elazar sat down, dumbfounded. "I would've thought she had left you a note telling you about it at least."

"Not that I've found. Feel free to start explaining," said Penelope, crossing her arms. She seriously doubted she could handle any more surprises.

"Did Nereus ever tell you how she came to be the Matriarch of the Citadel of Magicians?" asked Elazar.

"Not a peep. Neither did Alexis."

"Perhaps he doesn't know either. Nereus was a very private person, and I don't even know if the story she told me was the truth. I was a young man when she told me, and it was only after a substantial amount of ouzo."

"Truth or not, you can't say something like 'Poseidon's magic' and leave me hanging."

"I suppose the dead have no way of objecting. Nereus wasn't born a magician; she was made one. Like you were. She told me that when she was a young woman, she worked as a scribe in a seaport. She had a prodigious gift for languages and could write and work as a translator for the merchants from Greece, Persia, Phoenicia, and Egypt. One night, she was walking home along the beach when she saw Poseidon standing out in the water. Of course, she knew of Poseidon, even if she didn't recognize him. He was a great magician and king, as close to a god that the common people could imagine. She saw him performing magic out in the waves, calming the seas, and changing the course of a storm that was heading toward them from Greece. She actually had the nerve to demand to know what he was doing."

Penelope burst out laughing. "I can imagine her doing that. A young Nereus would have been a fearsome creature. How did he take it?"

"At first, he lectured her for being impertinent enough to question him, and then he realized that Nereus had seen through the magic he'd used to cloak his presence. He was overjoyed then, and relieved, because he knew he'd found the heir to his magic and the Citadel. No one was more surprised than Poseidon that his heir was a magicless, female scribe from an unimportant fishing port."

"Men! I can imagine the argument she would've had with him about it. He must have transferred his power to her in a vial, the way she did with me," said Penelope thoughtfully.

Elazar looked bashful as he replied, "Actually, he didn't. According to Nereus, he refused to leave her until she was convinced he wasn't trying to trick her, and that she really was destined to be the Matriarch of the Citadel. He gifted his power to her by other, more carnal means."

"Wow. Shagging Poseidon. Go Nereus!" Penelope's grin widened. "I suppose he was smitten in more ways than one."

"Yes, well, she was evasive when I asked her how long the affair lasted, but I know she never married, or took another lover after him."

"She was probably too busy looking after a tower full of obnoxious young magicians," said Penelope.

"Undoubtedly. I imagine it would've been too hard for a normal man to compete after Poseidon. His magic, or a part of it, was gifted to Nereus, and now shared again with you."

"But I'm not a magician! I'm an archaeologist."

"And Nereus was a scribe. Believe me, you're a magician even if you are untrained. It might take its time to manifest, but Poseidon's power is inside you now."

"It's not. Otherwise, it would've shown up on this." Penelope pulled the astrolabe out of its home in her pocket.

"Nereus's device. I had wondered what had happened to it," breathed Elazar. He had a look of such excitement and yearning that Penelope passed it to him.

"Hello, lovely," he crooned as he opened it. "I grew up watching Nereus using this. She never let it out of her sight." He twisted the dials on the side, and seven rings lifted up in silver-and-gold loops. "You see, Penelope, you are a magician." Elazar smiled widely.

"No, I'm not. Seven rings, seven magicians."

"That's right. There are still seven magicians."

"But the seventh ring is Nereus!"

"No, my darling, it's not. Nereus's ring was made of onyx. It's gone. It would have vanished with her death," Elazar explained slowly.

"Fuck me," whispered Penelope.

"I couldn't have said it better myself," said Alexis from the shadows, making both Penelope and Elazar start.

"How long have you been there?"

"Long enough to hear you're Poseidon's heir, as well as Nereus's," he said. Penelope had seen him face down Kreios without a flicker of fear or uncertainty, and now he was looking at her with both.

"If Nereus thought it was something to be concerned about, I'm sure she would've said so," argued Elazar, folding the rings back down and handing the astrolabe back to Penelope.

"Or she wouldn't have said anything, just to keep it interesting," muttered Alexis.

"Knowing my magic comes from Poseidon changes nothing. I still don't have any abilities, except translating languages, which came from Alexis's Tablet anyway," said Penelope, doing her best to shove the new knowledge aside and not dwell on it. She got to her feet. "I'm going to dig around and follow up on a lead."

"Pen—"

"I'm fine, Alexis. Help Elazar," she said, moving out of his reach and finding a far corner to sit in behind the stacks.

"One problem at a time," she reminded herself, bringing her knees to her chest. Where Nereus got her power from didn't change the immediate problem of figuring out how to stop Thevetat.

What's going to happen when the Tide rises and you have magic that you don't know what to do with?

"One problem at a time." Penelope straightened her legs and opened her eyes. The light wasn't as bright this far back amongst the shelves, but the golden title of the book in front of her caught her eye. Hebrew letters danced into a translation she could read. Penelope read it twice before pulling it off the shelf.

Then she started laughing.

"Penelope? Are you okay?" Alexis appeared around a shelf, wearing a concerned frown.

"Yeah, I've just solved the prophecy," she said and showed him the cover. He knelt down to read it, looked up at her with a huge smile, and unable to contain his excitement, kissed her hard.

"My wonderful Penelope," he said before helping her stand and kissing her again. "Whatever did I do to deserve you?"

"Something bad, I'm sure. You're not turned off by the whole Poseidon's magic thing?" she asked uncertainly.

"It would take much, much more than a dead magician's magic to scare me away from you. I was surprised, and then I wasn't, because everything about you is a wonder. We'll take it as it comes, Doctor Bryne, like everything else," he said, kissing her for a third time.

"Do I need to remind you two that this is a place of study?" Elazar asked, looking up at Penelope perched in Alexis's arms.

"I have been." Penelope freed her arm so she could pass the book to Elazar.

"What are you doing with the *Testament of Solomon*...oh."

TWENTY

I T WAS LATE in the afternoon when Penelope found Carolyn lying on a bed, reading a romance novel.

"Hey, how was shopping?" she asked, lying down next to her.

"Good. Exhausting. Aelia is out of control when it comes to a sale." Carolyn put the novel down. "How was researching? Get anywhere?"

"Sure did. Pretty sure I've solved the scroll prophecy. Elazar and Alexis are getting a proper theory together to talk about at dinner tonight."

"You have found the perfect nerd."

"Really did."

Neither woman looked at the other and Penelope had no idea how to fill the gulf that was widening between them.

"You scared me the other night," whispered Carolyn.

"I didn't mean to. I wanted to get you to safety. I wanted to help."

"You aren't like these people, Pen. You're never going to hang out of car windows and shoot at bad guys. You should stop trying to keep up with them. You've got nothing to prove."

"I know I don't. I might never be some kick-ass warrior, but I'm not going to act like a damsel at the first sign of confrontation. I refuse to be a victim," Penelope said, her hands bunching into fists.

"Why didn't you tell me you were kidnapped?" asked Carolyn.

"I see Tim opened his big, stupid mouth."

"He can be a clueless idiot, and even he's worried about you. That says something."

"Maybe I didn't tell you because you would've tried to guilt me into going back to Melbourne and I didn't want to. I wasn't ready to stand up to you and say no then, and I am now. I thought about walking away. I tried to. I got on a plane, ready to leave Venice. And I just… couldn't go. I belong there, with them."

"You barely know them! They have pulled you into their gang war or whatever the fuck it is, and they are going to get you killed."

"Maybe. It's a risk I've chosen to take, and you have to deal with that," Penelope said, trying to remain calm.

Carolyn found Penelope's closed fist and wrapped her hand over it. "I'm only acting like this because I'm so worried about you. I'm going back to Melbourne, and I'm going to leave you with them. It's going to turn me gray."

"Then don't go. Stay with us. Help us fight the priests of Thevetat," said Penelope, looking across at her. Tears were sliding down Carolyn's cheeks, silent and angry.

"I can't stay. I'm not like you, Pen. Not anymore. I don't want to fight people. I want my quiet corner of the university, and to terrorize my students, not run from crazy cultists. I'm not built for the pace of this *demimonde* that you've found yourself in."

"I thought you, of all people, would understand. That you would love having true magic in your life."

"So did I. But I love you, Pen. I'm never going to be okay with you endangering your life and I refuse to stand by and watch you willingly do it. What I can do is try and enjoy the rest of this unexpected holiday, before I get on a plane and try very hard not to dwell on the fact that my best friend is being hunted by demon worshippers."

"I can handle that. Is Tim going with you? Because if I had a choice, I'd send you both back to Australia until this is over. I never wanted you involved in the first place, and I don't want either of you caught in the cross fire."

"Tim will go back to the Dead Sea. That's where his heart will always be. I can't compete with it, and I've accepted that. He's fascinated by your new friends and what they can help him understand." Carolyn rolled over to face her. "I'm worried about him. He's pretending to be okay, but I know he's not. He's been writing on your laptop nonstop. I've never seen him write like that; he's never had that sort of laser focus. He's like Gollum with that scroll. If you think he's going to keep quiet about it and all of its implications, you're dreaming."

A spike of dread pierced Penelope's stomach. Elazar wouldn't let Tim expose his curse-breaking gifts or relinquish what he knew about the magic the Essenes wielded. She had seen him working at the laptop and had figured it was helping him sort out whatever was in his head, so she'd left him be. Penelope hoped for Tim's sake that he wasn't going to be stupid enough to argue about what he had to keep secret when the time came.

"I want to help you, Pen, but I can't stay. I don't have the courage to get shot at regularly," said Carolyn softly.

"Go home and be safe, that's how you'll help me. Don't feel guilty. I'll still love you the same," Penelope replied and pulled Carolyn into a hug. "Get it together and stop crying, Williams. Just think of those handsome men upstairs cooking for us."

Carolyn started laughing through her tears. "That's the one part I wouldn't mind taking back with me. You can keep the demon worshippers; I'll keep the hot kitchen boy."

"Good to know you still have your priorities straight," said Penelope, the gulf between them closing once more.

THE NIGHT was warm, clouds were building in the distance, and the winds brought the scent of rain up the valley. A table had been set on the terrace overlooking the fading sun on the mountains, and as Penelope and Carolyn made their way upstairs, the sounds of a violin filled the air. Carolyn stopped dead, her mouth falling open. Speechless, she cocked her head toward the sound.

"That will be Phaidros fighting the cats by threatening to make new strings from their guts," said Zo.

"You look adorable," said Penelope, pulling on one of the frills of his pink kitchen apron. Bright white letters across it stated, "If you think the kitchen is dirty, spend a night with the chef."

"It was a gift from Aelia. If I don't use it, she'll pout," he said.

"Tasteful as ever, I see," Penelope replied with a giggle. Carolyn was giving him a look like she was indeed imagining how filthy a night with the chef would be. Phaidros started another song, and like a fateful child, Carolyn followed the Pied Piper's music.

"Is she okay?" asked Zo, lifting a dark brow.

"Yeah, I think she will be. I'm sure the friendship will survive even though she thinks I'm insane."

"We all think you're insane, but with the magical tide rising, I'm glad you are staying."

"What's the tide got to do with me?"

"Not you. Alexis. He keeps a very tight leash on the power he has now, and that will get a lot harder for him the more magic rises."

"I saw him pull twenty iron floodgates out of the sea. I know how powerful he is."

Zo gave her a measured look. "No, *sorella mia*, you don't. Alexis tired and on low tide is impressive; Alexis on a high tide is an earth-shaker. Nereus said the tide coming will be the highest since Atlantis sank. Alexis was young and not as experienced then, so who knows what this tide will do to him. Having you with him will keep him steady and grounded."

"Are you trying to freak me out? What's brought this on?" asked Penelope. *Please God, no more surprises.*

"I can feel his magic growing. So can Phaidros. There are already signs it's starting to spark early, so be careful how far you push him, or you might very well end up locked in the tower until it's calm again."

"Don't be dramatic—he'd never lock me in a tower!"

"Last time the tide was high, he moved to a remote village in the Armenian mountains because he was worried about controlling his power and didn't want to accidentally damage a city. Unfortunately, he fell in love with a girl in the village and when her parents disapproved of the match and wouldn't let them marry, he lost his temper. Before anyone could stop him, he disappeared his house and the girl with it. It didn't reappear again for eighty years when the girl had died of old age. The crazy sorcerer had turned into an urban legend, and everyone was upset when he turned up again. *That* is Alexis on a normal high tide, not like what's coming, so don't tell me he wouldn't lock you up in a mad effort to protect you from Thevetat."

Penelope placed a calming hand on his arm. "You are being dramatic. I wouldn't do anything to worry Alexis. I have no intention of arguing with him or making him think I need to be placed in a tower. I did exactly what I was told the other night during the attack and—"

"And you tried to rush into a crack house in Tel Aviv to look for Tim without any of us with you. I'm not accusing you of anything, just trying to give you a heads-up. Nereus used to be able to take some of his magic and balance him when the tide started to rush in. She used to do it when she trained the new apprentices. It helped keep them steady when their magic was awakening and kept them from having too much, too fast. Nereus isn't here to help Alexis anymore, so you must find another way to keep him calm. He loves you like crazy and would never forgive himself if he hurt you, even accidentally."

"He doesn't love me," Penelope blurted instinctively, feeling ridiculous. Everything else Zo had said faded into insignificance.

"Come on, Penelope, you are smarter than that. Open your eyes." Zo flicked her nose gently.

"He hasn't said it, I haven't said it. It's not something we've discussed."

"And you think you have to put it into words? He told me you heard his heart song. You wouldn't have been able to do that if you didn't love each other deeply. Why do I even need to explain this to you?" he demanded, hands on his hips.

"We are courting?" Penelope said awkwardly.

"Courting death maybe, if you keep leaving him so frustrated and lovestruck."

"Shut up and get back in the kitchen. Stop trying to give me love advice like some sage *nonna*."

Zo placed his hand on his heart. "*Ah, love, that moves the sun and other stars...*"

"Don't you dare start quoting *Paradiso* to me!"

"*Love, which quickly arrests the gentle heart...*"

"Be careful quoting Dante to Penelope, it'll make her loins quiver, and you'll be the next man she runs away with to a foreign country," said Tim, as he walked past without looking up from the book in his hands.

"Shut up, Tim. You have no idea what gets any woman's loins quivering, least of all mine."

"Oh, *bella*, please tell me this is true," Zo said, wrapping his arms around her.

"Say another word, Timothy, and I'll get Elazar to put the curse back on you," threatened Penelope.

Tim gave Zo a serious look and whispered, "Loin quivering," before disappearing into the other room.

"Come into the kitchen with me, *bella*, and tell me more about what else Dante and his immortal words make you feel," Zo begged.

"Right now, Dante is making me feel wrathful," growled Penelope.

"Come, come. Perhaps my poetry can help your loins get into the mood so they can stop torturing Alexis."

"I hate you so much," Penelope said, following him into the kitchen anyway.

Carolyn was there already, staring through the sliding door that led out to the terrace.

"Look," she whispered, gesturing Penelope over. Phaidros was playing the violin again, moving in slow circles around Aelia. She was smiling in an open and sweet sort of way that Penelope had never seen on her before. Carolyn reached for the door handle, but Penelope stopped her.

"Wait...wait for it," she said.

An intense glow began to burn in Phaidros's golden, feline eyes as he teased Aelia, coaxing her to sing. As if waiting for the perfect opening in the music, Aelia broke out into a beautiful melody, her body moving around his in a slow and measured dance.

The hair on Penelope's arms rose, her pulse quickening as it always did when Aelia sang, the magic of her voice filling every part of her. Zo came to stand beside her, resting a forearm on her shoulder.

"Would you look at that? She's singing a very old love song, one from home," he said, and Penelope knew he meant Atlantis. "The peasant girls used to sing it in my village during springtime." Zo's face softened, sadness settling in with joy. "I thought I'd forgotten it."

"Phaidros hasn't," said Carolyn, unable to tear her eyes away from them.

"He's probably waited the last nine centuries for the right moment to play it to her. It's about time," Zo said with a sigh.

"You really are a hopeless romantic," said Penelope.

"There's nothing else worth devoting your life to. Believe me, I've looked. After all this time, it's only love that still surprises me."

"You make it sound like you're a thousand years old, and you're what? Forty at most?" asked Carolyn.

"Thirty-eight. It's old enough to know," Zo lied after a long silence. Penelope patted his arm in a silent thank-you and continued to watch Aelia and Phaidros let music say all the things they couldn't.

An hour later, Phaidros had convinced Alexis to pull out his cello, while Zo filled the table with seasoned lamb, fresh flatbread, couscous, salads, and multiple carafes of wine.

"He really does always cook this much, doesn't he?" asked Caro-lyn, eyes wide.

"My kitchen will be a sad and miserable place once he leaves," lamented Elazar.

"It shouldn't be. I taught you everything I know," Zo said, sitting down beside him.

"Except the willingness to actually do it," said Elazar.

Penelope smiled at their banter, full of love and gentleness. She couldn't imagine ever being so relaxed with her own parents. Dinners with Stuart Bryne were quiet affairs with minimal eye contact, while her mother did her best to fill the silence with single-sided conver-sations about her latest paper or discovery. It had become worse as Penelope got older with Stuart only talking to her in the form of crit-icism about everything, from her subject choices at school to what-ever fantasy novel she was reading. It nearly always led to arguments between them, her mother leaving the room as soon as they started at each other. By the time Penelope had moved away from home, she had to relearn how to eat with people, so she didn't internally cringe every time someone started talking to her with a fork in their hand.

Slowly, the magicians were getting Penelope used to loud, com-munal meals with food sharing, drinking, and laughter.

"Auntie, are you going to dance for us while they make all this noise?" Elazar asked Aelia.

"Are you going to tell us a story?" she countered.

"Only if you dance."

"I don't have a scarf or anything…" Aelia began, just as Phaidros dropped a gauzy, yellow scarf in her lap. He might have had it in his pocket the whole time, though Penelope strongly suspected magic had been involved.

"Something traditional. It seems like a night for it," said Ela-zar, and they all started slow-clapping until Aelia gave up with an exasperated sigh and stood, kicking off her shoes. Elazar changed the beat of the clap as Aelia twirled amidst loud whistles from Zo who ended up joining her, dancing steps to songs that the world was too young to remember. Carolyn, Tim, and Penelope sat back drinking and enjoying the show. The only time the music faulted was when Zo took the violin from Phaidros, shoving him gently forward so that Aelia could wrap the yellow scarf around his neck and drag him out to dance with her.

"Come along, Penelope, so they don't feel awkward and stop," Elazar insisted, taking Penelope's hand.

"I don't know how to dance—"

"You can waltz, everyone can waltz," Elazar said, before calling out loudly to Alexis in Hebrew. Instantly, Alexis and Zo changed the music to something gentle, and Elazar led her in slow circles. Penelope glanced up to see Tim bringing Carolyn out as well until they were one big, waltzing, laughing group.

Penelope could feel Alexis's eyes burning into her, so she got Elazar to dip her close enough for Alexis to kiss her upside down, all while still continuing to play.

"It's a delight to see you two together," Elazar said as he swept her away again.

"Not hard when he's so delightful to look at."

"It's more than that. Alexis can be hard to understand. You speak each other's language, and that makes it more than attraction. You couldn't be more suited for each other. Like another pair we know," Elazar said, looking over at Aelia and Phaidros. "It's certainly nicer than their arguments. I hope this time they finally get it together."

Phaidros still hadn't moved the scarf, letting Aelia keep him bound and close, their foreheads touching. Penelope quickly looked away, not wanting to intrude on their private moment.

TWENTY-ONE

"I THINK IT'S time for a story," Zo said, once the dancing had stopped and they had crowded around the table in a messy arrangement of chairs. Aelia stretched out a leg to poke Elazar with a pink toenail.

"Out with it, *maggid*! You and Alexis have been smug all evening, like you know something we don't."

"Penelope has had a healthy touch of that, too," said Carolyn on Penelope's left.

"Holding out on us, Bryne? Typical," Tim added from her right. Alexis smiled at Penelope from across the table, holding onto their secret a few moments longer.

"Hang on, did I just hear right? Are you a *maggid*?" Tim asked Elazar.

"I trained as one before I decided to get serious about my studies in Near Eastern mysticism and magic, and that took over everything else in my life," replied Elazar.

"He is an excellent storyteller, one of the finest *maggidim* I've ever seen," complimented Alexis. Penelope couldn't imagine how many he'd known over the centuries.

"I'm too tired and out of practice for a long story, so I will give you the abbreviated version. We will have things still to discuss afterward, so don't get too drunk, Phaidros," warned Elazar.

"I remember when you used to be fun," Phaidros complained. He was sitting on Aelia's right, close enough that their arms still touched.

"What story are you going to tell?" asked Tim, his eyes brightening as the academic in him became alert. Alexis picked up his cello again, and after a nod from Elazar, began to play a melody. It was ancient and haunting; it made Penelope's bones shake and the destiny knot tying her to Alexis hum. Unlike the other songs he'd been playing all night, there was now magic woven into the music.

Elazar cleared his throat and began.

THIS IS a story of a young man, Ornias, who was a member of the court of King Solomon. Ornias was the son of Solomon's personal scribe, and when he wasn't learning his father's art, he was a talented collector of stories. Every time ambassadors or travelers would come to Jerusalem, Ornias would go and sit with them to learn their tales and use his skills as a scribe to record them. He was a great favorite of Solomon's, who delighted in hearing Ornias tell him a new tale every week. That was why when Ornias started to lose weight and become sickly, Solomon was the first to notice.

"Am I not paying you enough to take care of him?" he asked his scribe. "Tell me, and I'll give you more."

"Of course you are paying me enough, sire. The more I feed him, the more he seems to waste away. I'll feed him in the evening and by morning any color he gained the day before is gone by the time he wakes."

"There must be something happening while he sleeps. Watch over him tonight, and tell me what you see tomorrow morning."

That night, the king could not sleep, worrying over his charges, and fearing a new sickness had unleashed itself on Jerusalem.

The next morning, the king was awakened by his steward, telling him that the scribe was begging to see him and that he was pale with terror. Solomon granted an audience to the scribe who was shaking in fear.

"Tell me, did you do as I asked?" Solomon asked.

"Yes, sire, but I fear you will not believe me when I tell you what I saw."

"Tell me, and I will do everything in my power to make your son well again."

The scribe began to describe how he'd made sure Ornias had eaten and gone to sleep early the previous evening, telling him to leave a lamp burning in the room. The old scribe had sat all night at the keyhole of Ornias's door, watching his son sleep. At midnight, a great shadow had filled the room. It had spoken words over Ornias before crouching down, taking his thumb into his mouth, and suckling. When the creature had grown to twice his size, he disappeared with the dawn.

"A demon," whispered Solomon, knowing that his dear, young friend was indeed possessed. "I will study and find a way to stop this creature from coming to your son. I will make sure it never harms one of my people again."

Solomon spent all day searching for the answer, and then the next, all the while fearing that if he didn't find an answer soon that Ornias would surely die.

On the third night, bleary with lack of sleep and a defeated heart, Solomon went to the Temple to pray for guidance and for a way to banish the demon from his city. He was about to give up all hope when an angel appeared to him. Solomon bowed, hiding his face. The angel was dressed as a mighty general and Solomon knew that it was the archangel Michael who addressed him.

"Son of David, the demon who harasses your kingdom is a prince of Hell, Ashmedai, and he will be cast down once more by your hand," the angel said and, taking Solomon's hand, he slid a signet ring made of bronze onto his finger. Solomon studied the carnelian stone engraved with symbols.

"How will I defeat a prince of Hell with only a ring?" he asked the angel.

"Carved onto this ring is the true name of Yahweh. Speak it in the presence of Ashmedai and the demon will be gone from this place forever."

Then the archangel left Solomon alone with the ring and the name he could not read. It was nearing midnight, so the king pushed aside his fear and hurried to the house of the scribe.

"Let me in, and I will release your son from his nightmare," he said, and the scribe, who feared the king more than the demon, did as he was told. Solomon went to Ornias's door and looked through the keyhole. At midnight, the room filled with the shadow of the demon, and while he was distracted by his feeding, Solomon whispered a prayer and opened the door. The ring on his hand glowed, and the engravings on the ring moved until he understood.

As Ashmedai attacked, Solomon spoke the true name of Yahweh, and the demon was torn apart by light until nothing remained, for in the end, only true light can banish darkness.

THERE ARE many stories of Solomon's ring, of how he used it to command demons to build the great Temple, how it was lost and returned to him when he deserved it again. Some stories claim that the ring doesn't have the name of Yahweh inscribed on it at all, but a word with no sound, a star or other symbols, that only the bearer can read at a time when it is needed. We may even know the truth, before this new war with a demon prince is over," finished Elazar.

Alexis stopped playing, and Penelope shook herself before she began to applaud loudly. The others joined in, with Aelia wrapping her arms around Elazar's neck and kissing his cheeks.

"There's my little bird who I missed so much," she said affectionately. "But why is tonight a night for Solomon tales?"

"Penelope?" Alexis looked to her expectantly, giving her the floor.

"I think the prophecy in Tim's scroll is telling us to search for the ring of Solomon," Penelope said. They all stared at her.

"But, it's a fairy tale, a talisman story. Most of the Solomon stories are in *One Thousand and One Nights*. There's not a historical thing to back up any of them," Tim replied, a deep frown creasing his forehead.

"And we need historical proof for it to be real? It fits perfectly with the prophecy. Honestly, I don't know why I didn't think of it straight-away, it's so damn obvious," Elazar replied. He gestured to Alexis who pulled out his journal and passed the translated page to Elazar.

"Look at this wording: 'The ancient ones'—meaning us—'will use a gift from the hand of the Prince of Heaven.' The Essenes always referred to the archangel Michael with this title; 'the seal of the King, who was blessed with the wisdom of all things'—the seal is the sig-net ring and the king who was blessed with wisdom was Solomon," explained Elazar excitedly. "Of course it was Penelope who made the connection."

"It was a total fluke. The *Testament of Solomon* almost fell into my lap."

"A pseudepigraphical text that was in all likelihood written by the Greeks as a popular fiction in the first century AD and has little-to-no historical evidence of being even a copy of an original Jewish text. It's as reliable for historical accuracy as *One Thousand and One Nights*," argued Tim.

"I remember reading *One Thousand and One Nights* over and over as a kid, wondering what happened to his treasure and the ring with it," Penelope said, the memory making her smile despite Tim's grow-ing outrage.

"Most of Solomon's treasure would've ended up in a Babylonian vault if there had been any left at all," said Phaidros.

"So you're really going on a treasure hunt to find a ring that might not even exist?" asked Carolyn.

"They said that about Atlantis, too," Penelope replied, her eyes narrowing in challenge. "And yes, I *am* going on another treasure hunt. If it's the only way to stop Thevetat, I'll hunt the ring to the ends of the earth."

"But the prophecy could be total bullshit!" exclaimed Tim, looking at them with a dumbfounded expression.

"You think that even after you had the vision of the scribe?" Alexis asked.

"I was six beers in and manic—who knows what the fuck I saw? None of it is verifiable or will ever be taken seriously. As for the scroll, it's a discovery. *My* discovery. I'm not about to take a two-thousand-year-old prophecy seriously. Actually, Penelope, I'm kind of surprised you could be roped in to believing it."

"No one is roping me into anything. You *know* that the people after you in Tel Aviv were followers of Thevetat. Do you really think they would go to that much effort if they weren't afraid of what the scroll could tell them? The scribe gave up everything for it. When all of his family and friends were getting slaughtered, he chose to bury himself alive to hide the truth. Do you really think anyone would do such a thing if they thought the prophecy could be wrong?" argued Penelope.

"Penelope Bryne, you have been the biggest skeptic your entire life. Hell, you thought this guy was one of your crystal-city nutcases when you first met him." Tim pointed accusingly at Alexis. "And now two months with him, and you want to go hunting a relic that might not exist, to wield power from a god you don't even believe in! You used to give Carolyn a hard time about auras and now you're one step away from buying a spangly robe and trying to do magic yourself. By all means, let me know what house you get sorted into for Hogwarts."

"How I choose to spend my time, whether it be curating a library or hunting a relic, doesn't concern you anymore," Penelope said. "I don't need you to believe in the prophecy, I need you to approach it as a scholar. If the ring once existed, where do you think it ended up? Come on, you know more Near Eastern history than I do." Penelope hoped giving him something he *could* process would dampen his outrage. She could handle him being a prick to her, but she wouldn't put up with him offending Alexis.

She risked a glance across the table. Alexis looked placid as Tim tried to explain historical events like the Persian army sacking Jerusalem, but his eyes were hard as they stared at him. Sensing Penelope's gaze, Alexis looked at her. Whatever he saw in her face made the hardness in his own soften.

"Alexis?" Elazar prompted.

"Pardon? Oh yes, I took some notes. As Elazar explained, there are some accounts that say that the signet ring had a star on it, not a name of God. Arabic magicians also put great amounts of energy into finding a way to replicate the ring. Even the Jewish historian Josephus talked of a ring being used during an exorcism in the court of Vespasian," he said, flicking through his journal. His hand stilled on a page, and his eyes widened in surprise. Penelope's heart began to race wildly. She recognized the half page of notes she had written. *Oh shit, wrong timing.* As Alexis read, the silence grew tense, the air pressure tightening around them.

"Alexis?" Phaidros asked nervously. He looked to Zo who shifted in his seat.

Alexis stared up at Penelope, locking her to her chair like a deer cornered by a lion. Pale-blue static began to crackle under his skin, the scent of cinnamon and firecrackers filling the air.

"What the fuck…" gasped Tim, shoving his chair backward.

The air electrified as light raced into Alexis's eyes.

Phaidros was on his feet, reaching out for Alexis. In a blink, Alexis was on the other side of the terrace. The rain that had been threatening all evening came down in a sudden downpour as if Alexis's magic had summoned it. He hadn't broken his stare with Penelope, the *moíra desmós* pulling tight in her chest making it hard to breathe.

"Alexis! Get out now before you hurt someone!" Phaidros shouted.

Alexis seemed to finally hear him. He blinked once slowly, before exploding into black-and-silver sand.

"It's okay, it's okay," said Zo, patting Elazar's shoulder reassuringly.

"No, it's not! What the fuck happened?" Tim let out a terrified groan as he clutched at his head. "I knew it. I knew you were the ones after me. Carolyn, I *told* you the ones in the streets that were tracking me, they just disappeared. They did that exact thing. They just vanished! Penelope, what have you done? They have tricked you!"

But Penelope couldn't hear him over the sound of her racing heart. She got to her feet and went to the place Alexis had stood, staring out at the rain lashing the mountains around them. *Where did you go?*

"What set him off?" asked Phaidros, picking up the journal. Elazar looked at Penelope.

"What did you write to him, Penelope?" he asked. Penelope didn't answer; she didn't have to. It was written all over her. Zo gave her a knowing look before swearing.

"I told you to be careful with the magical tide coming in. Alexis is not going to be able to control himself," Zo said.

"Look after Tim, he doesn't understand," she said, barely taking in the scene of her friend trembling. Tim was muttering to himself as Carolyn tried to calm him.

"Leave Alexis alone, Penelope. He needs to pull himself together," Aelia warned as Penelope ran to the door. She ignored their shouts as she raced through the house and downstairs to the door to the gardens. The rain pelted heavily as she tried to follow the path that joined the house to the bungalow. *Please don't disappear to the Armenian mountains again.*

"Alexis?" she called over the noise. She reached for the connection inside her, and it pulled hard. Pushing aside wet branches, she followed the magic, letting it lead her. Penelope slid in the mud, coming to a hard stop.

Alexis was crouched on the ground. Magic and light swirled around him, hot enough to make the rain steam. Penelope shuddered at the power he was feeding into the earth, thick and heady.

"Alexis? Are you okay?" Her voice was barely a whisper over the downpour. Somehow, he heard it and rose to his feet. Light still crackled on his skin as he loomed in the shadows.

"Alexis? I'm sorry, I didn't think…it was—"

"It's not your fault. I should have had better control, and it surprised me," he said, his voice distant. Penelope had heard him sound like that the night they faced Kreios when he was lost deep in his magic. "Did you mean it? What you wrote?" His blue eyes focused on her. At the time, Penelope had thought to cheekily get back at him for teasing her, as well as to find a way to voice the growing pressure of words inside her.

"Yes. The Living Language translated what I wanted to say and couldn't," she said, unable to lie or joke, not when he was so vibrant with power. The relentless, burning want that had been pressing her for weeks rushed to the surface, the touch of his power inside her pulsed hard before exploding through her veins. Before he could stop her, Penelope ran at him, throwing herself around him, her legs tightening around his waist as he caught her.

"I don't care how much magic you get. Don't ever disappear like that on me ever again," she said, before kissing his lips, her hands gripping his wet hair.

Alexis's arms tightened around her, pulling her body against his as his hands went under her shirt to touch her too-sensitive skin.

"I've always been incapable of going very far from you, my Penelope," he said, magic leaping from his skin to hers in a rush of light. Her head roared as Alexis carried her to the bungalow, the door blowing open with a crack ahead of them.

Once inside, Penelope clawed at his wet shirt, tearing buttons and cloth from his body as he pressed her up against a wall. Magic held her as her own clothes came off in hurried and desperate movements before she locked her legs around his waist once more. Glowing eyes locked her in an intense gaze.

"Your magic is burning you up," she said, running her hands down the hot skin of his chest. Alexis lowered his head to kiss under her ear.

"Then burn with me, Penelope," he whispered as he entered her.

Penelope bit into his shoulder to keep herself from crying out as he gripped one arm above her head, holding her, filling her, taking her until she didn't know where she began and Alexis ended. The twin magics inside her reached out for him, sliding through the destiny knot.

Alexis groaned as her magic plunged into his, drawing on the deep well inside him. Penelope could feel the pressure, the iron will that had been struggling to control the magic that had been increasing inside him for weeks. She knew what Nereus's magic had given her the ability to do.

"Let me take it," she gasped. "I know I can take it."

Alexis said something in Atlantean between his teeth as she drew on him, taking a small amount of magic from his well. Power raced through her, her desire unbearable as she took from him in every way that she could.

Alexis tore her away from the wall, to the bed where he fell to his back. Penelope cried out as she settled on top of him. She was dimly aware of the magic she had taken flaring up her hips and around her stomach, wrapping around her heart as she rode him. She reached for him, her disheveled hair falling around them in a curtain. Words and emotions flicked through her mind, but only one fell from her lips.

"More," she demanded and pulled on his magic again.

PENELOPE CAME back to herself hours later, entwined with Alexis. Outside, the storm had gone from torrential to a sulky drizzle.

Her cheeks were wet with tears, her skin damp and body satiated. She rested against Alexis's bicep as they stared at each other, both momentarily incapable of thought and speech.

The light flickered and pulsed, and her skin broke out in lines of text in a thousand different languages all saying the same thing: *I love you, I love you, I love you.*

She couldn't hide it and didn't try to as Alexis gently traced the words. As if he were a magnet, the words twisted up his fingers, moving and curling around his already tattooed skin to rest over his ribs, just above his heart. His hand moved to the small of her back so he could draw her to him, kissing the words on her shoulder.

"I love you, too," Alexis said, bringing her lips to his once more.

PART THREE

MANIAE

Greek, noun:
"Spirits of madness and insanity."

TWENTY-TWO

PENELOPE KNEW SHE was dreaming when she found herself dressed in a Grecian gown of red silk and standing in a palace of marble.

The night was warm, humid, and expectant, the long sheets of colored silks that hung from the ceilings and twisted around columns rustling in a light breeze. Penelope followed no direct route as she wandered, moving toward the sound of crashing waves. Eventually, she came to a high walkway that looked out on a dense tropical garden leading to the sea. A city of lights curved around the bay, shadowed by a ring of high mountains to protect its back.

"I knew you'd look stunning in red," a voice said from behind her.

Bitter fear coated her mouth and made her muscles coil tightly with rage. Penelope turned to the voice, hands fisted at her sides. She knew him, knew his height, his sharp profile, and straight, black hair. She had dreamt of his dark eyes and cruel smile, the way he had looked when he'd taunted her in the catacombs and attacked Alexis at the Lido.

"Kreios. It seems that the trauma of our meeting hasn't left me, after all," said Penelope. She had to stand up to him in dreams, where she felt she had some power, as opposed to their encounters in real life.

"I hate to disappoint you, Doctor Bryne. This isn't your dream. It is mine." Kreios stepped into the light of the torches. His skin shone bronze, and if she didn't know what an incredible bastard he was,

Penelope would've been able to acknowledge that he was as handsome and alluring as a snake.

"What do you want?" she demanded.

"An audience. The Defender has done something to stop you from leaving your body, so I had to come to you. Not an easy thing to do when you are surrounded by acolytes and a demon prince."

"So why do it at all?"

"Because this memory is the only place Thevetat can't penetrate." Kreios sat down on the balcony railing and looked out over the sea. "This was home before Abaddon came and destroyed my life and country."

"You worship Thevetat, too. Don't expect me to feel any empathy for your dumb life choices," said Penelope. *What the hell is this all about?*

"You are an educated woman, Penelope. Do you really think I would have allied myself with the likes of Abaddon if I had a choice?" Kreios asked. There was something different about him in this place. There was no sign of the snide cruelty she had seen in him in Venice.

"You brought me here so you could make me *pity* you?" she said in disgust.

"I brought you here so that I can tell you all is not as it seems. I don't expect you to pity me, I expect you to use your mind and consider what I have to say."

"Why me?"

"Because the magicians have thousands of years of distrust and misinformation shaping their opinion and you do not. I need an outsider from this war, a stranger to our history. I've been waiting for someone like you for centuries, who could give me this opportunity."

"You tried to fucking kill me!" shouted Penelope. "That's not the behavior of someone who wishes to be heard."

"No, that's the behavior of someone who has been controlled by an old man and a demon for the past ten thousand years. The magicians, even the valiant Defender, have never considered even for a moment that I was Abaddon's first victim," said Kreios calmly. He pointed to a temple on the edge of the mountains. It was an elegant construct, its marbled, gold façade illuminated by huge braziers—a beacon of light in the darkness.

"That was how it was meant to look, my temple to Poseidon. I had the gall to argue with the High King of Atlas over trade routes and how did he retaliate? By sending Abaddon, the disgraced High Priest of Poseidon, to my city. An unlooked-for honor, my advisors had said, a sign that the temple was blessed by Poseidon. Who better to oversee the construction than the High Priest himself?" Kreios began to walk, and unable to stifle her curiosity, Penelope followed.

"I knew the High King and the struggles he'd had with Abaddon. I knew it was a way for him to get Abaddon out of the capital, and to pass the problem onto me. He probably told Abaddon he could regain his favor by spying on me, a surly king from the East who could never handle the intrigues of court life."

"How did Thevetat come to be involved?" Penelope couldn't resist asking. "The story I heard was that you and Abaddon woke him together."

Kreios's laugh was sad and bitter. "I'm sure that's what the Citadel of Magicians thought. They had no idea that Abaddon found the key to summoning Thevetat in their own archives. He'd been searching for years for something to give him more power than Poseidon. He knew that Poseidon had been nothing but a very powerful magician and the founding father of Atlantis. Deifying him meant nothing. He was revered because of his magic, and Abaddon wanted it."

"Why choose to be one of his priests if he didn't believe in him?"

"Power and opportunity. He was a scholar with a minor talent for magic, and that small taste made him crave more. It wasn't until he was an old man that he found what he was looking for. Nereus had been suspicious of him for years. She had tried to keep the peace with the priests of Poseidon and had given him access to the archives as a sign of good faith. He found the book on how to summon Thevetat in her own library, buried deep on the lower levels where they kept the texts from darker times."

"Why didn't he summon Thevetat earlier? If he hated Atlas and Nereus so much, why wait?"

"He couldn't work that kind of magic where the magicians would have sensed it. My country lacked magicians. My people were artisans and sailors and merchants. Any of them with an ounce of magic left for the Citadel as soon as it manifested. Abaddon's banishment had given him the ideal opportunity."

"If you knew he was trying to summon Thevetat, why didn't you send word to Nereus about it? Why did you let them think that you had a part in it?" asked Penelope.

"By the time I knew what was happening, it was too late for me. I couldn't sleep so I rode to the temple site to inspect the work being completed. I had a habit of checking it every day, and I had been delayed because I had spent that day in session with my advisors about a new trade route to Egypt. It is strange the things you remember about the day your world was destroyed."

"You found him in the temple?"

"Out in the open for anyone to walk in on. I demanded to know what he was doing. Abaddon couldn't hear me, he was too far gone in the ritual. When the demon rose, it wasn't Abaddon's offered body that he forced his way into, but mine. I was in the prime of my life, and after a millennia locked in his dark prison, Thevetat wanted someone handsome and strong to create havoc in. I had no choice. I had stepped into the sacred space and had become bound into the ritual. That was permission enough for the demon to take me. I've been tied to him ever since."

"But I've seen Thevetat possess Abaddon and other Vessels," argued Penelope. "He's not a part of you all the time."

"And that gives me free will? I'm watched. Always. Possessed often. You can't imagine what it is like to not be able to have a single thing that belongs to you. Not even my own thoughts are safe."

"You seemed a pretty willing participant to me."

"I didn't have another choice."

"Everyone always has a choice." Penelope didn't have time to move as Kreios turned and grabbed her by the arms.

"I was dragged through all the hells that could ever be imagined. You think Thevetat would allow me to put a bullet in my head? You think I haven't tried? I've been waiting for you—a link, someone who can help me get revenge on Thevetat, and that fucking bastard, Abaddon. He made me into this monster."

"You seem to have benefited from it well enough. Why look for revenge when they will give you the world?" Penelope asked, and when she looked into Kreios's black eyes, she was surprised to find tears there.

"Because the world means nothing if you're not free, Penelope. I've waited so long for this chance. I know what I've done over the years. I know what Thevetat did to Aelia while using my body, because he made me watch all of it. I can't convince you that I wanted nothing to do with it; I could never ask that of you. What I can ask is for your help to stop them before the tide rises. They've had nine centuries to plan for this opportunity again, for the magic to be this strong. If we don't do something, the world will burn."

"You think the magicians are going to just trust you after all this time? That I'm stupid enough to believe this isn't some kind of way to fuck with my head?" demanded Penelope, shoving him away from her. She hated that she was suddenly torn, and that she had sympathy for the Devil himself, even after he'd terrorized her. It was too late, the doubt had been planted.

"I have a way to convince you of my good intentions," he said with a slow smile. "Tell your inspector he needs to have a closer look at the Ramo dei Muti sometime."

"Another trap?"

"There is no benefit to be gained by hurting you again, Doctor Bryne."

"Okay, if you hate Abaddon so much, tell me why he and The-vetat need the high tide? Don't tell me it is for something as mediocre as taking over the world. I didn't buy that when you said it at the Lido, and I don't buy it now."

"Of course you didn't. You are far too clever for that. Apart from being able to store magic, so when the tide goes down they have a sur-plus, why do you think Abaddon attacked Nereus?"

"Revenge. They were old enemies."

"True, but Abaddon has known of their palazzo in Venice for cen-turies and could've attacked it any time. Why else?"

"He wanted the Archives. It was why Nereus sealed it."

Kreios smiled at her charmingly. "It's not hard to see why the Defender likes you so much. Do you know Nereus has books from Atlantis? They are what Abaddon wants. He needs to ensure there's no knowledge on how to stop them. He needs to know what else is in there so he can ensure Thevetat's plan won't fail."

"And what plan is that exactly? What can a demon possibly want when he already has an army of followers to do his bidding?"

"Thevetat wants what all demons want: a real body of his own."

"It seems like a lot of magic stored up for only one body," Penelope pointed out.

"How much magic do you think is needed to create life, Penelope? I'm not privy to all of Thevetat's plans but this I know for certain. He wants his own body, and if he gets it, who knows what power he'll be able to wield."

Penelope had a million more questions, but she didn't have a chance to ask. Kreios smiled again. "This has been nice, to talk freely this way. Do tell the Defender I said hello."

Kreios blew her a kiss, and in that instant, Penelope was dragged up, flying backward through the air as the palace and the city fell away below her.

PENELOPE WOKE with a jolt, thrashing as if she was still falling into the night sky.

"I've got you, Penelope. It's okay. Wake up, *cara*." Alexis's voice cut through her terror. She opened her eyes, and he was standing beside the bed, a robe around his shoulders and a steaming cup in his hand. "Are you all right?" he asked, passing her his coffee as she sat up.

"Kreios. Fucking Kreios in my fucking dreams," Penelope managed to say. She sipped, letting the caffeine wake and comfort her. Alexis sat down on the edge of the bed and gently pushed her hair out of her face.

"Do you want to talk about it? Nightmares are common—"

"It wasn't a nightmare." Feeling like she was about to ruin his morning, Penelope told Alexis everything Kreios had said, giving him details that there was no way she could have known if it had been a dream of her own. Instead of dismissing it outright, Alexis listened and considered before lying down beside her.

"What are you going to do?" asked Alexis.

"What do you mean?"

"I don't like that he violated your dreams, but if what he says is true, he took a great risk to do the magic it would have taken to get to you," he said thoughtfully.

"Why are you so calm? I thought you would be furious."

"I am, though not for the reasons you imagine. I hate the bastard. I've always wanted to murder Kreios, since the war first began. Now you tell me that someone I've considered one of my greatest enemies could be a victim. If true, then we were all deceived," admitted Alexis. "I don't know how we are going to explain this to Phaidros and Aelia."

"I think we need to tell Marco to check out Ramo dei Muti. See if what Kreios told us was true."

"The street is in Cannaregio, right where Reitia said she felt the darkness growing."

"We don't have to like or trust Kreios. I would happily stab him again, given half a chance. Despite that, if he can give us an edge over Thevetat, we would be stupid not to take it because of hubris," said Penelope, lying back to stare at the ceiling. "I hate that Kreios ruined my excellent buzz. I guess after last night we know what that piece of magic Nereus gave me does."

"Poseidon and Nereus's magic, you mean. You balanced me last night when the magic was dragging me down. I don't know how you did it."

"Neither do I. Zo told me that the high tide messes with you, so if I can help you through it to ensure you don't run away to Armenia again, I'm going to do it."

"I can't believe he told you about that! I swear, I'm going to have to sew his lips together if he doesn't shut up." Alexis turned to face her. "Is that why you came after me last night? I felt your panic in the gardens. Did you really think I would vanish on you like that?"

"You would if you thought you were going to hurt us by accident."

"I'm not some fledgling magician that I lose all reason. If Zo told you all of that story, you should've remembered I didn't disappear alone, and if I *were* going to disappear for a hundred years, I'd take you with me."

"Now there's a tempting thought. Maybe we should do it, leave Carolyn and Tim to work out their shit, and the other magicians to take care of Thevetat." Penelope took Alexis's hand. "I'm ready, magician, let's go."

"You don't want to put any clothes on?"

"I thought the whole point of disappearing for a hundred years is so that I don't have to."

Laughing, Alexis gave her a whiskery kiss. "You're my kind of woman, Penelope Bryne."

"I suppose we can't leave them. They'd be lost without us." She sighed. "Dreams of Kreios, dire warnings, and dangerous leads to follow? This really isn't how I wanted to wake up this morning."

"It certainly isn't how I wanted to wake you up either," Alexis replied, the promise of sin in his voice.

Penelope rolled onto her side to face him. "Oh? How were you going to do it?"

"Differently."

"Do we have time for me to pretend to be asleep again, and then try it your way?" Penelope asked. A filthy chuckle emanated from Alexis, and her grin widened.

"We'll make time."

TWENTY-THREE

ZO AND ELAZAR were up and playing chess when Alexis and Penelope walked back to the house. After hearing about Kreios's offer of help, they had woken Phaidros and Aelia, both hungover and disgruntled at being moved before noon.

"We need to get out of Israel," said Zo as he put another egg on Penelope's plate. "If he can track Penelope to get into her head, he can find out where she's staying. I won't give them a chance to find Elazar."

"Don't overreact, Abba," said Elazar. "Even if they found the right mountain, they would never find the road. You and Alexis made sure of that years ago. You were held captive by Kreios, Penelope. It is more likely he's taken something from you like a lock of your hair that he can now use to link with you."

"That's even worse," Phaidros muttered.

"I don't care what he's been through, I'll never see that bastard as a victim, and I will put my sword through his throat if I ever get close enough to do it," hissed Aelia viciously. Penelope didn't blame her; she'd seen the scars, lived that night in Alexis's memory when Thevetat had carved her to pieces.

"He doesn't want forgiveness, he wants to get rid of Thevetat forever," said Alexis, as gently as he dared.

Zo turned to Elazar. "You should come with us back to Venice. Don't stay here alone. We could use your help."

"You don't need my help, Abba, you are just trying to keep me under your watchful eye," said Elazar. "Penelope is the Archivist. Nereus will have more information on the seal ring of Solomon; she may even have more recent accounts of its whereabouts." He turned to Penelope. "Know that you can call me any time. I will always help you when I can."

"If I do need you, will you come to Venice?" she asked. She didn't dare look at Zo. She didn't want Elazar to think it was only for his father's sake that she asked.

"If you really need me, I'll come. I'll have to believe it though. You have to stand your ground with these magicians, or they'll herd you about and call it protection."

Zo snorted. "Thanks, son."

"Have you talked to Marco yet?" asked Aelia as she paced the terrace. "He knows to call Lyca, right?"

"Dandolo is big enough to look after himself," said Phaidros, doing a poor job of hiding his annoyance.

"He is only human," Aelia replied, ignoring his tone.

"No, I haven't talked to him yet, but he knows not to move without Lyca. He promised," Penelope reassured her. "I don't want him getting hurt either."

"It's worth looking into Kreios's tip," said Phaidros. "It might be where Tony Duilio was doing his magic."

"Or it could be a building rigged to blow as soon as someone walks into it," Aelia snapped.

"Doubtful. Kreios acted like it was a gift," said Penelope, chewing her lip.

"Kreios isn't one to give gifts that do not end in fire and blood." Aelia made an exasperated sound before heading back inside.

"She just needs to process. Don't take it personally, Pen," said Phaidros.

"I knew it would be hard for her," Penelope said, "but I'm only the messenger."

Alexis took her hand under the table and gave it a reassuring squeeze. "You are forgetting something—or someone, I should say," said Elazar. "Two, in fact."

Penelope hadn't seen either Tim or Carolyn and hadn't wanted to wake them. "Carolyn said she was ready to go back to Australia. She doesn't want to help us, and I don't want her to be used against us by Abaddon."

"Tim was very distraught last night. He thought Alexis was going to kill you," said Zo.

"I'd never hurt Penelope," Alexis growled.

"He didn't know that. He only saw a scary magician lose his cool and then disappear. He saw Thevetat do something similar in a Vessel. We calmed him down, told him that he couldn't trust his memories from that time. He's still not convinced we aren't the enemy."

"He's not 100 percent sane either," Phaidros said under his breath.

"And Carolyn?" Penelope was almost too nervous to ask.

"She tried to remain steady to reassure him, but she was scared, too."

Alexis rested his hand at the back of her neck. "I'm sorry, *cara*. This is all my fault."

"No, it is what happens when you involve mortals in our life. I shouldn't have let it go this far. Lyca was right," Penelope said, pushing her chair back. "I'll deal with it, and I'll send them home."

"I'll try and find Aelia and talk her around," Alexis said with a sigh.

ALEXIS HEARD Aelia before he saw her. She was in the olive tree grove, hacking at an ancient tree with her *gladius*.

"Go away, Defender. I don't have the patience to listen to you try and be the voice of reason right now," she said, not turning to face him.

"If you want to fight something, fight me and make your training count for something. Stop taking it out on that poor tree. All you are going to do is ruin the edge of that blade and make Lyca furious when she needs to fix it," Alexis replied. Aelia wheeled around the sword in front of her, her face smeared with sweat and tears.

"Don't tell me what to do or how to feel right now. Kreios is our *enemy*, and you are talking about trusting what he says because he used dream magic on your girlfriend."

Alexis drew his *yataghan*. "I would never trust Kreios. You insult me just by suggesting it. If he's genuine, we use him as the pawn he is." Aelia's *gladius* came down toward him, and he moved to block it.

"He will feed us lies, lead us into a trap, and then laugh as we die screaming under his knife," she hissed, her violet eyes filled with fear.

"I won't let him get the chance to harm a hair on your head, I swear it. We will take what he has offered and see if it's genuine. We don't trust him—ever. And at the end of everything, if we are still standing and the demon is defeated, it will be your choice what to do with him," Alexis promised, moving his stance as they continued to spar.

"I vote we cut his head off," Phaidros said as he joined them.

"Too quick," Aelia replied, dropping quickly to her knee and swiping out for Alexis's legs.

"Penelope suffered at Kreios's hands too, the bastard is violating dreams, and she is willing to believe him only so far as it benefits us," said Alexis, jumping out of reach, so she didn't cripple him.

"Penelope doesn't know Kreios like we do. She can't even see her friends are bad for her because she cares about them so much. She's too innocent to play Kreios's games, and her friends are too soft to fight with us in a war. The sooner we cut them loose, the better it will be for everyone," Phaidros argued.

"We need Penelope. She will have to deal with them on her own, otherwise she'll never see for herself that they are not the same people anymore. So much for Carolyn being the one that was into magic. Penelope was so sure of her," said Aelia, resting her attack as they talked.

Phaidros snorted. "She couldn't have been more wrong. Carolyn is spiritual, and she doesn't actually believe in a damn thing. Tim's dedicated his life to research a dead people whose whole existence was founded on a God that he doesn't believe in. His energy says one thing and his mouth another. I want to trust him and I can't. Then there's Penelope, who's done her best not to believe with her head and yet believes in *everything* with her heart. They aren't bad people or company. I just can't figure out how they all became friends to begin with when they are so different."

"Loneliness," answered Alexis simply. "They are Penelope's friends, we shouldn't be talking about them in such a way. It would hurt her."

"Only because she's refusing to see the truth," said Aelia.

"It's her truth to—" Alexis froze as fear and panic flooded him.

"Alexis? What is it?" Phaidros asked as he steadied him.

"Penelope. Something's wrong." Alexis turned to where the *moíra desmós* was directing him and started running.

PENELOPE TOOK three deep breaths before walking downstairs to the basement apartment and knocking softly on the door.

"Hey, are you guys awake yet?" she whispered as she opened the door. She was still fumbling for the light switch when a gun muzzle pressed to her temple.

"Don't…don't make a sound, Hawkes. I mean it," said Tim.

Penelope lifted her hands, blood rushing to her head. "It's okay, Tim. I'm alone," she said as she turned toward him. He had one of Phaidros's handguns pointed at her. His hands were shaking, his eyes wild with fear.

"We can't stay here a second longer. These people have you completely fooled. I won't let them hurt us. I won't let them take us to Thevetat."

"They aren't hurting anyone, Tim. Trust me—"

"Trust *you*? You ran out after that psycho last night! He's got you under his spell. I'm going to help you break it. I'm going to get you away and then you'll be okay. You'll see I was right about them." He shifted the gun to his other hand, and Penelope saw the smear of blood on his shirt.

"Tim. Where's Carolyn? Is she…is she hurt, Tim?" Penelope tried to keep her voice steady even as fear licked along her bones.

"She argued with me. I was calling for help, and she got angry that I was using her phone. I have friends in Tel Aviv that can look after us, get us away from these people."

"Where is Carolyn?" Penelope repeated. Tim pushed his matted hair from his face.

"She was going to scream, so I…I hit her. I didn't mean to but she wouldn't stop crying, and I had to get her into the car. She's sleeping, she's okay," he babbled.

"Can you show me?" Penelope said, hands still raised. She had to make sure Carolyn was still breathing.

"Walk in front of me. Hands where I can see them," Tim demanded, waving the gun toward a door on the other side of the room.

"You don't need that gun, Carter. It's me, Penelope. You don't need to threaten me. I'm your friend, remember?"

"No, you aren't! I've been watching you the last few days. You aren't my Hawkes anymore. You would never have fallen in love with someone like that. These people aren't right. They have brainwashed you. I saw ones just like them in Tel Aviv. They aren't an ancient priesthood. They are demon worshippers like all the rest. I won't let you drink any more of their Kool-Aid."

Penelope opened the door to an underground garage. The black SUV they had arrived in was already running. Carolyn was slumped in the passenger seat, wounded head resting against the window above a streak of red. Books covered the back seat, and Penelope recognized them from Elazar's study.

"What have you done, Tim?" whispered Penelope.

"Carolyn's okay! I'm saving her! I don't care if you think I'm crazy. It's the spell they've put on you."

"Why do you have Elazar's books?"

"Because he's never going to tell people about what he knows about the Essene magic. He knows there is a *genizah* out there filled with their true treasures and I'm going to find it, because he won't. Knowledge is meant to be shared, not hoarded for the use of one man."

"Tim, if you do this, there's no going back—"

"Open the door, Penelope," he said, shoving her toward the back of the car. She opened the cargo area in the back, eyes searching desperately for something she could use as a weapon.

"Give me your hands," he demanded. Penelope did as she was told, and he slipped cable ties around her wrists and tightened them. "Get in."

"You don't have to do this, Tim. You are just confused by what you've been through. If you let me explain…" The gun muzzle pressed into the base of her neck.

"Get. In." Tim shoved her again, and she stepped up into the cargo hold. He slammed the door behind her and climbed into the driver's seat. "I know you hate me right now, Penelope. One day you'll see that I was right."

Tim put the car into gear and sped up and out of the underground parking to where the electric doors were already open.

Don't panic, just think. Penelope pulled at the inside handle of the door as she was jostled side to side, but it wouldn't unlock. The gates leading out of the yard sensed the vehicle and opened automatically.

Penelope braced herself against the back seat and kicked out at the door as hard as she could. Tim swore, the car swerving. Something heavy bashed into Penelope's hip, and she wriggled to see what it was. *The tire iron.*

Penelope gripped it between her hands and maneuvered it out from under the seat, pushing away the panic that threatened to overwhelm her.

Penelope didn't hesitate as she gripped the tire iron and smashed out the glass on the back window. Tim was shouting, but she couldn't hear him over the blood in her ears and the sound of the car's engine.

She reached out through the hole in the glass, shredding the skin on her forearms as she pulled at the handle. The door swung open from the speed of the car. Tim was driving as fast as he could on the dirt road, but if they made it to the main road, her fall would be harder on bitumen.

Penelope leaped out of the door, trying to tuck herself into a ball. She hit the dirt and gravel hard on her right shoulder and rolled into the grass and mud. Her head was ringing, but she still heard the sound of warping metal screech through the air.

Further down the dirt road, the SUV was no longer moving. The tires squealed, the engine roaring even as the SUV was lifted into the air. Alexis was standing in front of the car, hands lifted, his whole body crackling with power.

"Where is Penelope?" he demanded, his voice magnified and terrible. The engine went dead. Penelope groaned as she scrambled to unsteady feet. Her left ankle barked in pain as she tried to get to Alexis before he hurt Tim.

Metal screamed as Alexis slammed the SUV back to the road, his power ripping it in half like a sardine can. Tim took a shot at him, but Alexis merely waved the bullets aside.

"*Where is she?*" Alexis repeated, his *yataghan* appearing in his hand as he advanced on Tim.

Penelope's leg gave out, and she fell to the road. "*ALEXIS!*" she shouted. Magic rippled in waves around him as he turned and saw her. She blinked, and he was beside her.

"Don't—don't kill him, please don't kill him," she wheezed between tears. Alexis shouted a command in Atlantean and Phaidros appeared behind Tim, knocking him to the ground. Zo untangled an unconscious Carolyn from the wreckage of the car and held her tenderly in his arms.

"He hurt her…"

"She's still breathing, Pen. She'll be okay," Zo told her.

"There was so much blood, I didn't know," Penelope sobbed.

"Where are you hurt?" Alexis asked, his body still glowing with anger and magic.

"My shoulder and ankle are the worst. I'm okay. I just hit the road hard," Penelope explained as he lifted her up into his arms.

"What happened to your arm?"

"Glass. Smashed out a window so I could get the handle. It would take more than a crazed best friend and the door of a moving car to keep me away from you," she tried to joke even as she wept against his chest.

"My brave Penelope, I can't leave you alone for five minutes. Rest my love, I've got you," Alexis reassured her as he carried her back to the house, leaving the smoking wreckage of the car behind them.

TWENTY-FOUR

PENELOPE WINCED AS Alexis rolled her onto her good side and ran his fingers over her ribs.

"I thought so. Two of these are broken," he said gently.

Two broken ribs to go with her sprained ankle, grazed arms, and a mild concussion. She was ready to beat the shit out of Tim herself.

Warm tingling heat spread from Alexis's fingers as magic knit her wounds back together. She breathed deeply without any pain, and she swallowed the rush of tears in her throat.

"Where's Carolyn?" she asked.

"On a couch in the house under Zo's watchful gaze. He's assured me that her head wound was minor and he's made sure that she won't be sick when she wakes," he said, resting his palm on her ribs, as though feeling for her heartbeat.

"And Tim?" Penelope almost didn't want to know. She'd only ever seen Alexis angry like that on the night Venice had almost sunk into the lagoon.

"He's knocked out downstairs. Phaidros is keeping an eye on him to make sure he stays that way. Elazar has insisted on going over him again for traces of the curse."

"I'm sure Caro will know what set him off this morning. I don't know what to do—"

"You don't have to do anything yet, except let me heal you and maybe have a shower to get all this mud off you," Alexis said, looking down at her smeared jeans.

"Lucky it was something as soft as mud. I can't believe I jumped out of a moving car."

"I can." Alexis kissed her forehead before going back to work.

Now that she was safe, the shock of what had happened was setting in. Her best friend had tried to kidnap her, he'd assaulted the woman he'd loved for most of his adult life, tried to steal another academic's research, and now she had no idea what she was going to do with him.

If they let him go, Tim wouldn't have any qualms with telling the world about them thinking he was doing the right thing. He wouldn't be allowed to take the scroll with him, not with the secrets it contained.

"This is such a fucking mess. How did you even know I was gone?" Penelope whispered, tears coming despite how hard she was trying to present a strong front.

"I felt your fear and arrived at the garage too late, so I caught you on the road. As usual, you didn't need my help," Alexis said, with a smile. He finished healing her ankle and Penelope sighed with relief as she rotated it.

"Tim thought he was doing the right thing and that you've got me under some kind of spell," she said, sitting up slowly.

"He pulled a gun on you, frightened you, tried to take you like... like you were some trinket that belonged to him. I will leave it up to you to judge what to do with him. He's your friend and believe me, you don't want me making the decision." Alexis helped her to her feet, and she pulled him into a tight hug.

"Thank you for coming after me," she said.

"I'll always come after you, Penelope. That I can promise you."

IT WASN'T until later, in the middle of a warm shower, that Penelope's shock caught up to her. She gripped the cold tiles, fighting off nausea. She tried to focus on her breathing, to keep the shaking at bay, but all she saw was Carolyn in the front seat, blood staining the window.

"She's okay," she reminded herself over and over until her heart stopped racing. She needed to be there when Carolyn woke up, and the thought helped her focus enough to wash the mud and blood away from her skin.

Back at the house, Penelope found Carolyn still unconscious on a couch. Zo handed Penelope a glass of whiskey and vacated the chair so she could sit beside Carolyn.

"It was nothing. Only a nasty bump," Zo said, answering the question Penelope was about to ask. There was a dark bruise coming up on Carolyn's forehead, but otherwise no sign of the cut. "I wasn't sure if it would upset her more if I fully healed her, so I left the bruise."

"Thanks, Zo. I appreciate you coming to the rescue."

"I have to take advantage of every opportunity to be valiant," he said and kissed her head. "I'm glad you are in one piece. Alexis told me you jumped out of the car which is very impressive."

"I try," she replied halfheartedly. Penelope sipped her whiskey and held Carolyn's hand. She was just beginning to doze off when she felt Carolyn shift.

"Fuck, my head," Carolyn said, groaning.

"Hey, try not to get up too quickly. You've got a nasty bump," said Penelope as she helped her sit upright. She gave Carolyn a glass of water and watched her carefully to make sure she drank it all. "Do you remember what happened?"

Carolyn touched the spreading bruise on her forehead, her skin going even paler as she took a shuddering breath.

"Tim attacked me," she said, her eyes welling with tears.

"Yeah, me too. He tried to take us back to Tel Aviv," Penelope explained.

"That bastard! He stole my phone. I heard him talking to someone, telling them that he had the scroll and that we were being held by a cult."

"Do you know who he was talking to?"

"No idea, but he sounded like he knew them really well. I think it was someone from the dig site. He told them that he needed to tell Professor Schaal he was okay. He was really freaking out. When I tried to talk sense into him, he pulled the gun on me, and when I refused to get in the car, he hit me with it."

Penelope handed her the glass of whiskey and told her what had happened next, glossing over Alexis's anger and the fact that he tore a car in half to stop them.

"Tim must have seriously lost his mind if he thought he could pull this shit off," Carolyn muttered, swallowing more whiskey.

"Elazar checked him. There are no side effects from the curse. Tim has been through a trauma, and it has left his head all messed up. He thought he was saving us." Penelope didn't know how to approach the subject of what to do with Tim. Carolyn's face grew still and cold.

"You told me that Alexis once wiped your memory, right?"

"Yeah, he did," Penelope said uneasily.

"Get him to do it to Tim."

"What? Caro, you don't know—"

"Pen, when have you known Tim to ever let anything go? The only reason we don't have the IDF on our doorstep right now is because he has no idea where we are. I seriously doubt Alexis is going to let Tim waltz out of here to blab to the world about Essene magic and the seal ring of Solomon."

"You can't just wipe his memory, Caro. There needs to be something there to account for the time he missed, something to fill the gap."

"Then we get Alexis to plant some memories while he's at it. We create a new story for Tim to believe. It's the only way he'll be able to be let go. You think your god-magician boyfriend is going to let Tim go after what he's done? With the damage he could still do? I'm not an idiot. The only reason Tim is drawing breath right now is because Alexis knows you care about him."

Alexis himself had hinted as much. Hearing Carolyn say it made it so much worse, even if it was the truth. If it had been anyone else, Alexis wouldn't have hesitated for a second.

"Even if Alexis wipes Tim's memory, you'll still have to remember it all. Can you live with that? I mean, *really* live with it. It'll be a huge burden to bear alone."

Carolyn's mouth formed a thin, tight line. "Yes. I can help corroborate whatever story Alexis spins him. Tim hurt you, Pen. He *hit* me with a fucking gun. He did that to *us*. The people who love him the most. A fresh slate will help him go back to who he was before he found that fucking scroll. It's better than he deserves."

ALEXIS SAT in the corner of the sunroom, his cello resting between his knees and his hand gripping too tightly around the neck. He needed to play, needed to let the feelings inside him out; rage, worry, love, fear, violence. They swirled around him in a vicious maelstrom, even as he determined to be calm for Penelope. She needed him to be calm even if he could've torn Tim Sanders apart with his bare hands. Phaidros was still downstairs, and Alexis had let Penelope believe it was so Tim didn't hurt himself or others, not because there needed to be someone powerful enough to stop Alexis from cutting his head off.

"*Don't kill him*," had been the first thing Penelope said to him as she lay broken and bloody in his arms. Maybe she had known he wanted to.

"Are you going to stare at the cello all day or are you going to play me something?" demanded Elazar, sitting down in a chair opposite him. Alexis said nothing.

"Come now, Uncle. Penelope is fine. Looking at the pair of you, I think you are worse off than she is right now."

"He hurt her, and he stole your work," said Alexis numbly.

"I know. I'm not an idiot. I do back up what I work on, and being kidnapped didn't stop Penelope either. Seems to me she was doing just fine before you stepped in. She's going to be more heartsore than anything else. Magic can't fix that. The man she loves may be able to ease it a little if he pulls himself together."

"I'm going to have to kill him. Penelope won't love me after that."

"It wasn't so long ago that you were moping over the decision to kill Penelope. You found another way then. You can do it now."

"I told her she has to decide what we do with Tim."

"That was wise. She has a kind heart and a steadier hand than you, magician. It seems love has knocked a healthy amount of sense out of your thick head."

Alexis managed a smile. "It has been…a while. I almost forgot what it felt like."

"You are lost deep in the Sefirot of *Chesed* now, my dear uncle. Perhaps what Abba says is true: only love has the power to surprise you anymore."

"Zo's right, even though I'll never admit it to him." Alexis picked up his bow, enjoying the sound of Elazar's laughter, the only thing about him that time hadn't altered.

"Play for me, Uncle. You'll be gone soon, and that cello will be neglected."

Elazar knew the playing would calm Alexis, and the small tyrant who had demanded songs for hours knew as a mature man what manipulative buttons to press to get what he wanted.

Unable to deny Elazar anything for long, Alexis began to play. He surrendered to it, let the music and movement lull him into a meditative state, to a place where he didn't feel like a bag of jangled nerves. He wove the rainstorm of the previous evening into it, the crash of magic and emotions, bodies, and love. He expressed the feeling when he had seen a thousand versions of the same message stretching along Penelope's skin, a result of the magic he had first placed into his Tablet. Just another piece of him that belonged to her.

When Alexis came back to himself, Aelia was sitting on the arm of Elazar's chair, and both looked weepy.

"If you played for me like that, even I might fall in love with you," Aelia said, and Alexis laughed. "I came to see how you are. I didn't expect...that."

"I told Alexis to play for me," said Elazar, with a dreamy smile.

"Does Penelope know you feel that way?" asked Aelia, rare tenderness in her expression.

"She knows," Alexis said with a hidden smile.

"No wonder you overreacted this morning! It was dramatic, even for you."

"This from the woman who wiped out the Ninth Legion on her own because they took her boyfriend as a slave after a battle," argued Alexis.

"That was different."

"Sure it was."

"We need to talk about Kreios," Aelia said, shifting the conversation without warning.

"I know, and we will. We need to deal with Tim first."

"Kreios is a little bit more important than the nutter in the basement. We can't believe anything Kreios says. We don't even know for sure that Penelope's head didn't conjure the whole thing as a result of stress."

"Kreios did promise to prove it to her."

"By giving her an address that could be another booby trap!"

"Aelia, I *know*. Let me handle the immediate situation with Tim, and we'll go back to Venice and figure out what to do about Kreios, yes?" Alexis said, his patience wearing thin.

"Well, handle it already, Defender."

"Is Penelope still with Carolyn?" he asked, trying to avoid the inevitable argument.

"Yes. That was the other reason I was coming to find you. They are hatching a plan, and I think you might need to step in before they get too carried away."

Penelope saw Alexis waiting outside the kitchen and gave him a small, relieved smile.

"Aladdin's here now. I'm sure he'll agree that it's a good plan," said Carolyn. A half-empty bottle of whiskey sat between them. Not a good sign.

Alexis let the Aladdin comment slide and joined them at the bench. "Dare I ask what you two are arguing over?"

"Tim. What else?" said Penelope.

"And what is your plan, Carolyn?" asked Alexis. He placed his hand on the tense hunch of Penelope's shoulders, and she relaxed fractionally.

"Wipe Tim's memories of finding the scroll and the madness, and replace them with new ones. You can do that, right?" said Carolyn with a hint of challenge.

"I can. It's not a bad idea. But you'll need something very convincing to replace memories with such a strong resonance," Alexis explained.

"Exactly what I said," mumbled Penelope.

"Change the whiskey to coffee and then we'll talk about it, Carolyn. I need you sober and focused. You will be the one who will have to act as an anchor for the memories and convince him they are true."

Alexis ended up making the coffee as Penelope and Carolyn designed the memories and the way to set the scene for when Tim regained consciousness. The women were detail oriented, and more than a touch diabolical in their thoroughness. Alexis knew exactly why Tim would've risked everything to save them, even if it was from the wrong people.

Two hours and two pots of coffee later, Alexis went downstairs. Phaidros was pacing, his fingers releasing combinations on his violin without using a bow, carefully not making any noise. Tim was lying on the carpet, hands comfortably bound and still asleep.

"Defender," Phaidros said coolly, his body suddenly alert and ready for a fight.

"I'm calm, and have no intention of hurting him, so stand down."

"A rather dramatic change of heart for a handful of hours," said Phaidros suspiciously.

"He's Penelope's friend. She's decided his fate; I'm only here to carry it out. He's going to be placed somewhere he can get help, where they can do proper scans and see what lasting damage the curse has done to his brain."

Phaidros placed his violin down and crossed his arms. "It's a nasty business. The whole thing sits uneasily with me. This is exactly why I hate prophets, even dead ones. They see so much, yet more often than not, they leave a trail of human wreckage behind them. The scribe didn't consider for a moment that an innocent could stumble across that blasted jar," he said, looking at Tim's broken form.

"The scribe wouldn't have had time to consider it. Every one of his actions was driven by fear." Alexis crouched next to Tim and took his head in his hands.

"You are very lucky to have the love of two good women. When you wake, you'd better treat them better," Alexis said before letting his magic seep into Tim's memory.

It was the kind of magic Alexis truly hated doing, no matter how important the cause. A man's mind was all he had. Tim's short-term memories were a horrific mess of twisted moments, bleak colors, and emotions. Alexis scanned them before at last arriving at the day that Tim was alone in the cave, the sunburn on his legs killing him. Then, moment by moment, Alexis recreated Tim's world.

When Alexis came back to himself, Penelope sat watching him from the other side of the room. She wore her emotions on her face, the grief so fresh that his chest ached.

"Is it done?" she asked, her voice small and pained.

"It is. Tim will sleep more peacefully now." Alexis moved to sit beside her.

"Tell me this was the right thing to do, Alexis," Penelope said, not looking at him.

"It was the best of only bad choices."

"This is a part of staying on as Archivist, isn't it? I'm going to have to make these kinds of decisions all the time."

"You can't blame yourself for his actions, Penelope, even if you are the one who has to clean them up. I know the pain you're feeling. Take comfort in the fact that he will be safer not remembering. He and Carolyn will go back to Melbourne and be out of harm's way."

"I hate that I'm relieved about that. I can't keep lying to them. I feel like I can't be myself around them anymore. Carolyn can barely look me in the eye," said Penelope, her voice choked with tears. Alexis wrapped an arm around her, holding her in silence because there was nothing he could say that would make her feel better.

"I texted Marco the address Kreios gave us. I told him to take Lyca and expect the worse. I couldn't sit on it anymore. We need to start thinking offensively and get ahead of them somehow. We can't let them use the tide to make Thevetat a body."

Penelope's mind had shifted gears, locking away the helpless feelings regarding her friends, and focusing on what she could change. Alexis knew it wouldn't work for long as a coping mechanism. She wasn't wrong though.

"I've never heard of such a ritual, although it makes sense that Thevetat would need the power of a high tide to complete it. They've waited a long time for this moment; they aren't going to go down easily."

"All the more reason we can't sit on our asses crying over our losses. We need to start looking for Solomon's ring."

Alexis loved her intensely at that moment; her determination and ferocity replacing her fear. It was that love which also forced him to ask the one thing he dreaded an answer to.

"Are you sure you don't want to go back to Australia with them? This isn't going to get better, Penelope. A war means making decisions worse than this. It means losses worse than a few rearranged memories. I love you. I would find you when it's over."

Penelope took his hand, her expression furious. "I know you feel you have to give me an out here. But let me be very clear: I chose to be here, I choose to stay here, so don't ever fucking ask me that again."

Alexis lifted her hand to his lips. "I love you."

"I love you, too. Now let's get Tim to a hospital. I want to go home."

TWENTY-FIVE

O N A QUIET corner in Cannaregio, Marco lit a cigarette and tried to calm his nerves. He had received a message from Penelope, a street address from yet another unnamed and no doubt dubious source. He had called Lyca and left her a voice mail asking her to meet him that evening.

It was only April, yet the night was unseasonably warm, with a hot breeze blowing from the south. His *nonna* used to call it "ill winds from the desert" and would shut herself in her room until they were over. She claimed the winds carried whispers and made people restless enough to do stupid things.

All it did was fill Marco with a tense expectation that he usually associated with the magicians.

Speaking of magicians, he was about to message Lyca again when she peeled away from the shadow of the building opposite him.

"*Dio!* You scared me half to death," he said.

Lyca lifted the black hood that covered her silver hair. "Not being seen is the point, Inspector. You don't seem to have much self-preservation, standing out in the open and smoking. A good tracker would be able to find you from the scent alone," she said.

Marco quickly dropped the cigarette and stepped it out. "Thank you for coming. I wasn't sure if you got my message."

"Alexis told me I must protect you for Penelope's sake. She told you to come here?"

"Yes, though she didn't tell me why."

Lyca's silver-gray eyes narrowed to slits. "Yes, there are a lot of things not being said at the moment. Something has gone wrong in Israel. I feel it in my bones. But the other magicians are not our immediate concern right now. Let's get moving. I'm itching to kill a priest of Thevetat tonight."

Usually, Marco would've objected, making the argument that they needed to keep any suspects alive for questioning, to process them through the proper channels of the law. But Marco knew if he tried that with Lyca, he would end up at the bottom of a canal, right alongside the dispatched priest of Thevetat.

They walked silently along the Fondamenta dei Mori, Marco stealing glances behind them every few meters, the itchy feeling between his shoulder blades growing with each step. Lyca's footfalls barely made a sound, so when she stopped suddenly, Marco almost crashed into her.

The magician held out an arm to stop him from moving past her, a wickedly curved dagger in her hand.

"What is it?" he whispered.

"Something is wrong. I can feel some kind of magic at work around us. Stay close."

With careful steps, they turned into the Ramo dei Muti. There were lights on in the buildings around them, music drifting from a rooftop terrace where people were having a good time. To Marco, everything seemed calm and normal. Lyca let out a low hiss when they came to a wall covered in hanging ivy. The moonlight glinted on steel as she made a quick swipe at the wall. Marco was about to ask her what was wrong when he saw it. A *patere* made of marble had been hidden behind the plants, the motif of a snake with a crown in its dripping fangs. Lyca ran her fingers over it before slicing her finger and rubbing blood on the serpent's mouth. The air around them charged before the pressure broke, making Marco's ears pop.

"Lazy wards," Lyca grumbled and turned to a weatherworn, red door that Marco could've sworn wasn't there a moment beforehand.

With expert precision, she jammed the dagger into the door edge and popped the lock.

"Keep close behind me, watch our backs, and do everything I tell you." Lyca handed him a dagger. "Use bullets to slow them and the blade to kill them." She stepped into the shadows of the house before he could argue. Marco gripped the hilt of the dagger in his sweaty palm and followed.

There was a light burning somewhere on the other side of the house, giving him just enough to see Lyca moving ahead of them. They searched room by room on the ground floor before coming to an inner courtyard.

"There doesn't seem to be anyone home," whispered Marco as they looked about the small gardens. Lyca ignored him, every inch of her alert as she moved along the flagstones. The light was coming from the other side, the walkways leading to a set of wide double doors that led into a study.

A shadow flicked across the light, and without warning, Lyca shoved him hard out of the way as two knives sank into the wooden pillar where he had just been standing. Lyca bolted toward the study, her knives drawn. Marco caught up just in time to see her clash with a hooded figure, blade and shadow meeting. Red mist hissed from the priest, and the light above them died. Lyca swore, pulling Marco down as the red light exploded into flame. Lyca threw up a wall of magic, and the flames died, sucked into nothing.

Then she was running again, leaping over fallen furniture as the priest hurried to get away. Marco tried to keep up, but he only caught a glimpse of silver hair and heard the clang of blades before they were running again.

"Outside!" Lyca called to him, and he made for the front door. A figure leaped over the stone wall, and Marco fired two shots, just missing the priest as they dropped to the street. Lyca was a flash of darkness as she came over the wall behind them. Marco followed Lyca as she chased the fleeing priest down the Corte dei Muti. People were blocking the bridge in front of them, the priest not slowing as they jumped onto the wooden railing, racing past them along the beam.

"*Polizia*! Out of the way!" Marco shouted, and the people hurried to one side as Lyca and Marco ran past.

"Try and get them to go to the marina," Lyca said, barely a hitch in her breathing.

Marco slowed long enough to fire a shot at the buildings ahead of them. The priest dodged it, turning sharply into the Corte Vecchia. Marco caught up to Lyca as they crossed the Ponte dela Saca, the hooded figure a blur ahead of them as they headed down the nearest jetty of the marina. The priest halted, realizing too late that they were cornered between the magician and the lagoon. Lyca replaced her dagger with a sword.

"Stay," she said to Marco before closing in on her prey.

A sultry laugh echoed across the water, and Marco's blood went cold as he recognized it. A hand pulled back the hood, and he saw the beautiful face of Francesca Garcia.

"Inspector, are you going to allow me to be murdered in cold blood?" she asked, even as her hand reached into her jacket and pulled out two long knives.

"You don't really need a civilian to save you, do you, priestess?" Lyca countered, raising her sword. She ducked as Francesca threw fire toward her. Marco watched in horror as the two women clashed, both moving in swift strikes and blocks that he could barely track. He never thought he would see someone match Lyca strike for strike, but Francesca held her own, throwing magic and knives with a ferocity and speed that left him breathless. Lyca pushed her further down the pier until she neared the edge.

"Tell me where your master is, and I'll make your death clean," promised Lyca.

"I'm not as disloyal as you filthy magicians. My prince and my master mean more to me than my own blood. Torture me, kill me, it matters not. I'll tell you nothing," Francesca snarled, blood dripping from her nose. Lyca readjusted her stance and met Francesca's attack with an almost bored easiness.

The jetty shuddered beneath Marco's feet as if something had brushed against the pylons. The water rippled at the edge of the jetty and Marco bit down on a scream as a head rose up from the waves. His mind struggled to take in the fangs and scales.

Francesca tried to run, but the creature was faster. Its massive head struck, the serpent's mouth cutting off her screams as powerful jaws closed over her. Marco heard a sickening crunch of bones breaking, and that was all. After, the creature cleaned its maw with a long tongue.

Thank you for honoring our arrangement, a strangely deep and feminine voice echoed in Marco's head. Lyca sheathed her sword and bowed to the serpent, offering the back of her neck to it.

"It was my honor, Reitia. Thank you for letting us know that there was still such evil in your great city," Lyca said reverently.

Reitia, the goddess of Venice. The great serpent that Marco had heard so many fairy tales about growing up. Marco's stomach shuddered as the serpent's glowing eyes fixed on him.

Come here, human.

Marco's legs were rubber as he stumbled down the jetty to stand next to Lyca. She made a small sound at the back of her throat, and Marco bowed, praying to all the saints that the creature didn't devour him, too. Water dripped onto his hair as hot breath steamed over him. He didn't dare move or look up.

I thought I smelled a Dandolo.

"He's a friend of Penelope's who's been helping us," Lyca explained.

Marco's mind raced for something to say. "Thank you for coming to our aid, great goddess."

The serpent let out a sound that may have been a laugh. *I like this one, assassin. He smells trustworthy.* With that, the serpent slid beneath the water, the boats in the marina knocking against their pylons as Reitia moved out to deeper water.

"That…that was the Serpent of Venice," Marco managed to say as he straightened.

"The one and only. Reitia asked to be the one to deliver justice. I wasn't in a position to deny her, otherwise I would have slain the priestess back at the house." Marco managed two steps before he leaned over the side of the jetty and hurled his guts up into the water. Lyca gave his back a pat.

"Don't be so frightened. She liked you."

"How could you tell?" He coughed and spat before straightening.

"Isn't it obvious? You are still alive."

His stomach still shuddering, Marco followed Lyca back to the house on the Ramo dei Muti. She began flicking on lights as they entered, in case anyone else decided to jump out at them.

"That priestess tried to burn the study," Lyca said as they crossed the inner courtyard. "Her first fire spell wasn't aimed at me. It was aimed at the walls, and I want to know what she was getting rid of." She turned on the light and Marco could see why Francesca had tried to burn the office down. Tacked onto the walls were maps, plans, photographs of people, and shots of places. Stacks of papers sat on the large desk next to a laptop.

"No wonder she tried to get rid of all this. It looks like their whole operation," he murmured, staring at the office.

Lyca pointed. "You start on that pile."

"Are we looking for something in particular?" Marco asked.

"Any information on Israel and the Dead Sea. Alexis and the others were jumped while they were in Tel Aviv, and the priests were onto Penelope's friend before she even knew he was missing. They *must* have had priests already stationed in Israel."

An hour later, Marco found a file that made his heart pound. Without hesitation, he pulled out his phone and dialed Penelope's number. He didn't want to risk waiting.

"Marco! Did you find anything?" Penelope answered. She sounded exhausted and upset.

"Where are you?"

"On our way back to Tel Aviv. We have a red-eye back to Venice."

"You need—" he began, but Lyca snatched the phone from him.

"Penelope, you need to get back to the hospital. Put Alexis on the fucking phone now," she snapped before delivering a terse message in Atlantean. Marco heard Alexis swear and the squeal of brakes. Lyca hung up the phone and passed it back to him.

"Stop gaping at me and help me pack all this up. We need to clear the house before you call in the property to the police," Lyca instructed.

Marco waged a small internal struggle before agreeing. "I'll try and find some suitcases."

TWENTY-SIX

CAROLYN HELD ONTO Penelope too tightly before finally saying her goodbyes and shoving her toward the door of the hospital room. They had brought Tim to the Hadassah hospital, not far from Elazar's house, and Alexis had managed to get him checked into a room with an ease that would've been suspicious if it wasn't for the magic Carolyn knew he wielded. Carolyn hadn't said it to Penelope, but Alexis Donato scared the absolute shit out of her. He loved Penelope, though. It radiated from him whenever he looked at her, and Carolyn knew that his scariness would never be directed toward her.

"You aren't going to feel this way forever. Do your duty to Tim Sanders and then go and find your joy again. You have a heart that was made to love; you just need to find someone who will return it with the same passion and devotion. Don't let this incident harden you," Zo had said as he hugged her goodbye. She had kissed his cheek and waited until she was alone before bursting into tears. That guy saw *way* too much. She hoped he was right.

Under the fluorescent hospital lights, Tim's weight loss was even more obvious. He was a scrawny, unshaved version of the man she had fallen so hard for. Despite still being angry with him, Carolyn sat down and took his hand. It was dry and calloused from digging in the desert, and there had never been any violence in them until he had found that blasted scroll. She'd always known the Dead Sea would break him. It was a land made for those stronger than the sweet dreamer that had been Tim Sanders.

Tim sighed as he stirred. He looked blearily around the room with bloodshot eyes before finally noticing her.

"Carolyn? Why are you here? Where am I?"

"Shh, take it easy, honey," she crooned, pushing his sandy hair back from his face.

"What happened?"

"You were out on a dig—do you remember?"

"Ah…yeah. Cave 12. I was looking after the site while Schaal and the others went on holiday."

"That's right. You got sick. You caught a bug that turned into viral meningitis. The hotel staff in Kalia called the doctors after you collapsed while getting out of your Jeep. The doctors called me because I'm still listed as your emergency contact," Carolyn explained, calmly stroking his head. "You scared the shit out of me, so I got on a plane and came straightaway."

"But that doesn't…I can't remember. I was at the site…I was going to camp in the cave," Tim stammered, pressing his palms to his eyes.

"That's right."

"There were lights, and something happened."

"Tim, you were hallucinating. It's a symptom of meningitis. The doctor said you might be remembering all sorts of weird stuff that never actually happened. You were so sick when you finally got here, they thought you were going to have brain damage."

"Fuck, Caro. I can't remember anything," he said, true fear filling his eyes.

Carolyn squeezed his hand. "Hey, look at me. It's going to be okay. I've called your Professor Schaal and let him know you are safe. You had him really worried, too. Apparently, you called him when you had a fever and scared the hell out of him. He's happy to hear you're okay and promised to come in and check on you soon. You made everyone panic, by the sound of things. I wish you could've thought of a better way to drag me back into your life, to be honest. Lucky I still have a soft spot for you, even though you're a high-maintenance pain in my ass."

"Take it easy, love. I've been super sick. You can't be angry at me," he said, and they managed a quiet laugh. "God, I think I dreamed about Penelope. I remember being really worried about her."

"She's okay. I told her what happened and she went on a really big rant about you drinking too much beer and not enough water when you're in the desert."

"Sounds like her. I'm all messed up, and she's still riding my ass about a few beers," Tim said with a smile. "I'm sorry for dragging you into my drama, Caro. Thank you for coming all this way. I've really missed you. God, I was such a prick before. You never deserved it, and I'm sorry. Really."

Invisible knives of guilt stabbed into Carolyn as she forced herself to reply. "It's okay, Tim. We both made mistakes. I'm always going to give a shit about what happens to you. No matter if we are a couple or not."

There was a quiet tap on the door. Two men were studying them, and Carolyn didn't recognize either of them.

"I hope I'm not interrupting," the old man apologized.

"Professor Schaal! Come in," said Tim. Professor Schaal looked like the quintessential academic with wire-framed glasses perched on his nose, a slightly rumpled dress shirt and pants, and unpolished loafers.

"I was just speaking with Doctor Solon and convinced him you could have visitors," said Schaal. The doctor, Carolyn couldn't help noticing, was drop-dead gorgeous. Tall, with dark hair tied back, and dressed in a pristine doctor's coat. He looked at Carolyn and gave her a wide smile.

"You must be Carolyn Williams. The nurse said you would be in here and that visiting hours didn't apply to you," the doctor said.

"I thought it better Tim have a familiar face when he woke up. It's nice to meet you finally, Professor. Tim has always spoken very highly of you," Carolyn said, shaking Schaal's hand.

"The pleasure is mine. You are exactly how I imagined you," Schaal said.

"Tim, you wouldn't mind if I step out with Carolyn while you catch up with the Professor, would you? There are a few things I need her to sign off on regarding your treatment. The boring paperwork side of things," Doctor Solon said.

"As long as it's okay with Carolyn," said Tim.

"She doesn't have to go. I'm sure paperwork can wait a night," Professor Schaal argued, giving the doctor a deep frown.

"No, I'll be happy for the walk. I need to stretch my legs and get a coffee. Besides, I know you two will start talking about the Dead Sea, and I'll be forgotten," Carolyn said, getting to her feet. She gave Tim a kiss on his cheek before following the doctor out into the too-bright hallway.

"Your boyfriend seems to have been through quite an ordeal," commented Doctor Solon.

"He's not my boyfriend, Doctor," Carolyn objected a little too quickly.

"Call me Adam, it's easier. Boyfriend or not, he's going to be unwell for quite some time. Have you considered taking him back to Australia?"

"I want to, but I doubt I'll be able to convince Tim to leave. Trying to pull him away from the Dead Sea has always been a trial," said Carolyn, heading for the coffee machine.

"As a doctor, I can't let you drink that," Adam said, placing a gentle hand on her arm. "Come with me to the staff room, and I'll make you a decent coffee on the espresso machine."

Carolyn smiled gratefully. "Thank you. Are you sure the other staff won't mind?"

"No one will even notice us. It's late. There's only a skeleton staff working right now. I'm on call so I might have to dash away if I'm needed," Adam told her.

Carolyn thought it was weird to be having coffee with a total stranger and talking about the drama that was being Tim's closest friend, but the longer they did, the easier she felt. Adam was intelligent and warm and made them both coffee as they chatted. After the crazy two weeks she'd had, talking to a normal, good-looking Israeli doctor was exactly what she needed. An hour had passed, and she still hadn't seen a single piece of paper to sign.

"We should be getting back, I suppose. I doubt they have even noticed how long we've been gone," said Carolyn.

"And I have rounds that I need to do. This place is a maze, so I'll walk you back," Adam offered.

When they stepped out of the lifts, Carolyn noticed that the floor was eerily quiet. *Everyone is sleeping but you,* she reminded herself. Spending so much time talking about cultists had left her paranoid. It was definitely time to go back to Australia.

When they got to Tim's room Carolyn was hit with a wet, meaty smell, and she froze in her tracks. Someone had pulled the privacy screen around Tim's bed, and there was no sign of Professor Schaal.

"Tim?" Her voice was tiny as she pulled back the screen.

There was nothing recognizable about the congealing mess of blood and flesh in the hospital bed. She opened her mouth to scream just as a strong arm came around her neck. A hand clamped firmly over her sobbing mouth. Adam's breath was hot on the back of her neck.

"Listen carefully, Carolyn. You tell Penelope Bryne that she owes Kreios a life debt and that the only reason you are now drawing breath is because he saved you. Understand?" Carolyn nodded quickly. Then he was gone, and Carolyn finally scrambled out of the room, screaming for help.

TWENTY-SEVEN

By the time Penelope arrived, the hospital floor was in chaos and Carolyn was fighting with nurses who were trying to sedate her. She saw Penelope through the crowd and pushed her way over, collapsing into her arms in tears.

"I've got you, honey. Let's find somewhere to sit down, okay?" Penelope tried to soothe, even as her own tears smeared her cheeks.

"In here," Alexis said, gesturing toward an empty office.

Between shaky breaths, Carolyn told them about the visit from Schaal and the man posing as Tim's doctor, Adam.

"He...he said to tell you that you owe Kreios a debt for saving my life," Carolyn sobbed. Penelope gripped Carolyn tighter to her as if holding her would stop her world from crumbling.

"I tried to get here as quickly as possible. I'm sorry—"

Carolyn shoved her away. "You knew they were coming for him?"

"We received a call from Marco," Alexis explained. "He found one of the priests' safe houses in Venice. He and Lyca found information on the digs that the priests of Thevetat were funding. Was this the man you saw?" He held out his phone to her.

"Yes! That's Professor Schaal. Tim's been working for him for ages."

"His real name is Abaddon, and this Adam you met was one of his men, Kreios," said Penelope. "As soon as Marco sent us the picture, we turned the car around."

"And you were too goddamn late! Tim was torn to p-pieces because of your fucking war with these creeps!" screamed Carolyn through her tears. She turned on Alexis. "Take away my memories of seeing it. *Now.*"

"Caro, you don't know what you're asking—" Penelope began helplessly.

"You don't get a say in this! I don't want to have my last memory of Tim to be…that. I can't live with that memory. I can't." Carolyn covered her face with her hands, unable to control the grief and rage inside her. Alexis took her in his arms, and she clung to him, begging him to erase her memory.

"Breathe, Carolyn, you must keep breathing," Alexis said gently.

Penelope wrapped her arms around herself to keep from shaking as the air filled with the smell of firecrackers and cinnamon. Alexis would take the nightmare from Carolyn, reshape the last few weeks into something she could handle, leaving Penelope to carry the memory of it forever, alone.

When Alexis was finished, he passed a drowsy Carolyn to Penelope who held her gently.

"Stay here. I'll make sure the rest of the staff know the new cover story," Alexis said and stepped outside.

Without him there to witness it, Penelope broke down into heart-wrenching sobs. When Marco had called, she'd known that someone would get to Tim and Carolyn before she did. The world had dropped out from beneath her and she didn't know how she was going to make it right again.

Penelope stroked Carolyn's golden hair over and over, reminding herself that she was still alive. Carolyn might not have understood the significance of what Kreios had done, but Penelope did. He'd saved her when Abaddon had been ready to kill them both. Penelope had kept the scroll that Abaddon would have come looking for, and when Tim couldn't produce it, it had sealed his fate.

The noise in the hospital outside the door quieted, and a little while later, Zo opened the door. He took one look at Penelope cradling Carolyn, and sat down beside her, taking both women into his arms.

"This isn't your fault, Pen. Don't shoulder the guilt of his death," he said softly.

"Of course this is my fault. Abaddon went after them because of me."

"That's bullshit. It sounds like Abaddon was involved with Tim and that Dead Sea site long before he even knew you existed, Penelope. From what Lyca has said, the priests of Thevetat have been funding digs at the Dead Sea. Abaddon wanted the scroll, and any Essene magic he could find, and that's why Tim died. It was a message to intimidate and break us, because that's how Thevetat has always operated."

"Carolyn is never going to forgive me for this."

"She's not even going to remember it."

"But I *know* she blames me. I'm always going to know."

Carolyn stirred in Penelope's arms, and she opened her brown eyes. "Pen, I'm so glad you're here."

"I wouldn't be anywhere else," Penelope assured her.

"How many times did we tell Tim not to drive drunk?" Carolyn said, sitting up and wiping the tears off her cheeks. "He had so much to live for, and now he'll never find his scrolls, all because he thought there would be no danger on a desert road."

Unable to find the right words, Penelope wept for her dead friend, and for Carolyn who'd never remember the truth. Penelope didn't know if the lie was worse, only that she needed to find a way to set aside her grief until she'd gotten her revenge.

THE FOLLOWING days passed in a blur. Phaidros and Aelia returned to Venice to help Marco and Lyca, while Alexis and Zo made arrangements for Tim's body to be cremated. Penelope was on autopilot as she ate and slept, all the while trying to comfort Carolyn. Alexis held Penelope at night until all of her grief had turned into a cold lump in the pit of her stomach. They had driven to the Dead Sea, carefully avoiding where the dig site was, and sprinkled Tim's ashes.

"It would be where he wanted to rest," Carolyn said, looking out over the water, her puffy eyes hidden behind dark sunglasses. "I hate this place so goddamn much."

"I know," Penelope replied. Despite how much Carolyn had loved him, Tim had always loved this stretch of desert and sea more than anything—or anyone—else.

Goodbyes had been brief at the airport in Tel Aviv. Carolyn was still cautious around Penelope as if, deep under Alexis's magic, she still knew that they had fought. Penelope hoped she wouldn't feel that way forever, that somehow they could salvage their friendship. At the same time, she knew things between them would never be the same again. *She* was never going to be the same again.

Once they landed in Venice, Penelope gulped down the warm, salty air and stared across the water at her city. Even with her heart pulverized, the sight of La Serenissima didn't fail to lift her spirits. Alexis placed his arm around her shoulders.

"I'm so relieved to be back that I'm almost ashamed of it," Penelope said.

They hadn't discussed her going back to Melbourne with Carolyn, even though Penelope could see the question in Alexis's eyes. There would be no comfort back there for her. Carolyn would go to her parents, and they were far better qualified to help her through her grief and get her life back together.

"There's nothing shameful about wanting to stay where you feel most at home," Alexis replied, steering her toward the docks where Phaidros would be waiting for them.

"I don't know how to process what I'm feeling. I'm so angry, I could choke," Penelope admitted.

"I know, *cara*. The only thing you can do is find a way to live with it." Alexis pulled her closer. "We will get justice for what Abaddon has taken from us. I promise you, Penelope. I promise."

TWENTY-EIGHT

ESPITE EVERYTHING THAT needed to be done, Penelope spent the following two days in bed. She was aware of Alexis occasionally checking on her, leaving tea and food if she wanted it. He didn't pressure her to move, and he made sure the other magicians left her alone. Nightmares waited for her whenever she closed her eyes, the days in Israel blending together in a montage of destruction and death. Carolyn's accusations and the hard look in her eyes as she blamed Penelope for Tim's death would haunt her forever.

By the third day, Penelope had had enough of her own self-pity and grief. She couldn't handle her own thoughts and company a second longer. Turning on her phone, Penelope found messages from Carolyn saying she'd arrived back in Melbourne and had gone to stay with her parents on the farm for a while. Carolyn would have the support that she needed while coming to terms with Tim's death, and being so far from Penelope would hopefully make Thevetat lose interest in her friend.

No matter how much the thought pained her, Penelope had to admit that Kreios had saved Carolyn's life at the hospital. She only hoped that he'd given Abaddon enough reason not to go to Australia and finish the job.

Taking a croissant and a cup of coffee from the kitchen, Penelope headed to the Archives. As soon as she stepped out of the glass elevator, the smell of leather and paper welcomed her, and the ball of ice in Penelope's stomach that had formed in Israel finally began to melt.

"Home," she said aloud. Floating orbs drifted down around her, encasing her in light as they gently pushed against her like affectionate cats. "I missed you, too," she told the Archives.

A quick look at her office revealed that her laptop, the journal she'd started in Israel, and the scroll had been placed neatly on her desk. She wasn't ready to deal with them yet, so she walked through the stacks, listening for the sounds of metal that would take her to Lyca's forge.

Penelope had barely passed the rack of javelins when Lyca looked up from her workbench.

"Hey," Penelope said by way of greeting, never knowing how to begin with Lyca. She didn't know how to express how glad she was to see the warrior magician, hard at work creating beautiful items of death. Lyca was silent, giving her space to continue.

"I wanted to say that you were right about Carolyn and telling people about you..."

"Us," corrected Lyca, putting her tools down. She pulled up a wooden stool and pointed to it. "Sit down, Archivist."

Penelope did as she was told. Lyca pulled out a flask and tipped some of its contents into Penelope's coffee.

"To fallen friends, may they be at peace," Lyca said, and Penelope drank with her. She didn't know what the liquor was, but it burnt her throat, heating all of her body.

"Just so you know, I didn't want to be right about telling them," Lyca said, pulling another stool up opposite her.

"I honestly thought they would understand. Carolyn was frightened by her brush with a magical *demimonde*, and Tim was torn between wanting to mine us all for information that would lead him to Essene magical texts and thinking that I was under a spell of Thevetat's. It was a great big fucking mess." Penelope took another drink.

Lyca took a moment before replying. "It has been my experience that sometimes even your closest friends only like the things you can do for them, not who you are. When they see the real you, when you act in a way that they don't understand, they lash out because you have changed the status quo. I'm not going to pretend to understand your friendship with Carolyn. From where I'm sitting, as soon as you made decisions that benefitted only you, she didn't like it. She was jealous of you, even if she didn't know why. I saw it in her eyes. I'm not saying that you won't ever work it out and be friends again. If you are true friends, it will heal and become something new. She needs to learn how to love the person you are becoming. Otherwise, your relationship will never regain its balance."

"I guess only time will tell."

Lyca poured more liquor into her mug. "Alexis told me that you jumped out of a moving car and that you didn't panic when priests attacked you in Tel Aviv."

"And?"

"It proves that you know how to keep a cool head and adapt, not burst into tears like a fucking damsel. I can respect that. There's no room for damsel theatrics in a war."

Lyca is trying to be nice to me, Penelope realized and tried to hide her surprise.

"Thanks, Lyca. Tell me about the priestess you killed," said Penelope, attempting to meet her halfway and keep the conversation going.

"I didn't kill her. Reitia ate her."

"No way! In front of Marco?"

"She scared the shit out of him." Lyca grinned with feral amusement.

"Oh, God. How did he take it?"

"He kept his Venetian cool until she was gone and then he vomited everywhere like a frightened child, not a seasoned police officer."

Penelope laughed for the first time since Tim had tried to kidnap her. It felt good to laugh again.

Lyca shrugged. "Marco stuck around. I can't fault his bravery." She opened a cabinet and pulled out a polished wooden case. "I've made him these to reward him." Inside were freshly minted bullets, shining with magic.

"Priest-slaying bullets?" Penelope asked, lifting one and turning it over in her hand.

"If Marco insists on tagging along on our hunts, I'd prefer him to be armed with something useful. I gave him a dagger the other night and spent the whole time worried he was going to cut himself."

"I would've been more concerned with him cutting you," said Penelope.

"He kept up and followed orders, and that was good enough for me to make sure nothing killed him."

"Did you find any sacrifices at the house?" Penelope almost didn't want to know the answer.

"No, there weren't any bodies. Perhaps they wanted to keep it purely as a safe house or a training place for the acolytes. We did find a room full of Tony Duilio's plans and records."

"Any books of magic? Or does Thevetat have a book of scripture or something?"

"No, the priesthood has always been an oral tradition. It used to be one apprentice to every master."

"Like the Sith," joked Penelope before remembering her audience.

"I don't know about the rules of the Sith, but Thevetat has always covered his tracks. That is why they have been able to remain hidden for so long."

"Where did Marco put all the paperwork? That would be a good project for me...you know, to take my mind off everything," Penelope said. She really wanted to know how the fuck Abaddon had gotten his filthy claws into Tim.

"Marco and I put it into an office upstairs, seeing how I didn't think it was wise to let him into the Archives without the Archivist being present. He wants to see you. Maybe you should invite him around to help you set it all up. He took photos of everything before he allowed me to touch anything. The man is pedantic."

Penelope smiled. "He's a cop. They are trained to photograph a scene, and I think I put the fear of God into him with the walls on the Duilio crime scenes."

"He's the one to help you put it all together. Come on, I'll show you."

"Show me what?"

Lyca got to her feet. "The Archives has been renovating while you were away. It must've sensed you were on your way back."

Penelope walked on slightly unsteady feet, following Lyca past her weapons and to the pillar marking the history section. Behind the last shelf of books, next to the bare cavern wall, was a brand-new door. It looked like a tall, wooden cabinet. Penelope gave Lyca a confused look before Lyca pulled open the red-and-blue painted doors to reveal another elevator.

Penelope smiled. "Hiding in plain sight. I love the magic of this place." She stepped inside with Lyca and pressed the button.

When the doors opened again, Penelope was in the upstairs library, surrounded by warm wood and spring light.

"I'll never understand why you look at books that way," Lyca said with a shake of her head. She led Penelope to a large room with wooden shelves and a long wall of Byzantine windows looking out over the water. There was a large desk on one side and a fireplace. What caught her attention most were the piles of boxes, stacked suitcases, and rolled maps.

"Let's get started," she said.

Penelope was slowly unpacking the second box when Alexis came in wearing a magnificent *entari* robe of burnt-orange silk and embroidered with golden suns. Penelope had missed his never-ending supply of robes in Israel, and a little more normality crept into her mind to comfort her.

"At least that is a look I understand," teased Lyca, from her spot at the desk.

"You'll never believe who I found loitering along the Calle dei Cerchieri," said Alexis, moving out of the way to reveal Marco Dandolo.

"If any of you would answer your phones occasionally, I wouldn't have looked so pathetic," Marco complained.

"And where would be the fun in that?" said Alexis. Penelope was on her feet in moments, wrapping her arms tightly around Marco.

"I missed you, too, *Dottore*," he said, kissing her cheeks. When she refused to let him go, he gave her back a gentle rub. "Easy now. Everything is okay."

"I'm really glad to see you," Penelope said, brushing tears off her cheeks. "I'm sorry, I can't seem to stop my stupid face from leaking at the moment."

"Penelope, you don't have to apologize. Alexis told me Abaddon killed your friend. I'm so sorry, *amica*."

Lyca and Alexis had disappeared from the room, giving them space to catch up and begin sorting through the mess around them.

Penelope and Marco ended up in the gardens, sitting on a stone bench that looked out over the Grand Canal, a bottle of wine between them. Penelope released all the thoughts that had been bottled up inside her since Tim had tried to kidnap her and steal Elazar's research. Marco poured wine as she tried to untangle the painful knot of feelings. She told him of Carolyn's accusations and Tim's death, and the horrible, shameful anger that she had at the both of them.

"I suppose that makes me the worst person in the world, right? To be pissed off at a dead guy and my best friend?" Penelope said, draining her wine.

"You have a right to your feelings, Penelope. I can understand your anger. They both failed you, in their own ways."

"According to them, I was the one who failed them."

Marco sat back with a sigh. "Tim betrayed you, stole from your friends—he hurt you after you had saved him. I don't care what his reasons were; he could've talked to you about his fears and suspicions without resorting to violence. Alexis would've been able to straighten out every misconception he had. No excuse can change the fact that Tim was in his right mind enough to try and steal another academic's research. What do you think he would've done with all that information if he had gotten away? Tim made his own choices and they didn't have anyone's interests in mind except for his."

They watched the boats for a while before he finally continued. "Carolyn is more complicated. You trusted her with your secrets, opened yourself to her because you expected she'd be able to have your back and be your ally. Instead, she panicked, and instead of admitting that she didn't understand why you chose this life, she retaliated with hurt and anger that you had gone somewhere she didn't have the courage to follow. You didn't fail Carolyn or get Tim killed."

"Abaddon killed him because he didn't have the scroll. I kept it."

"Don't be naïve, *amica*. Abaddon would've taken the scroll and killed him anyway. By keeping the scroll, you now have the upper hand against Thevetat. Not only that, you solved an ancient prophecy. You suffered terrible losses as well as had an immense victory in Israel. It's the nature of the war we are in," said Marco. He squeezed her shoulder gently. "I know it's not going to comfort you, even though you struck a good blow to Thevetat. With the information we collected from the Cannaregio house, we'll strike many more."

"I know you're right, but the victory still feels hollow," said Penelope sadly.

"Do you think you're going to be able to trust Kreios?"

"Trust? No. He saved Carolyn and led you to Duilio's house, I can be grateful for that. If he insists on interrupting my dreams, then I'll use him, and get Lyca to cut his head off when it's over. That is, if Aelia doesn't get to him first."

Marco didn't blink. He wasn't surprised or horrified by her harshness and the talk of inevitable violence. It made Penelope want to hug him again because at least Marco understood. He'd seen the sacrifices. He knew what violence Thevetat's priests were capable of.

"Maybe it's what Kreios wants," Marco said.

"What do you mean?"

"After ten thousand years as the slave to a madman and a demon, wouldn't you want to die?"

PENELOPE AND Marco spent the rest of the day, and much of the evening, using his photos to reassemble the walls of information taken from the Duilio house. Penelope felt good doing something useful, and Marco's pragmatic personality and advice were finally breaking through her gloom.

When they were finally finished, the magicians joined them, all staring at the massive wall of information.

"Holy shit," said Zo, breaking their contemplative silence.

"This can't be their whole operation," Aelia said, eyeing it skeptically.

"Maybe not the whole thing. It's an excellent start, nonetheless," replied Alexis. He was studying the list of dig sites and the various aliases and businesses funding them.

"That's how we found out about Abaddon being Schaal," explained Marco, pointing to the list of names. "It's one of his many established covers. He has articles and multiple books published. He's even legally married." Marco pointed to a photo of a stunning woman with black hair. "This was Tony Duilio's lawyer, Francesca Garcia. She was Abaddon's wife."

"Gross," said Aelia.

"She has at least seven other aliases," Marco added.

"Is that the laptop you found?" Galenos asked.

"It is. I turned it on, but it's password protected."

Galenos gave him an amused smile, picked up the laptop, and disappeared from the room.

"He'll sort it out," Alexis said with a dismissive wave.

"Looks like Kreios wasn't lying, after all. Maybe he does want to help bring Abaddon down," said Zo uncertainly.

"It doesn't mean I won't kill him if I'm given half a chance," muttered Phaidros, his golden eyes filled with old fury.

"Let's clear up this mess." Aelia pointed at the wall before linking her arm through Phaidros's. "And then we will kill him together."

"Abaddon first," Lyca and Alexis said at the same time.

"Where do we start?" Penelope asked, staring at the walls.

"We can worry about this. You and Alexis are the academics so you can track down Solomon's ring," said Zo.

Penelope let out a cynical laugh. "Sure thing. People have only been searching for it for the last three thousand years. We should search for the Ark of the Covenant while we are at it."

"You found a piece of Atlantis from ten thousand years ago," Marco said. "Three thousand should be much easier." He gave her a confident pat on her back.

"I don't even know where to start. My field has always been the Mediterranean and Aegean, not the Near East," Penelope pointed out.

"Maybe you should have a look and see what Tim wrote. You said he was working on a document of everything he remembered. There could be something there that can point you to a starting place," suggested Zo.

"I don't think he was sane enough to know anything of worth," said Phaidros, earning a sharp look from Alexis.

"Never underestimate the ravings of madmen," Zo said. "They see things far more clearly than we do."

"Ignore them, *cara*. Start where you want to. The Archives will keep us both busy enough without Tim's document," Alexis said gently.

Penelope had already filtered them out, already puzzling over her next impossible archaeological challenge.

TWENTY-NINE

I T WAS DECIDED that the upstairs library would be devoted to the hunt for Thevetat's priests while Penelope's office in the Archives be reserved to her and Alexis's search for the seal ring of Solomon. As soon as it was agreed, another desk had appeared on the other side of her office with Alexis's journals.

"Don't get used to the special treatment, Donato. I'll be kicking you out of my office as soon as this ring is found," said Penelope, leaning back against the desk, careful to not disturb his piles of books. Alexis placed his arms on either side of her, leaning down until they were at eye level with one another.

"I wouldn't dream of it, Archivist," he said.

Penelope grinned. "I could get used to you calling me that. It makes me sound like I'm the boss."

"You are, most definitely, the boss," agreed Alexis before kissing her. Heat traveled up her spine, and Penelope gripped the edges on the desk to stop herself from pulling him closer. *Think of all the priceless manuscripts behind you that will get damaged.*

"I'm starting to rethink my decision to have you for a study partner," she said against his lips.

"I'm an excellent study partner!"

"You're an excellent distraction from studying."

"Says the woman sitting on my desk so I can't work."

"The boss gets to sit where she likes," Penelope pointed out.

"Well, the boss better move unless she wants me to start telling her where I want her to sit next," Alexis threatened, a sinful gleam in his eyes. Penelope reluctantly slid out of his embrace and headed for her own desk.

"Don't make me review my employee sexual harassment policy," she warned, making him laugh in a way that made her feel like maybe she'd like to be harassed a little bit more.

"Where would you like to start, Archivist?" Alexis asked.

Reaching for a pad of Post-it Notes, Penelope wrote down "990 BCE" and stuck it on the wall of glass windows beside her.

"We start at the beginning with Solomon. We review all the stories of the ring, his rule, and heirs, and move on from there."

IT WAS another three days before Penelope dared to open the file that Tim had named "Tim's Awesome Adventure."

"You're such a douchebag, Carter," she couldn't help muttering even as she wiped the tears off her cheeks. "Okay, Penelope, don't be lame, you have work to do."

Four hours later, Alexis arrived with a bottle of wine and bowls of pasta. "Zo insists we eat," he said, placing the food down on a small table next to her chaise lounge.

"What time is it?" Penelope asked, rubbing her eyes.

"Nearly 11:00 p.m. Come and sit with me. Tell me what you're working on."

"Tim is what I'm working on," Penelope said, moving from her chair to collapse on the lounge.

"I see. Anything interesting yet?" Alexis passed her a bowl of pasta and sat down beside her.

"Part of it is clear. It reads almost like a diary. The days leading up to the find, how excited he was at being left alone, and how he had known that he was close to finding something. Then there are other parts that were Thevetat's acolytes following him and how he began to have visions. He saw the scribe and the night the community members were killed over and over again, almost like the memory was playing on repeat. Do you think Thevetat did it because he knew that a prophecy about Solomon's Seal would come from them?" Penelope swallowed a mouthful of wine, letting it soothe her fried thoughts before she began to eat.

"It could be possible. Who knows what insight Thevetat and Abaddon could have? Whatever the reason, it worried them enough to take drastic action against a peaceful people. Did you find any references to the Roman emperor he kept speaking of?" said Alexis.

"I was just getting to Rome when you came in. He seemed to have visions from various time periods. He wrote *a lot* in those three days he had my computer. He had so much going on in his mind that he never spoke about. He pretended that he was back to normal. I should've known better, looked closer." Penelope skewered an olive with her fork, contemplating the jumble of stories and glimpses of courts and battles and desert seas she had read for the past hours.

"He could've talked to you, or Carolyn, or any of us. He didn't. You need to let the guilt of it go. It doesn't serve you in any way. Grieve for the man he was. Don't blame yourself for what was out of your control."

"I don't know when I'm going to stop feeling this way," she admitted.

"You need to learn to move with your grief. It's not something you can get over like you would a cold. Nobody can get over a loss this quickly, not even saints."

Penelope's fork stopped halfway to her mouth. "Saints..." she said, putting her pasta down.

"What is it?" Alexis gave a startled laugh as she kissed him hard.

"Saints!" exclaimed Penelope. She ran back to her desk and grabbed her laptop. "Tim, Tim, Tim. Where is it...?" She sat back down next to Alexis, scrolling through the document, searching for the reference. Alexis sat patiently while she mumbled to herself.

"You remember when Elazar was working on breaking Tim's curse, and Tim kept talking about 'purple and gold and laurel leaves?'"

"You and Carolyn thought it strange because he didn't like Roman history," recalled Alexis.

"Hated it. We were debating who Tim was talking about, and then today I read this part: 'Tiers of seats and hawk-eyed men. There was one who came amongst them, dressed in purple and gold and stones. A huge man built for a battlefield, not a court. Dignified. You could tell that the onlookers were impressed and humbled and kind of scared. This guy was the boss, and they felt it, even though he acted as if he was deferring to them. He opened the council, and it was Latin, so I only caught every couple of words. There was another guy translating into Greek. The hawk-eyed men went on arguing loudly about having one faith, and a lot of other arguments I couldn't follow. There was something about the Christian Arians. The big guy, who I think was an emperor, watched and listened and sort of let them rant, while all the time he had this smile on his face, like even though everyone else was running their mouths, they really weren't in charge. He was.'"

Penelope looked up at Alexis. "Then you said 'saints' and it clicked because I studied Later Roman and Early Byzantine history as an undergraduate. The Oration to the Assembly of the Saints. I think that Tim saw the opening of the Council of Nicaea. Which means the emperor—"

"Was Constantine," Alexis said, his expression darkening as he muttered Greek curses under his breath.

"You're not a fan? I thought he was one of the better emperors, to be honest. Thirty-two years as Caesar would've taken a special kind of man," Penelope said, scrolling down and searching for more.

"He was certainly special."

"You sound like you knew him." Penelope looked up sharply. "*Did* you know Constantine?"

The look on his face said it all. She vaguely remembered Phaidros mentioning Constantine had tried to marry Aelia.

"Yes. We had a bad falling-out. It's a long story," Alexis admitted, reaching for the wine bottle.

"I bet. Okay, you knew Constantine. Any idea why Tim would've seen him in a vision?"

Alexis got to his feet and began to pace, a frustrated lion in a cage. "What's the common thread in all of Tim's visions?"

"I haven't gotten that far with them. I've only been reading through it, not really looking for patterns. As you can tell from the description of the Council, he didn't go into a lot of details because it wasn't his field. He didn't always know what he was looking at."

"Why do you think he had visions of things he had no interest in? It isn't as if his memory could have dredged it up if it was never there to begin with." Alexis frowned at the growing wall of information.

Penelope chewed on her lip. "The scroll curse. I don't understand Essene magic, but what if it made Tim into a seer or something? Is that possible? I know Elazar said it could be."

"Constantine's reign was over two hundred years in the future from when the scroll was written," Alexis pointed out. He stopped pacing. "Unless it wasn't the scroll, so much as the scribe."

"What do you mean?"

"We know this scribe was extremely gifted with magic and that he had powerful visions. He was running out of time to physically write down everything he had seen in his vision of us finding the seal. What he wrote was short, only a few paragraphs of what he considered the most important information. His vision could've been much longer. He didn't have the resources to record everything in its complete form so he could've used magic to embed the scroll itself with his visions."

"Which means Tim wasn't cursed at all. He was just...what? A vessel for a dead scribe's visions?"

"Exactly. Tim had no idea what was happening, so he acted like he was losing his mind. Elazar's the only person I've known that has been able to understand Essene magic and even he thought it was a curse. He had his suspicions that there was something off about it. How did he put it? 'A note of discord in a symphony.' He didn't realize that Tim was writing visions, or he would have investigated it differently. Instead of curing him of a curse, he cured him of the visions."

"And Tim wrote them down because I asked him to. He might not have even completed it all or remembered everything." Penelope looked at the document and tears filled her eyes as she realized something far worse. "If there was no curse, that means once he was cured of the imprinted visions, he had no brain damage. He was erratic and exhausted from his ordeal, but he wasn't crazy. He knew exactly what he was doing when he tried to kidnap me and steal Elazar's research."

Alexis sat back down and placed an arm around her. "I'm sorry I didn't realize sooner."

"You couldn't have known it wasn't a curse. You said yourself that even Elazar didn't pick up on it." Penelope sniffed her tears back. "No time for regret or anger. Okay. They are visions, and we need to find out what links them. Why these periods of time? What made the scribe see them?"

"It wasn't any of us, or Tim would've recognized us. He knew what Abaddon looked like, so I doubt Thevetat would've been the link either."

"Then it's the seal itself," reasoned Penelope. "That's the only other thing it could be. You don't think that he saw where it traveled to or when it was found?"

"It is possible. Tim's descriptions aren't very detailed as you said, so it might be hard to tell for certain who they are speaking about."

"What about Constantine? Do you remember if he wore an unusual ring?"

"He was emperor. He wore lots of different jewelry." Alexis finished his wine, a faraway look in his eyes.

"Wasn't his mom like an early relic hunter? Tried to find the True Cross and stuff like that?"

"Helena converted, and it was a very intense faith. Constantine gave her as much money as she wanted when she went on her tour of

Israel. She destroyed a temple to Venus that Hadrian had built over what she believed was Jesus's tomb, and Constantine ordered that the Church of the Holy Sepulchre be built in its place. I never heard of her finding any ring during her visit. That's not to say that she didn't."

"I don't suppose you could check somehow? What about going back into a memory?" asked Penelope. His expression clouded over, and it was like every single wall he had came up behind his eyes.

"I'll have to think it over. Some memories are better left in darkness," Alexis said. He gathered up their empty bowls, kissed her forehead, and disappeared, leaving her wondering just how bad the falling out with Constantine had been.

THIRTY

PENELOPE FOUND HER way back upstairs before dawn. Her mind was a haze from staring at her laptop for so long, searching every database imaginable for stories about Constantine and holy relics. She was stepping out of her bathroom when she spotted Alexis sitting on her balcony, staring at the still, dark lagoon.

"Hey, I thought you'd be sleeping," she said as she joined him.

"Not without you. I'm sorry about walking out on you before."

"You don't need to explain. Constantine was your friend, and it doesn't take a genius to figure out that he hurt you. Let's face it, friends can be the worst." Penelope rested a hand against his shoulder, and he moved so he could gently pull her into his lap.

"I will show you our last meeting, and we can see if he had the ring on. Otherwise, we will have to dig into the other visions Tim had to confirm your theory about the ring linking them," Alexis said. He kissed the groove of her shoulder. "Are you ready?"

"Only if you are." The scent of firecrackers and cinnamon warmed the air around her, and suddenly she was standing in a richly decorated room, with marble pillars surrounded by silk hangings and rich, wooden furnishings.

"Where are we?" she asked Alexis.

"This is the Palace of Daphne, the emperor's personal palace located inside the Great Palace of Constantinople. This section is the Octagon, the emperor's bedchamber," explained Alexis.

The doors opened, and Penelope saw Alexis's shadow memory of himself walk into the room. He wore a winter military uniform consisting of a long-sleeved tunic under a metal breastplate and short leather trousers tucked into high boots.

"I do not see you for two years, Alecto, and then you sneak into the palace like a thief? I sent for you months ago, and you ignored me. What could be so pressing now?" a deep voice said. A tall, well-built man joined him. He would've been in his early sixties, with silver streaking his curly, black hair and shortly clipped beard. Despite that, his muscles were still strong under the purple of his toga, and he stood straight as he sized Alexis up.

It was a face Penelope had seen represented in marble and bronze and only some of the details had come close; dark eyes, high cheekbones, a cleft chin. What all the artists never rendered was the authority and power he wielded that made her feel like she should be bowing. *Constantine.*

"I beg you, don't get into a pissing contest with Shapur. No good will come of it, and your empire does not need another war to pay for just for the sake of your Roman pride," Alexis said, wasting no time on words.

"It is not for my pride that I do this! It is for the safety of the Christian lives I've sworn to protect, who are being persecuted across Persia!" argued Constantine.

"Is that what your priests tell you? That a war will save people? Think of the thousands of innocents who will die because of it."

"I must act, Alecto. Prince Narseh has already invaded Armenia, a Christian country under Roman protection. I can't sit back and take such an insult. The generals will see it as weakness and come like wolves to my door."

"They know better than to try to challenge you. This is folly, Constantine. All that you will find in the East is your death."

"You dare threaten your emperor?"

"I warn my friend. Leave Shapur be, and look to the empire you've managed to hold together for thirty years. You've been one of the greatest emperors Rome has ever seen. You don't have the time left to try and be an Alexander of Macedon as well."

"I will if you relent and allow me…"

"Man was not meant to live forever, Constantine. Especially not an emperor."

"Very well. You came to give me counsel and I've heard it. If you will not support me when I need you most, you are no friend of mine."

"Any simpering courtier can tell you what you want to hear. Only a true friend will tell you what you *need* to hear." Alexis bowed low. "Farewell, *Emperor*." He had almost left the Octagon when a strong hand stopped him.

"I will go to the Jordan River to be baptized before the campaign begins in the spring. Meet me there, if you change your mind. Fight with me one more time before I die, Alecto," said Constantine.

Then Penelope saw it: a signet ring of carnelian stone with symbols set in thick bronze. It was on the hand that gripped Alexis's forearm. As she stared at it, something tingled through her. The symbols began to shift and change, but then the Roman Alexis blocked her view.

Alexis turned to him and clasped the emperor's forearms in a final embrace. "I'm tired of fighting, Constantine. If you want a final piece of advice, save the baptism until after your war. The pure and godly have no place on a battlefield, and you won't survive it with your soul unsullied. You never do."

And with that, Alexis walked away from the emperor forever.

THE MEMORY faded and Penelope was once again sitting with Alexis on the balcony in Venice, the sun slowly turning the sky pink.

"That was the closest to begging I ever heard from him. Even knowing that, I never went back and joined the Persian campaign.

Constantine became sick over Easter and canceled it. I should've stayed and kept arguing with him to keep him from future follies." Alexis sighed.

"That sounds familiar." Penelope rested her head against his shoulder. "Constantine had the ring on, even if he didn't know what it could be used for. That confirms Tim's visions, at least."

"Then we go through the visions, piece by piece, identify what we can and try and locate the ring that way."

"The first thing we need to do is tell the others. We will need them to see what we can't, perhaps they will be able to guess identities from the descriptions," Penelope pointed out.

"You're right. I will give you prior warning: Constantine is a touchy subject with all of us. Especially Phaidros."

"He said that Constantine tried to marry Aelia, so I guess that pissed him off."

Alexis smiled. "It gets worse. Aelia wasn't just playing with Constantine. She was in love with him."

"WOW, HAVEN'T you two already made a mess," said Aelia as she stepped into Penelope's office. More Post-it Notes covered the windows as their timeline filled up. Soon, Penelope was going to get started on printing out sections of Tim's visions and trying to match them with the proper period.

"I hope you haven't had sex on this yet," Phaidros commented as he stretched out on the chaise lounge.

"Too late to warn you now," Penelope couldn't resist saying from her desk.

"Move over already," said Aelia, shoving Phaidros so she could sit down beside him on the chaise. She quickly made herself comfortable, throwing her legs over its curved arm.

"You seem to be making quick progress," Phaidros said.

"Not nearly quick enough. The longer we take to find the ring, the longer Thevetat and Abaddon are free to walk the earth," Penelope replied.

"We've had a breakthrough, so it's coming together," Alexis explained as he came in with Galenos, Lyca, and Zo. He gave a slight, deferential bow to Penelope. "The floor is yours, Archivist."

Penelope grinned. "Okay magicians, this is what we know…"

She explained the timeline they had been constructing, Tim's visions, and the revelation that there had been no curse, only a form of memory spell.

"Oh, Pen, I didn't even think the Essenes were capable of such magic," Zo lamented. "I'll have to tell Elazar, though he's not going to take the news well."

Penelope cleared the lump in her throat before she continued. "It's too late now, so we use what we have."

"Which aren't the rantings of a madman, but the visions of a dead Essene prophet," said Phaidros. "Even better."

"Tim didn't have the skills for creative writing, but we've still been able to confirm that his visions were linked to the ring. It really is made of carnelian and bronze, by the way," Penelope added.

"She's wearing her smug smile. What are you driving at, Penelope?" asked Lyca.

"I figured out that one of the visions was of the Council of Nicaea. Alexis helped me confirm that Constantine once had Solomon's Seal in his possession." Phaidros went very still, and Aelia lifted a brow at Alexis.

"And how did you do that, Defender?" she asked.

"I took Penelope into my memories of him when he was still planning his Persian campaign. He was wearing the ring," confirmed Alexis.

"He wore lots of rings. It could've been any old trinket," Lyca pointed out.

"It was Solomon's seal ring. My magic reacted to it, even in the memory. The engravings on it began to change," said Penelope, secretly marveling that it had worked at all. "It has given us firmer ground to start on. According to Eusebius, Constantine was entombed at the Church of Holy Apostles. It was designed for relics, so it is possible he was buried with it. We know that the original tomb and church were sacked by Enrico Dandolo and his rampaging bastards during the Fourth Crusade, before it was finally demolished in 1461 by the Ottomans. We need to see what else Tim's visions say, and I've got a hunch that if the ring was taken from Constantine's tomb by Crusaders, it might have ended up here in Europe. We could—"

"We could just ask Constantine where he put the damn thing and save ourselves some time," interrupted Zo. "For all we know, the handsome devil is still wearing it around."

"Uh—what?" Penelope stared. "What do mean, *ask* him?"

The magicians' heads all swiveled in Alexis's direction. He twisted the ring on his thumb uncertainly before finally admitting to Penelope. "Constantine is still alive."

EPILOGUE

THE DEMON PRINCE placed a hand against the cavern floor and whispered soothing tones to the rumbling volcano beneath him.

"Calm yourself. Our time hasn't come yet. Soon," he crooned, letting his power funnel down into the layers of rock, dampening the growing pressure.

Around Thevetat were statues of every size and shape, made of bronze, marble, wood, and glass. Some were of humans, or animals, or fantastical combinations of both—nightmare creatures.

A large worktable stood in the middle of the cavern, blocks of wet clay stacked beside it. Thevetat picked up a block and began to knead it with a potter's precision. He dipped his hand into a bronze dish of blood and used it to wet and soften the clay. He had spotted a man at a beach earlier that week who had the most beautiful feet he'd ever seen, and he knew he must have them. Yes, he would start with the feet this time.

It had been a long time since Thevetat had worked with clay. Sometimes one had to go back to the old ways to get it right. He took more blood and dripped it over the earth. He'd had the last nine thousand years to experiment with the body he wanted, the cavern a museum of early failures and ideas. His glorious body would only be the first part of his true vision.

The tide was finally rising, and this time, everything would be perfect.

ABOUT THE AUTHOR

Amy Kuivalainen is a Finnish-Australian writer who is obsessed with magical wardrobes, doors, auroras, and burial mounds that might offer her a way into another realm. Until that happens, she plans to write about monsters, magic, mythology and fairy tales because that's the next best thing. She enjoys practicing yoga and spending her time hanging out with her German Shepherd, Duke in the beautiful city of Melbourne.

Her upcoming Firebird Faerie Tale series combines Russian and Finnish mythology with legends, magic, the mysterious firebird and her love of reluctant heroes. *Cry of the Firebird*, book one in the series, is slated for release fall 2021 from BHC Press.

CPSIA information can be obtained
at www.ICGtesting.com
Printed in the USA
LVHW041929021122
732207LV00001B/166

9 781643 971346